P9-BZI-569

THE MOTHER-IN-LAW DIARIES

The
MOTHER-IN-LAW
DIARIES

A NOVEL BY

Carol Dawson

ALGONQUIN BOOKS
OF CHAPEL HILL
1999

Published by
ALGONQUIN BOOKS OF CHAPEL HILL
Post Office Box 2225
Chapel Hill, North Carolina 27515-2225

a division of
Workman Publishing
708 Broadway
New York, New York 10003

LIBRARY OF CONGRESS CATALOGING-IN-PUBLICATION
DATA
Dawson, Carol, 1951–
    The mother-in-law diaries : a novel / by Carol Dawson.
        p.   cm.
    ISBN 1-56512-127-9 (hardcover)
    I. Title.
    PS3554.A947M68   1999
    813'.54—dc21

10   9   8   7   6   5   4   3   2   1
First Edition

To Michelle, and the girls:
Annette, Becky, Cynthia, Donna, Jessica, Joyce,
Linda, Marilyn, Marsha, Virginia, my mother,
and all you ladies out there, with love

With special gratitude to Kathy Pories, Kerry Grombacher,
Justin, Nikos, and Mike

You Americans! You think if you sleep with them,
you gotta marry them.

—A FRIEND OF LULU PENFIELD'S

The Mother-in-Law Diaries

April 1, this year

Good God, Treatie. What have you done?

Ever since your call I've been so upset I can hardly think, although the whole time we were talking I was trying to corral my feelings so that you wouldn't guess how wild they are. Over the phone that wasn't so difficult, since the only expression you seemed to expect from me was stun. Which is what you got. You can never know how much consternation lay dammed behind it. It'll be over my dead body if you ever do know.

Of course the minute I write this, wondering if you will ever read it, I keep feeling I should be addressing you as my dearest Tristan. Dear son. My sweet boy. Your little surprise has triggered so many emotions that I've simply got to talk to you somehow, write what I would never dream of saying out loud, and how could I possibly call you Tristan for that? That name was your father's idea anyhow. Well, maybe it was both of us, being the romantic students of literature we were, but at least you've never complained, being the brave stoic you are—being, in fact, the treat God misdirected to me in a fit of absent-mindedness and then failed to cancel despite my many follies. So how in the sam hell could you have committed such a folly yourself, without telling me first?

I'm sorry for the scream. Right now I'm praying you took it for shocked delight. I hope your earache's better. It's too bad it was the holey one. But that's another thing: that eardrum should never have been on a jet flight to San Francisco—not with a cold coming on after ten hours Alitalia from Rome. Didn't you *know* six year olds have no business as stoics? Or were you just too tired to cry? Whatever was your mother thinking of that she didn't pay closer attention?

But you got me now, haven't you?

Marriage! *Elopement!!* Treatie, I don't understand. We've been so close. We've been through so much together. Living with Swalla was one thing, but *this!!!* Besides which, I have to confess to feeling deeply hurt by your silence. Couldn't you have at least called and told what you were planning to do even if you wouldn't extend an invitation? Only one other time in your whole life can I remember you deliberately hiding your purpose from me. And when I think of how much you've confided, sharing minutes and thoughts and epiphanies, I'm struck dumb. Your blueprints for tattoos and orifice piercings. Your Twisted Sister tapes. Your crush on that cold little Mill Valley girl when you were thirteen. Your poems. Your desire to join the Special Forces. Remember the time you described getting stoned on the mesa and falling facedown into a compost pit? And the Saturday morning that I took one look at you and knew like lightning—"Treatie," I said, "I've never talked with you about sex much, have I? We've not yet had a proper little chat?" and your face convulsed involuntarily into that sheepish grin—"Mom, too late." And later when girls started phoning and I relayed the messages and Heather who'd just graduated from Princeton with an honors degree in economics fell in love with you? "But honey," I said, "he's only fifteen years old." "I don't care," she said. "He's man enough for me." And when you finally told her, "No, Heather, we'll have to break up, I've already got a mother," she came and sat at the kitchen table while you were at school and cried and cried while I patted her shoulders, thinking, Poor thing. Poor thing. Thank you, Lord.

And now what?

You've gone and changed a major life condition— *secretly*. And it's the big one. You may not realize it, but short of birth and death, this is the SS *Lusitania*, Treatie. Well, if you can't trust your own parent with a sacrament, whom can you trust? For goodness sake, *look* at me! Didn't I show you by example? Didn't you get it? You weren't even baptized. How many sacraments are left, besides Extreme Unction? What do you need *this* one for?

Maybe it's your No Rites History that actually prompted you to hire the hearse to drive you and Swalla in her funeral veil and matching gown to the judge's chambers—

3

sort of a "This isn't really happening, ha ha" and "Just covering every step at once" grab-bag. Not that I'm knocking judge weddings, God knows. Yours probably sat behind his desk the way mine usually did, in his robe color-coordinated to the bride's outfit; perhaps a white boutonniere for contrast. Swalla holding a lily. I'm glad that Swalla's got an interesting sense of style, but what an occasion to show it.

Oh, my Lord. Swalla! I've just realized. Treatie, on top of everything else you've changed *my* life condition. You have actually reached across two thousand continental miles and tampered with my life condition. Do you realize what this means?

You've turned me into a mother-in-law.

1970: *Walking After Midnight*

All women become like their mothers. That is their tragedy.
Men never do, and that is theirs.
— OSCAR WILDE

Mothers-in-law.

If there's one species I know about, that's it. Forget men. Forget dogs and parakeets. The women who give birth to future husbands: those are the creatures I've recognized since the age of five, when I met my very first one in the nursery of the Bernice, Texas, Central Baptist Church when she came in to pick up the four-year-old boy whose hair I'd been stroking lovingly for an hour in the corner. My first, conceptually speaking. Then and there I could tell, from the way her son leaped from my arms and flung himself into her skirt folds, that I was up against a force beyond any I'd ever reckoned with before. This was the woman who counted.

The thing is that despite my wide field experience, the mother-in-law principle has remained until now one-sided. You can stand one hundred years on a river bank painting the opposite view without getting your feet wet, but you won't see the perspective behind your own back until you've thrashed through the water, clambered up the other bank, and squinted, that is if the rapids don't drown you first. As you know, I've rolled over coughing and spluttering plenty.

Do you happen to remember your sixteenth birthday, Treatie? Looking back, I think that was when I should have had my initial glimpse of things to come if only I'd been smart enough to realize. I can see it now. There I stood cooking spaghetti for your all-time favorite meal when you asked if you could invite a friend over to spend the night. I said, "Of course you may. He can come to dinner. Who is it? Michael?" And you said, "No, Laurel Ann Goodwin."

It was then that she should have come back to me. Mrs. Barnes. Murleen.

Murleen Barnes.

My first mother-in-law, carnally speaking.

YOU KNOW, TREATIE, we girls pick the women we'll join by picking the boys we love.

The boy stands there in all his tender glory. You only have eyes for him. Meanwhile a woman whose existence you acknowledge only in principle starts seeping into your life the moment you say 'I will,' whatever it is you happen to be willing: time, fidelity, hitchhiking around the Mediterranean. Of course, I'm not sticking to the strict legal sense of the term. Marriage doesn't even have to be involved. In fact the more I consider it, the more I'm beginning to think that the whole concept of mother-in-law has a breadth that can only be truly appreciated in retrospect.

Time reveals all things; or at least a few. How could I have guessed way back when I was in high school that Murleen Barnes, a woman I met rarely (twice in the course of a whole year, even though I was inside her house four nights out of seven) was connected to me on deep subterranean levels just as surely as tap roots are connected to subsoil? It's now been over twenty-two years since I've given her a thought. Yet back on that sunny white winter's day in Durango, Colorado, as you waited there beside the stove while I stirred the Bolognese sauce, and asked, "Can Laurel Ann come stay overnight, please, Mom? We'll get up early, I promise," Mrs. Barnes should by all rights have come slamming back into my consciousness with hurricane force. "She can ride on the school bus with me tomorrow morning," you said, your voice falling mild, your smile curving in sweet reason, your eyes shining bright with loaded, unspoken freight.

And through the distant air around us I should have heard a sound.

A COUGH EXPLODED. The scuffling feet made a dry rasping along the floor. Once in a while a pop filtered through the wall as her toe joints released a step and seized another. The image of her nylon nightie slithered through my thoughts which were chock full of static electricity; I imagined it clinging to her bare-legged stride.

The instant we heard the cough Jack froze above me in midarch. How long had all those noises been happening? us not hearing?

"Who is it?" I whispered, and he slipped his hand over my mouth and shook his head.

I prised the fingers away for a second. "Burglar?"—the word barely leaking from my throat.

"Mom," he breathed.

The hand clamped down. Smelling our mingling chemistry and his musty gas-station scent, I wanted even then to bite it. Fear sparkled through my veins. The terror intensified heat like a craziness. I saw his eyes lock on to mine above the fingers' blunt tips—those tools of miracle competence that could knot a tiny fishhook onto a hair-thin fly or change gears like a snake shifting or slide up my thigh until—and then I bit his fingers because I just couldn't help it.

"Ow!" He flinched. For a second the hand jerked away.

"What's she—" I mumbled. The fingers mashed down, harder.

It was dark. The room melted without edges on the darkness and his shoulders rose against it, pale blurs. My eyes switched back and forth. All at once there was the feeling that we were in an old-fashioned train depot stuck in time way off the main line with wooden benches and an empty ticket window and dust motes hanging in the sunbeams. From the other landscape we'd been exploring only seconds before, mapping every square inch of forest, hill, and canyon that we could reach with our tongues, we'd now been dragged away to this room by this single sound.

I lay waiting, impaled, like a moth chloroformed by fear. I could barely make out his jawline dusted with bristles. He'd only recently begun to shave. The hollow of his throat beat just above my eyes like a tiny bird—that pocket of life, those blood vessels so available under thin silk. His mother stepped, paused.

In the instant silence hung definition: from now on for all time, this act of love would be the ultimate profanity.

ONE HOUR BEFORE I'd stolen through the moonless blocks and houses, past window units throbbing and one lone bulldog that shoved his face against the chain-link fence and barked. For months now I'd sneaked out of the house nearly every night like an outlaw, killing time until my parents went off to bed and the central air switched on, then raising my window, climbing out onto the balcony, scrambling down the rungs of our giant TV aerial, and touching earth in the rose garden opposite the ancient oak tree. Sparky would run up and down the garden, squirming like a trout with excitement, her tail whacking my arm. "Okay, girl," I'd whisper. "You can't come. Stay here." We'd stand a minute together under the jasmine, getting used to the pulsing world—star-fixed, burgeoning, dense as a realm on the ocean floor. Moths flittered through the air. Fireflies burned holes in the azaleas. We could feel the twitches within the void, the spiraling movements across stillness, darkness wheeling into a spatial arc swarming with lone migrations. The neighborhood no longer existed. No elderly couple next door watered their daylilies or stooped toward the newspaper or kneeled to pluck crabgrass or called out that dinner was ready. All over town lay bedrooms trapping people in sleep, and I was the only one out, the only one connecting, the only one alive.

Sparky skipped along beside me as I darted from tree to tree across the wide front lawn. On these nights she knew; she'd stop at the curb by our driveway and watch me head off toward the new adventures I had now discovered within my own skin—the exciting voyage across town, the flesh my ship of limitless possibilities. Two miles away the blocks opened up a different universe. Everything looked strange. Grass grew scanty and closer to the dirt. Weeds stood by the front steps. Secret lives as mysterious and arcane as those of Bedouins were contained within these walls. On the corner near Jack's house a scraggled old chinaberry tree flung berries into the gutter every time the wind shook it. This street, which should have have been called Eighth Avenue, had somehow been inserted out of order where it didn't belong, and it sidled between Seventh and Eighth like a bastard child in hand-me-down clothes. The houses on it were dingy, the curb no more than a gravel hump; the asphalt itself seemed just a thin black smear over hardpan clay. But it had a name.

Roland Lane.

Five blocks up I crept on to the porch of a tiny house with two front doors. Turning the knob of the left one I slipped inside and went groping through the dark. Bedsheets met my hands, rife with the odor of sleeping boy. I fumbled around, finding his arm and shoulder warm as sunny marble, then I came across muscles, ribs, a flat belly, and ran my fingers up his neck to catch in the wavy hair. Slowly he began to wake up. I felt the breath leave his parting mouth. Limbs stirred. Then, all at once, steel hands grabbed and pulled me down, and his lips were everywhere.

YOU SEE, TREATIE, I know.

NOW, LYING THERE, with Mrs. Barnes paused just beyond the wall, I began to receive her thoughts like radio signals of great clarity. They burned tracks, parsing across my brain: *Scorched that casserole. Macaroni tuna. Country preacher's pay puny as witches' spit, what are they dreaming? they may as well not give him a red cent. "Oh, your husband, we think he hung the moon." Then they expect the whole world! Sundays, Wednesday evenings, revivals August and Easter, sickrooms morning and midnight ready to catch every disease and bring it home, never mind that there's only fifty-two members in the whole church, hardly a wedding anytime, no easy forty dollars, nuh-uh!——just baptizings in that scummy old cattle tank claiming they can't afford a pool. Use a play pool! Sears Roebuck. Backyard special. At least something you can drain! Even since he started the second job with Firestone it's still not enough to scrape by on. Could not afford to ruin a whole supper. And, oh——Maria's two black teeth on the front which they're babies which she'll lose them but still. An arm and a leg just for cavities. And as for braces! Then Lannie Lynn trying to tell me she didn't roll across that garbage can backing out her drive yesterday and smush it flat as a cookie sheet, does she take me for a chicken-head?*

Between her and us was only a thin double-wood panel with a brass knob. It could have been clear as glass.

Did the pause mean she was about to open it?

A sound broke out. In panic I clenched against Jack's arms. He didn't move. It broke like a fist punching through a paper shell—another cough.

Somehow it sounded so lonesome. So small. Actually she was tall and rail thin, gaunt as a heron. Sometimes I'd hear her talking to Jack in a worried nasal whine, while we were on the phone: "Jacky, you better not stay out so late tomorrow night or this time your daddy might whup you, Jacky, are you going to take your little sister Maria to that Little League game like you said?" I'd wait a moment and sure enough, the voice would drop back down to a gravelly mezzo pitch: "Is that shirt new? Are you spending that hard money you work for in the filling station on fancy new shirts instead of saving up for the junior college? How come you think you have to dress up all the time? For who?"

After one long *harrumph* she finally started again— step, step, scuff.

I could feel her debating the choice of opening the door as she circled the living room, perhaps not yet ready to see what she'd find. Had her footsteps, once capable of ranging whole frontiers, kept on shrinking until this strict pine floor was now as deep into the night as they dared go? Did this happen always as women grew older? Got married? Had children? Certainly my mother didn't gallivant off through the midnight hours, nor, so far as I knew, did teachers, country club golf players, church organists, grocery checkers, or the female relatives of friends.

The fever hit me like a lance. Goosebumps rose on my skin. As I lay there under Jack's weight the terror increased, this time from an entirely new source: Where *was* she going? Where would I?

"I've got a cramp," Jack breathed into my ear.

The footsteps suddenly stopped. But instead of hinges creaking, a sighing sound wheezed under the door. I realized instantly what it was. She'd sunk into the vinyl armchair directly facing us. I heard a rustle, then a metallic click. After a quarter of a minute the scent of cigarette smoke came curling along the dark.

I couldn't see Jack's eyes now. He eased down flat beside me, his lips nibbling my neck. I hadn't even known she smoked! It was against her religion for sure; no one in my family had ever so much as touched an ashtray butt. In fact religion was the only real thing Jack and I had in common, the slender thread I'd been counting on all this time ever since we'd started going steady six months before and he'd given me his senior ring and then around about Valentine's Night we'd parked down the country road next to Babyland Cemetery and there in the backseat of his 442 demolished my virginity, and I knew that I was now a goner for sure, tangled in barbwire, and no Armageddon was likely to come along and save me.

"Dad?" I'd said two nights after my defloration. "Did you know that on Sundays Jack Barnes's father preaches at a Baptist church? Just like your father did?"

Dad looked blankly down from the distant height of his grim intellect, chewing a piece of fried chicken breast, saying nothing.

"I thought he worked in the tire store," said my mother.

"Only during the week," I turned to her. "On weekends he leads a whole congregation. And Mrs. Barnes teaches Sunday school, just like Grandmother did."

Carefully Dad took a swig of iced tea. Then another bite, his jaw rotating. My grandfather's published works occupied an entire shelf in our home library. Some, like the United Nations Charter on religious liberties he had helped to draft, were mere monographs. Others—the volumes of philosophy, history, and sermons—were beefy doorstops.

"Isn't that good?" I pressed.

But Dad's silence couldn't disguise the judicial cool in his eye. He was being tactful.

We both knew Jack was not good.

Yet what other link seemed strong enough to justify the fact that, although we shared no mutual interests whatsoever, he didn't read so much as a Cliffs Note, make jokes, or laugh, or care about a tenth of the things that grabbed my curiosity, I was nonetheless hip-deep in lust with the Number One Bernice High School hell-raiser from across the tracks?

And now his Southern Baptist mother sat outside his

door all by herself at two in the morning, smoking like a nightclub singer.

OUR SWEAT-DAMP bellies made a sucking noise as Jack nudged himself out. The Trojan slipped off. It stuck to my thigh. He turned his head so that his eyes caught the light. It was then, at that moment, that I realized: he recognized these sounds. They were not news. The fact gleamed, familiar as breakfast; he'd lain in this bed alone in the dark listening to the footsteps slog through the wee hours many times. As a little boy struggling from a nightmare; as a twelve year old festering on the note from the teacher he'd stuffed down the side of the couch; as a teenager scheming for gas money, or flexing over a girl in a dream; through fall and spring, ice storms and mosquito weather, her insomnia had bound his nights together. And now he was finally sharing it. This, the secret of his most profound silence, was the real intimacy, the new thing we had in common.

I felt my mouth go dry. A knot filled my craw. I bucked against his chest, hard as a boulder. "Jack!"

He shook his head.

"Let me up," I whispered. I was starting to feel desperate.

She wasn't going to open the door. I knew that now. Whatever she thought, whatever she did or didn't know, she wasn't going to risk a look. I could just jump right up and leave through his outside door—I would lever myself from the bed this minute and silently crawl across that darkness and twist the knob and walk out onto the front porch the same way I'd come in and shut it behind me quietly, quietly; and then run through the blocks back across town to the gracious two-acre lawns and silent blank housefronts and ancient oak trees that I had come from, run toward the future of a good college with my junior year spent in Europe and summers in the green countryside, plus a riveting career as a writer, writing plays and novels and poetry, and islands across the ocean spread out for coconut palm hula dance research vacations and bazaars in strange lands ringing with barter and laughter and cloths striped crimson and gold and hot curried dishes from roadside stalls and brightly colored birds and anthropology and museums and concerts and jeep rides into the jungle. I pictured my parents getting up to use the bathroom, opening my door, checking through the empty bedspread. Phoning the police. For a split second I thought I saw the first gray streak of dawn edge the window.

I tried to move.

"You can't go yet."

"*I have to!*" The footsteps dragged slowly around. On each circuit she hit the same loose board somewhere in the region of the TV console, and it creaked as she left it behind.

"She won't hear me. I *promise.*"

"Yes she will." He breathed it into my ear. "She hears everything."

His arms braced to hold me tight. It was then I saw his eyes.

He knew.

He knew she wasn't going to open the door. He'd known all along.

Something scraped on the wood-plank floor. The cushion huffed, inhaling. The soft slapping began again.

"Shh, baby," he whispered, his breath lingering in my ear.

I felt his penis stiffen and go hard, rolling across my thigh. It knocked the empty Trojan to the mattress.

"*Jack! Stop!*" I hissed.

His lips found mine. His tongue darted into my mouth. With one limber swing he rose and climbed against my body, pinning me in place, and slowly, inch by inch, rammed himself inside, probing, nailing, plunging, in and out.

There was no rubber.

I twisted my head: "Stop! *No! Stop it!*"

"Shh," he whispered, and then he went on driving, hammering me fast, and all at once I heard her thoughts again, as sharp as light, etching into my mind: *No money. No hope. Can't even buy Maria her new dress for the school recital. Not to mention our only boy, the high school senior, our Jacky we've tried and tried bringing up so good, rassling in his bed this very minute, straight through the wall, under my very own roof, with a whore.*

That girl. A whore.

No matter whose daughter.

And the footsteps scuffled and flapped, and then the terror bloomed up my sides and through my belly where any minute the seed was going to spurt and make a baby, getting me pregnant at the age of sixteen, tying me down and trapping me there for the rest of my life on that little bastard of a street, in the little Texas town, on the pine floor of a tinderbox living room where I would trudge every night circling my cage like a wingless bird.

ONE WEEK LATER I told Jack I was going away to boarding school and couldn't ever see him again.

The next day I bought my first pack of Salems.

1971: The Heiress

*And Ruth said, "Entreat me not to leave thee, or to return
from following after thee . . . thy people shall be my people,
and thy God my God.*——RUTH 1:16

To regard a mother-in-law as a wellspring is to stomp on
convention, not to mention five thousand years of comic
permafrost. How the title grew synonymous with *foe* is not
so hard to figure out, but I find its dimensions a little claus-
trophobic. Plus, the wording itself seems confusing. Legally
it carries no weight in either a guardian or property sense.
So once you eliminate "in-law" and are left with "mother,"
you're faced with a lie. I mean, where's the real maternity?
Where's the nourishment? What's left besides irony?

Plenty, as I shortly found out.

When Mark Brune and I started dancing toward each
other up in Dallas the summer of my junior year at boarding school, I knew pretty quick there must be a decent
woman hovering in the background. Somebody was teaching him manners, training his brain, and schooling him in
easy chat with females. Our first real conversation started
off with a critique of John Fowles's *The Magus,* which his

mother had passed on to him, along with Jung's *Man and His Symbols,* the *Collected Poems of T. S. Eliot, Cycladic Sculpture,* an illustrated tome on Egyptian deities, a tour guide of Greece, *The Tempest,* and some reproductions of Bonnard paintings, all of which she'd gradually gathered beside her as she unraveled the novel. The minute I saw the references stacked on the bedside table beneath *The Magus* a bolt of intuition struck: I knew exactly why they were there. I stood peering down at a full-scale topographical map of a mental country.

Later I would discover that this was Bo's habit: to weave a tent of knowledge around the act of absorption, so that she sat snug inside its bright tapestry and experienced not only each image the author mentioned but its invisible relatives connected by webs and palettes and dead languages across the world. Extensions would form labyrinths in her scribbled margins: the polo *maidan* in *A Passage to India* telescoped into a discourse on Afghan horseflesh (adjuncted by Kipling's *Kim*), leading to the sports of seventeenth-century hill maharajahs, to hunting miniatures, to pornographic miniatures, to palace *purdah* screens (which looped back on Forster's Indian women guests at the Bridge party) to Shiva, musings on reincarnation, and the Bhagavad-Gita. These histories accreted around the literary nucleus like oyster spit around a pearl. They became the scaffolding she would then hand on to whoever happened to ask for something new to read. It never occurred to her to dismantle the additions, to peel it all back down to a single original volume. She shared the whole building. This was her idea of fun.

She was my kind of mother.

But of course in the beginning I didn't know all that. I just knew that Mark was witty, curious, solemn, and that his kisses were as sweet as chocolate-coated mangoes. He was a brilliant cocaptain of his school soccer team, urged on by maternal approval of a.) the Greek ideal, b.) the vigor and balletic grace of athletes, and c.) the Dallas Cowboys. He spoke decent French. He painted his dreams. I mean it: *he painted his dreams!* In abstract motifs that captured some essence far deeper than the usual surreal tragicomedy films playing nightly in my own inner theater. He showed me the Arches boards that same first afternoon as we sat on his bed talking and talking and moving toward each other's hands. By the time he'd turned ten his mother had taught him to use watercolors —how to grade a wash, reserve paper for white, which paints were glazes, which ones would warm skin tones from beneath, which ones would make mud. The kissing came natural. He'd learned that all by himself.

The strange node of fate was that I'd heard of Mark at least three years prior to the summer afternoon when his younger sister Perky introduced us. One of my childhood girlfriends from Bernice had a Dallas cousin who'd shown us Mark Brune's eighth-grade photograph, drooling like a puppy over his manly virtues—something she encouraged us small-towners to do also. Judging from the snapshot he was pretty cute. But at the time definitely out of my immediate galaxy.

Boarding school changed all that.

The July of my junior year I was taking a summer-school drama course. I played the dupe servant girl in our play, *High Tea and Cyanide*. Perky Brune, a girl I'd just gotten to know better, played one of the elderly ladies who employed me. Throughout the cool, dim auditorium lay an acreage of plush seats engulfed by shadow. One afternoon I noticed a boy in one of them, lazing there with his feet propped up as if he'd been sitting for hours, watching us quaver through our lines in the chittering cries of marsh creatures. I hadn't seen him come in, and his identity seemed a mystery. He was this boy out there in the lofty darkness. A one-guy audience.

Instantly I contracted stage fright.

"Lulu, I didn't hear you. You've run in, you've just eavesdropped on a plan to kill nice old Mrs. Lupus—louder, Lulu, squawk. Squawk!"

"Yessir," I answered the drama coach, a florid queen from Oklahoma with marvelous stage gestures and a violet seersucker suit that complemented his green and purple Sulka tie and flaming saffron hair. "Yessir" struck me as a contradiction in terms. "*Ack! Eeee-eeee!* Mrs. Lupus, marm—*murder, there's murder aflop!*"

I broke off. Slowly the boy set his feet down, leaned forward, and propped his chin on his fist.

"Aflop?" said Mr. Rankin.

"Yes," I said.

"Are you making that up? Are you under the impression that you can re-create some sort of nineteenth-century working-class Yorkshire dialect all by yourself?"

There was a silence. "That's what the script says," I answered weakly. My throat began to close.

"It says 'aplot.'"

The silence extended. "Mine said 'aflop,'" I said.

"I doubt Messrs. Samuel French and Company would permit so out-*ra*-geous a typo to elude the copy-editor's eye—given the fact that the original word is an awkward *enough* piece of dramaturgy—dramatur*gidity*, ha! ha!—" he chuckled acidly. "*God help* the playwright." With a weary snarl he held out his hand for my script. I turned and pounded into the wings to fetch it.

"Oh. The mimeographed copy." Regally he returned it, swopping his brow where it had flushed an unbecoming red. "It's smeared."

"Yes."

"You must have spilled something. Or perspired on it. Have you been carrying it around in your hand? In the hot sun?"

"No, sir."

"Tucked under your arm, perhaps? In your armpit?"

The cast stood spellbound, breathing through their mouths. In the audience the boy had cocked his head in attention.

"No," I said with great hauteur. "Not even inside my bra."

"Well!" He tossed up his chin. "Bravo. Ha! *Bra-vo!* Heh, heh! Get it?" and then stopped suddenly as a round of hard, stony applause broke out, echoing through the vastness of the auditorium. It took me a moment to realize where it came from.

The girls turned. I followed their eyes, straining through the gloom. The boy was sitting straight up with his hands raised high in the air beating together like wings.

"Thank you." Mr. Rankin puckered his mouth and arched an eyebrow.

"I'm applauding her," the boy explained.

"Are you?" For a second Mr. Rankin didn't speak. Then he rolled his arm, shot the cuff, and looked at his gold-encrusted slab watch. "That's it! Time to go! Be back at twelve sharp tomorrow with all your blocking memorized. And *correct lines, please!*" He sent a wry yet withering glance my way.

As soon as his back was turned I sagged and started shuffling toward the wings.

"Hey, Lulu. Where are you going?"

Perky Brune stood tapping on my elbow.

"Home, I guess," I muttered.

"I've got a better idea. Why don't you come over to our place for dinner?"

"Oh." I was pleased and taken aback. "Wow. Thanks." Perky had never asked me over before. "But I've got to get back before dark. My mother doesn't like me on the road late." The boarding dorms were shut for the summer, so every day after rehearsal I drove the thirty-five miles south to Bernice.

"You could spend the night. We'll come in together to-morrow morning."

I thought about it. "I could phone Mom."

"Do it from our house, why don't you?"

"Where is it?"

She pointed to the boy who had now stood up and was waiting in the aisle. "We'll show you. Follow us."

Once through the glass doors and out into the blast furnace of the parking lot she said, "This is my brother Mark. He goes to Saint Luke's. This fall he'll be a senior. Like you."

"Hi," I said.

He smiled. "Nice squawking back there."

"Thanks."

"We only live ten blocks away," said Perky, climbing into the passenger seat of his red M.G. "Our grandmother's staying with us right now while Mother and Dad are gone on a trip to New Mexico. She'll be glad to have you."

I unlocked my old Chevy. "Okay, I'll follow you."

"See you there," said Mark. And it wasn't until we were rolling down Hillcrest toward Lovers' Lane through the bright humidity rising up from the grass lawns that an old memory whapped me and I finally added two and two: *Mark* and *Brune,* as in Perky Brune, as in the boy in the photo Susie Rosenberg had been toting around all through that whole long-ago visit, for whom she'd stripped totally buck naked during a game of strip poker in his pool cabana and been proud to do it; Mark Brune, the star of the Saint Luke's Middle School for Boys soccer team; Mark Brune, the Apollo of Highland Park, Dallas, Texas.

IF PERKY FELT neglected that evening she didn't show it.

"I've got to do my Algebra homework," she said as soon as we entered the house and she led me to her bedroom. "If I don't get it done before dinner I won't be able to do French. The phone's over there, if you want to call your mom." It took all of five minutes for Mark and me to defect to his room on the opposite side of the house and commence a dialogue that would continue solidly for the next eleven months.

"Is that a Rouault poster?" I asked, glimpsing a black-outlined Christ glowing like half-shadowed stained glass on Mark's far wall as he slid the dream images back into their portfolio. Thanks to my parents carting me around to every art gallery in every city we ever entered, I recognized the manner.

"Not a poster, no," he said.

"Oh. A lithograph?" He shook his head. "You mean a— real Rouault?"

He nodded.

I blinked. Next to his bathroom hung a portrait of a misty-edged girl holding a rose bouquet like wads of pink velvet. "So then, is that really a Renoir?" I asked, embarassed, expecting him to laugh.

"Yeah," he said.

Although this was Dallas, where any tangible thing

becomes not only possible but probable, I was suddenly astounded that I could be lounging in a teenage boy's suburban bedroom with the sun beating on the basketball hoop outside and a genuine *Head of Gabrielle* sniffing flowers in a nineteenth-century French country garden. From *that* French country garden.

"God. I mean——God! It could just as well be—— Giverny!"

"In the dining room it is."

"You have a *Monet?*"

He nodded again.

"I——" I closed my mouth.

He shrugged. "The Renoir's in here because Perky claims it's too sweet. She won't allow any Impressionists to enter her room."

"Well, damn. Who would?"

He grinned.

"She and Mother like Cubists better. Vlaminck, Braque. Picasso. Also Cezanne, of course. And the Fauves. Mother calls the Nabis too eggy for her taste. Except for Bonnard."

"How about you?" I asked after a pause. He'd spoken shyly, not realizing he'd long overreached my lone little peninsula and set right on out to sea.

"I kind of lean to the surrealists."

"Oh. Yeah. Sure."

"Mother thinks that Monet's late work heads more toward early Expressionism."

"Really?"

"What do you think?" He looked sincere. "Frankly I

just can't equate him as the forerunner of, say, Jackson Pollock."

"Well—possibly." Did I like fried chicken? Was the Pope Methodist? Was Kirchner an utter stranger?

"Perky said you'll be at Winlawn all year now."

He had gray eyes. Gray eyes and long black lashes. In shorts and a tank-shirt he looked like a half-concealed *David*, scaled down from the Palazzo Vecchio. "Yes," I said. "I was there last year, too. I'm a boarder."

"Hey. Doesn't that mean they let you spend the night at other students' houses on weekends?"

"Yeah, it does."

"So if, say, Perky asked you to spend the night sometimes, it wouldn't be a problem? I mean—if you wanted to?"

"Those are the rules. If the day student's parents sign a permission slip." My pulse began to quicken.

"In that case, I guess maybe you need to meet my mother," he said.

I WAS THERE when Mr. and Mrs. Brune returned one week later. "Call me Bo, honey," she said as Mr. Brune and Mark heaved the suitcases in through the service door. "I don't even know who Mrs. Bearden Brune is except on my charge plates."

"Okay."

"Besides, Perky told me over the phone we've already met."

"Yes, a long time ago at Camp Mer-de-Bois, when you

and Mr. Brune came to Field Day," I explained. "Perky and I used to go to the same session. We didn't know each other very well then, though."

"Uh-huh. Were you a member of the Comanche tribe, by any chance?"

"Caddo."

She nodded. "Yep. Perky and I were, too. I went to camp there when I was young."

"So did my mother and sisters. They were both Caddos."

"Well hell, it's in the blood, then, isn't it. All us good old team girls rowing away."

"Except for my sister Dyllis. She was a Kickapoo."

"Kickapoo. What a pity. Well, God delights in inconsistency. It's literally the luck of the draw that we-all wound up Caddos, you know, since we choose by lot." She looked as fine-boned as Audrey Hepburn, her hair pulled back in a black chignon that shone with the iridescence of a crow's wing. Her gray eyes were set in waxy pale skin. A smile lifted the corners of her lips. "Did you ever hear much about the real Caddo Indians, that they were pacifists?"

"No," I said.

"Conscientious objectors, every one. They designed towns around their agricultural and artisan society in the piney woods, which is why the old Rangers found them so easy to exterminate. No resistance, especially against white men's germs." She smiled once more. "But Comanches were a slightly different matter. As any settler would tell you once his women got raped and his children dragged off. There's balance in the world, make no doubt. However—" She paused, weighing something. "Perky thinks it'd be a good idea if I phone your dorm mother when school starts and put our name and address on your permission list for the weekends." She glanced quizzically sideways over at Mark playing checkers with his six-year-old brother Oliver.

"Oh, ah—thank you, Mrs. Brune," I said. "I mean—that is, if—"

"No problem, honey. I'll be glad to. But for Christ's sakes Almighty call me Bo."

"Okay," I said.

Perky asked a languid question. "While you were in New Mexico did you manage to meet Georgia O'Keeffe like you wanted?"

"Yes, darling." Bo turned. "She invited us on up to Ghost Ranch for the afternoon, so we drove over to Abiquiu from Santa Fe. Can you imagine? the entire daily diet that woman eats consists of one tiny charred hamburger patty and a glass of orange juice. She's no bigger than a doodlebug. I swear to God she looks like some kind of martyred fifth-century saint." She shook her head, fitted a Marlboro precisely into her apple green jade holder, tamped it down, and lit it.

WHEN SCHOOL STARTED in September Mark and I knew just where we stood.

Every weekday morning he drove Perky to the Winlawn Academy parking lot, where I'd meet him for a quick smooch as the teachers arrived and climbed out of their cars. After school, on the days he didn't have soccer practice, he'd drop by the auditorium where I had drama rehearsals and together we'd sneak into the women's rest room and lie down on the chaise lounge occupying the corner of the powder room. We spent much time on this chaise. I acted in a lot of plays. *The Crucible. Oklahoma. Much Ado About Nothing.* If I wasn't screaming, "There's a bird on the beam!" I was painting flats for London parlors and cornfields with my new best friend Miriam and fetching pick-me-up chocolate bars for the cast. At night Mark and I would tie up the phone hour after hour while the girls with families in Venezuela and Saudi Arabia and Austin and L.A. milled around the TV lounge and battered on the booth door in frustrated fury.

THE FIRST TIME I ever laid eyes on an erotic Japanese woodblock was in Bo's company.

"Utamara's *Uki-yo* records of Edo always remind me of the Weimar Republic," she pronounced one Sunday morning, opening a heavy clothbound book and flattening the centerfold with one palm while she sipped her coffee.

I only knew fragments from history class: one loaf of bread equaled one wheelbarrow full of depression money in 1922 Weimar Germany. I dumped several teaspoons of sugar in my cup. "Dosing yourself up on White Death again, Lulu?" said Mr. Brune as he walked past on his way to clean his shotguns for the opening of dove season.

"Here. What do you think?" Bo shoved the book across the table. "Look at those lines. One whack only, get it right or lose it. Exquisite, aren't they?"

Carefully I scrutinized a geisha with her legs flung wide in welcome and her face modestly averted, then a farm wife offering her breast to a lover while her tooth-gnashing husband spied on them both through a bamboo fence. Certainly I'd never seen anything quite like those lines. Bo turned the page. Opposite a courtesan arranging her combs sprawled an extraordinary sight: the ink painting of a penis-measuring contest. "By Anonymous Master" said the caption, but there was nothing anonymous in the entries: huge tuberous stalks supported with slings, long floppy cables flung over the shoulder; capped mushrooms as stout and veined as redwood trunks anchoring their owners in place; cleft tree branches employed as a crutch for that helpless third leg, and sure enough! a wheelbarrow stuffed full of male member rolling toward the giggling prostitute judges' tools (yardstick, scales) while the owner heaved sweatily from behind; you could hear the girls whispering, "I think we've got a winner!"

Bo looked sidelong at me. I swallowed my shock. "That's, uh, pretty—inventive," I ventured.

"Joie de vivre. What you get when a culture embraces its own sensual instincts." She'd already skipped ahead to the next illustration.

"So, sex is okay over there?" I was still trying to digest the full implications: Had those whoppers actually been based on precedent? Or bravado? Was there really this much variety in the world?

"You might say their 'proper circumstances' are a little more broadly defined than ours." She thumbed through another section, studying each plate with a magnanimous detachment while I admired the gymnastic ingenuity and tried to figure out what she might really be trying to tell me. I was all too used to covert agendas from my own parents, the message lying beneath the word, coiled and ready to strike. But Bo focused, as if unaware, on the aesthetic understatement—the spare stroke evoking an eye, the twists of shining hair, the clever drape of a split kimono. And that was when I finally caught my breath at the latest revelation she was offering me: the wealth of diversity with which God had endowed the world.

"Well, *hmph,*" she said then. "This one might be a little ripe for youthful consumption," she pointed to a woodblock that featured a sprawling woman whose pudenda looked (as Bo demonstrated by cropping the picture with her hands), like ikebana ready for exhibit. She sighed. "I suppose I'd better to keep this book locked up so Oliver won't find it."

"Oh. Right." I nodded, squinting down. My parents would have locked it up tight as a vault so *I* wouldn't find it. But of course my parents wouldn't have owned a copy, much less known that I knew what a penis looked like. Much less somebody else's son's.

Or an entire nation's.

"But then, just look here. Notice how Mary Cassatt copied the same lines." Bo pulled out another book and tilted her head fondly. "One single stroke for the back. Bang! gotcha. The same damn technique she learned from the Japanese." She smiled narrow-eyed at the woman standing over a dresser washing herself, oblivious.

I MUST CONFESS: I got lucky.

Growing up in Bernice I'd always felt my exclusion sharply—where was the pleasure other girls found in Barbie's Dream House and Convertible? Why couldn't I join right into grade school twirling class? What kept my wrist from that knack of flipping the baton high, or even catching it at all? I tried, I brooded, but I couldn't fake interest where interest didn't live, and the dregs of solitude can be bitter. Bo provided their replacement. The first time I ever ate genuine beluga caviar was when she served it to us early one Saturday evening as a special treat with lemon slices and Melba toast on a crystal bed of ice. "Don't bother with lumpfish," she said. "It's a waste of time." Bo was my tutor the first moment I comprehended Freud's definition of the id, which she had first understood as a psychology major at Bryn Mawr; it was Bo who taught me to distinguish T'ang porcelain from Sung. She made me my first cherries jubilee, for my birthday. She also served my first real French champagne (although she herself never drank anything but ice water or coffee). Through her I learned the meaning of the Japanese concept *shibui*. The story behind Sargent's *Portrait of Madame*

X—that dropped evening gown strap he'd had to repaint back into the upright position.

I took to wearing simple, streamlined outfits, not an eyelet ruffle anywhere. I adopted a new haircut, combing my hair with a safety razor, an effect that looked very chic, never more than two inches long.

Late at night on weekends, I'd rise from the twin bed in Perky's room and creep through the stuffy gloom. The tiny pinpoint bulb on Perky's radio bloomed against her sleeping face like the halo around a Raphael infant, and often while fumbling past her footboard I'd pause to look at that veil of light. One weekend when I'd asked her how she could stand to have a radio bleating in her ear all night and could we please turn it off she'd answered in plaintive indignation, "I've had it since when I was little. I *have* to have it."

"Why?" I asked.

She just shook her head. "It was on the scary nights. When Mom——" and then she stopped and refused to say anything more.

So relief as well as excitement spurred my escape from the starched Swiss embroidery wilderness and the wash of red noise to Mark's bed while Bo and presumably Mr. Brune slept, beyond moral judgment, beyond Fundamentalism, scarcely registering the whispers of my bare feet in the tidal pool of faint night sounds. If Bo suffered insomnia she never dropped a clue.

By mid-autumn she'd begun addressing me with that same light, dry affability she used toward her own three children. I felt like I'd been waiting for her all my life.

"**THAT WOMAN'S MEANER** than a water moccasin," she said one day as we drove past Mrs. Frank Carmody's stucco mansion set back inside landscaped grounds on Turtle Creek.

"Why?" I was startled. Never before had I heard her comment about somebody's character. Gossip she left strictly alone, although I'd started realizing from tiny allusions here and there that she knew the stories of everybody in Dallas—the gambling wildcatters, the property developer descended from a gunslinger, the kidney specialist who'd slowly poisoned his wife, the whisky-throated ranching dowager who took up with a gigolo and put a contract out on her husband, the Baptist department store tycoon who left everything to his coon dog when his son emerged from the closet wrapped in the arms of a Miami Dolphin, the insurance frauds, the jeweled queens, the loud social climbers, and the charitable old patricians who knew that you must put back what you take out. Social politics weren't Bo's style; she occupied a plane far above petty chitchat, too aware of the human condition to judge. I stared at the rolled lawn and leafy bowers sliding past my window. A topiary obelisk erect between two green spheres guarded one end of the stone terrace. Against the hedge a Mexican gardener teetered on a ladder, clippers snapping. "What does she do?"

"Damage," she answered.

"What kind?"

She wheeled the Mercedes to the end of the street past mounds of fallen leaves, and turned the corner without speaking.

"Do you know her?"

"Lord God, yes. I've known her since high school. We boarded in Winlawn together. She's one of Bearden's clients." She reached into her purse with one hand, jockeying around for her Marlboros. "Treats her maids like slavery never got abolished. Tried to charge the art museum cash last year to show her dead husband's Frederic Remington, for Christ's sakes." Despite the expletive she spoke levelly and without heat; I'd heard her use the same exact tone clocking the merits of the museum's new Pomodoro or approving a spunky debutante for holding her Undersea Dance in the Fair Park bandshell instead of at the Fairmont. "She's got more than one surgeon. Her body's an entire archaeological reconstruction. Like the plaster ash casts at Pompeii." She jammed in the lighter. "Seems a little premature since she's only thirty-nine." She kept her dark glasses trained on the road.

"Isn't her son in Saint Luke's?" I asked finally.

"I believe so."

"I think I met him at the Soccer Dance." I paused, collecting myself. "Mark said they used to live next door to you when you still lived over in Highland Park."

"Uh-huh."

He'd been one of the boys in the pool cabana applauding Susie Rosenberg's crucial moment at strip poker when she failed to draw to an inside straight. He'd gone to kindergarten with Mark and attended all the young Brunes's birthday parties, even Oliver's when he'd turned one, and every morning their mothers had drunk coffee and swapped childbirth stories and marital annoyance, and carpooled for swimming lessons and Cub Scouts and cotillion. The two boys had built a tree house and caught toads behind the goldfish pond, and the parents had all caravanned the boys down to the hill country each summer for camp, and this whole picture he'd reminded Mark of while we hung around outside the gym waiting for the band to start the next set. He'd splashed a bottle of Bacardi into a paper Coke cup as he ranted, his seventh Cuba Libre without any lime—no, the eighth since he'd *finished* the limes. His corroded cheeks bubbled with acne. The debate captain pin hung askew on his lapel. His voice rose in truculence. Once long ago he'd been Mark's best friend.

"The problem with that woman is she's the kind of person who uses other people's troubles as a conversation piece. No matter who gets hurt in the process."

I stared down at my brown knees poking out from under my white tennis skirt, disturbed.

"Gossip is a deadly tool," Bo added. "I've seen it wreck more than one family." But her tone had gone flat and detached once more; she now sounded merely instructive.

"When was it exactly that you-all moved to North Dallas, to the house you're in now?" I asked.

"Four years ago. Why?"

"No reason. I just wondered."

She pulled on her cigarette, ovaled her lips, and exhaled a tail of smoke. "Have Mark or Perky ever shown you our old house?"

"No. They've hardly even mentioned it."

But I'd watched a home movie filmed in its back gardens: two small children chugging around fat-legged, hunting Easter eggs; a girl, a boy, and a lusty baby splashing watery glitter inside the swimming pool beside reefs of nodding daffodils. We were speaking of another world. Never had I heard Bo so much as phone other women to trade duck marinade recipes or share long PTA *klatches*. Most days she spent fully dressed, black pants, black cashmere turtleneck, perched on her bedspread reading Jung and Dickens and Li Po.

"Let's stop at the bakery for those gingerbread squirrels Oliver likes so much," she said, parking the car in Highland Park Shopping Center and pulling on the emergency brake. I watched as she smiled and, lifting her hand with a practiced sweep, adjusted her dark glasses.

"HOLD STILL," SHE said to me. It was the Thanksgiving holidays; we were staying in a beach house down at Aransas Pass on the Gulf. Outside the wind tore at billboards above the empty shops while waves crashed against the sand dunes. "Don't move for a minute."

She sat opposite me after breakfast, a large pad propped against the table's edge. I was rereading *Jane Eyre* and too engrossed in the stiff-necked proposal of Saint-John to pay much attention. Dutifully I held still.

"There," she said at last, and turned the pad around.

I stared at myself.

"It's that pensive look you get sometimes," she added as my heart began to dilate with revelation: this was a picture of me. This sketch she'd been diligently laying down line by line proved that she perceived me, and what's more did so truly, in a way no one had ever demonstrated in the past—not my father who had once painted me grinning the grin of obligation he always required ("*Smile!* You can smile, can't you? Look happy for once?"), not the school photographer, nor the street cartoonist at the State Fair who'd captured my little brother and me looking urchin-eyed and crazed with pleasure, with balloon heads set on flea bodies, nor the college student my mother had commissioned to render us in pastels for my grandmother's upstairs hallway. Bo saw me as an adult. She saw me as her equal.

A person like her.

She rubbed the drawing with a fingertip, then held the pad up once more. The unsmiling girl gazed obliquely to one side, but her sadness leached out from the paper as pervasive as coal gas.

ONE NIGHT NEAR Christmas Bo stood in the foyer dressed for a rare dinner out. A black strapless Balenciaga bared her white shoulders underneath a sable cloak while Mr. Brune fussed with his black tie. So seldom did they go places together that the sight of them both stopped me in my tracks. She was always home in the evenings. I didn't think to question why.

"What is that perfume you're wearing?" I asked, breathing in.

"Joy," she said.

Suddenly the word quivered on my mind: a syllable summing up everything the world promised at that moment.

"I always used to wear it when the kids were little, but I haven't bothered in a long time. I keep it for winter. Chanel No. 19 in summer. Otherwise you should just squeeze a lemon on your hands and trust to nature." She smiled dryly. "Well, come on, Bearden. Let's go."

BY ELEVEN P.M. when they came home Perky and Oliver had long since fallen asleep. Mark and I still sat up in the library toying with cognac snifters and discussing the movie we'd gone to that evening. Occasionally my eyes would wander along the crimson leather walls past tall bookcases to snag on a picture—Braque's angular trees faceted like tourmaline, or the powdery points of Seurat. On the side table near my chair lay a recumbent water buffalo carved in muttonfat jade. A Bernini terra-cotta graced a dark corner with its muscular struggle; two wrestlers hung banked in shadow, a Florentine figment adrift on the ether. This was all Bo, I thought. She'd made it all appear somehow—through her choice, her magnetism, her mysterious acquisition, through her inheritance or skill or whatever had created the possibility for such works to be transplanted into such an unlikely location. I was pondering how this might be when distantly I heard the back door unlatch; we heard the key rattle, clumsily scraping inside the dead bolt even after the tumbler clicked. Then Mr. Brune and Bo swept in on a tide of cold air, Mr. Brune swaying to some inward music while talking in an uncommonly loud voice.

"That fool Scotty Montgomery claims all the javelina are hunted out! The hell with him!" He thrust his head around the room toward no one in particular although Mark inclined his ear. "I'm telling you, down in South Texas they got them like bedbugs. Good grief, they got them like grapefruit, gored an old boy just last year halfway through his knee. You just got to know the scrub." He eyed me. "They hide in scrub, eat anything alive."

"They do?"

"Do you know what Scotty *said* when I told him that?"

"No, sir."

"Dom Perignon's grabbed holt of his tongue," explained Bo. "It always makes him this way." She stood looking beatific, focused with utter sobriety below the lamplight. In the back of her eyes lay a dead calm. With the smallest shrug she slipped out of her sable cloak and instantly released a personal atmosphere; Joy floated through the room, haunting corners, the undernooks of furniture, the bookshelves, as evocative as when she'd first left the house.

"*Dom Perry* my left *hinie!* I'm the only person gets holt of my tongue and I can prove it," bellowed Mr. Brune.

Her eyes shut and opened.

"Well?" Mr. Brune turned on me. "Do you? Or don't you know?"

"I don't," I answered.

No expression marred her face. When Mr. Brune spoke again she half pivoted like a waiting dancer.

"He said, 'Bullshit, Bearden, what are you, an Aggie?' Now what Aggies have to do with javelinas I've got no idea in the wide world, but I can tell you a fact about Scotty Montgomery's spleen'll make you keel over; he was in this car wreck——"

"Good night," sighed Bo, suddenly looking very tired. As if from inside a dream she dropped the cloak onto the rug and glided from the room.

Mr. Brune stopped. He frowned. The heap of huddled fur lay darkly abandoned against Persian jewel-tones, blue, red, saffron, like a pet run over by a truck.

"Hey, Dad," Mark asked. "Can I make you a cup of coffee?"

"Some people got no respect for property," Mr. Brune said, touching it with the toe of his shoe.

"Or maybe, some warm milk?" said Mark.

"You don't need to start offering that pablum to me. I'm not the one ever had to get taken care of by you," Mr. Brune barked.

Mark went very still. His look turned blank, as if he'd just been slapped.

"Oh, hell," mumbled Mr. Brune. "Hell. Heck. Well. No, son, thank you. No coffee." He frowned again, jerking on his scarf. "I'm sorry. I think I'll——I'd better just roll on off to bed." Tucking his chin into his starched collar he shuffled through the library doors, pausing only to close them awkwardly behind him.

We glanced at one another when he'd gone. After a second Mark looked away.

"Please don't start wearing it," Mark whispered late that night in bed.

"Why not?"

He'd often read my thoughts. Throughout our months together so far we had not had one single argument or even a differing opinion. Mark didn't know how to fight. It was an art no one had ever taught him. "Just don't."

The smell kept silvering through my brain like a drug. I'd already decided to ask for a bottle early for next year's birthday. "But I love it."

He lay back crossing his arms behind his head, not replying.

"I want to wear it to the Christmas Dance."

He would appear royal in his tuxedo, as I'd already noted when he'd tried it on. I imagined my cream and gilt formal, the gold pumps, the wide burgundy velvet shawl.

"Please," he murmured, and I wrapped my legs around him. A little while later he whispered, "Please, Lulu."

"Don't you want me to smell wonderful?" I asked.

"No," he muttered. "No."

Every memory corner I turn in that most electric spring of my high school years reveals banks of azaleas, jonquils clustered under the oaks, the sunlight filling landscape like clear gold in a grail. The sense of being included in a family I adored rather than the contentious clan I'd been born into seemed like one of those wooden Russian dolls that keep twisting open at the waist to surprise you with a smaller and ever more perfectly detailed replica; my happiness went on and on, seamed with ever richer intensities. At school Miriam and I spent lunchtimes learning to play the harmonica together, or practicing lines from *The Importance of Being Earnest*. Sometimes Mark and I doubledated with her and her radical activist boyfriend. Usually on weekends Perky and I went shopping, wandering for hours through the shoe department and Young Miss Designers at Neiman's. Meanwhile Bo continued to steer clear of everybody, marooned in her cool bedroom behind the book barricades, occasionally emerging long enough to give the maid the instructions for supper.

Two weeks before graduation, time seemed to start looping back on itself. On the first of September Mark would be heading north to Brown. I was going to the University of Texas. During the summer months while I vacationed in California Mark planned to bicycle through Wales. We hadn't so much as alluded to what would happen between us when the fall came. No promises. Not once had Mark said, "You should come up to see me at Halloween. Then I'll be home with you for Thanksgiving, and we won't have spent much time apart," or "I'll miss you so badly I'll probably fly down every other weekend." Not once had he asked, "How can we stand to be that far away from each other?" Or said, "I'll phone and write every single night." Or "I'll write." Each mention he made of future life at Brown seemed concerned only with what classes he would take, or what sports he might play. He spoke to me as if I, too, was of course already planning my life in Austin, as if I knew exactly where I'd be three months from now, what I'd be doing, eating, studying, wearing, who I'd be meeting. Dating.

When I caught Bo watching us over the supper table a reflective look floated deep down behind her eyes.

Two days before graduation I spent the night with another girlfriend from Drama class.

Mark had his end-of-year French Club banquet, Perky was off to her sophomore prom. We'd agreed to meet up at his house in time for lunch the next day. This girl Lori was one year younger than I, a junior. Her older brother Eddie was somebody I knew well, my age and also graduating from Saint Luke's. He'd starred as the imported male lead in a couple of Winlawn theater productions. We'd played opposite each other in *Present Laughter,* and parents and teachers often speculated on how he would probably whiz straight from Harvard to Broadway.

After Lori went to bed Eddie and I settled on the sofa in his parents' big game room, reminiscing as we balanced on the cusp of the future. That's when Eddie suggested we replay our big solo scene from *Present Laughter* together. This particular scene required the curtain to fall one second before a kiss, hitting the boards just as our lips actually touched. Sitting there we laughed until our stomachs hurt, racking our brains for old lines. When we'd finally reached the scene's end, and the gap between our mouths narrowed tighter and tighter, and our eyelids began drooping slow, slow, we moved at last into that long-impending collision behind the invisible velvet folds and then just kept right on kissing.

THE NEXT MORNING I had a car wreck. A lady ran a red light in her El Dorado and crushed my Chevy as I drove to graduation rehearsal. I hit the windshield with my head but was otherwise okay. Bo picked me up from the intersection a few blocks south of her house after the police called her, lay me down in Perky's room, phoned their family doctor who was also a close friend and asked him to drop by at lunchtime and examine my concussed skull, and went off to brew tea, leaving me in the darkened room with my swelling self-loathing.

The tinkle of silverware came from many miles away in another state. Spots crowded before my vision. "You can't allow yourself to doze off, now," Bo warned, but there was no chance of that. Seconds oozed by like hours. Perky got home from wherever she'd been and announced to me that one of my classmates had just now accidentally killed a motorcyclist as she was leaving the Winlawn parking lot after commencement rehearsal; the guy hadn't been wearing a helmet, he was still lying mangled in the road this very minute beside her Jaguar grille unless the ambulance had already arrived. All I could think was, what had *she* been up to last night? It must have been one hell of an unspeakable act to deserve that kind of payment.

When Bo brought in the sugary tea, I had to screw my

eyes straight on her without blinking in order to hide the fact that I couldn't look at her at all. "You seem a little glazed," Bo said. "I think I ought to get the doctor to come on over sooner than lunchtime."

"No, no, don't worry," I begged. "I'm not sleepy. Truly. Please don't bother him."

She frowned slightly. "I've called your folks, of course. They know you're safe and sound. Your dad asked about the damage to both cars, but I told him I didn't think that mattered a whit, compared to possible head injuries."

"Thank you," I murmured. The house seemed to be filled with molecules splitting, icebergs breaking apart, matter fracturing and diffusing: the rifle report of betrayal. Bo's fingers grazed a burn on mine as she placed the cup and saucer in them. I tried to sip. "Your forehead looks like the Matterhorn," Perky marveled; but the one I'd really crowned with horns wasn't home yet and wouldn't return for another hour. By the time he did, the doctor was examining my skull. "You just stay quiet," he said. "No talking. Mark, Bo, you folks had best leave her alone for now. She needs to rest."

It took until Saint Luke's graduation night for me to finally tell him.

Unable to say a word I walked around in a daze, stupefied by the unreality of our celebrations. Guilt disconnected me from everything. It created such a schism between what was happening and my senses that even now I only recall those rituals through an amnesiac's gauzy scrim. I don't remember my postgraduation party at all.

Mark's took place out on a ranch where we had wound up after many a night drinking and running wild and making love until two in the morning. Driving there Mark was happy, a little subdued after delivering his saluditorian speech. Occasionally he paused at stop signs to glimpse at me with concern, since the concussion appeared to have blunted both my attitude and speech capacity. Perhaps he was wrapped up, too, in his own thoughts. As we waited for a light to change he let go of the gear stick and laid his hand on mine. "Lulu," he murmured, "I love you." He looked imploringly into my face. Feebly I nodded. The whole senior class of Saint Luke's would be at the ranch, and I knew Eddie wasn't bringing a date—only the phantom of what we'd done, the invisible perfidious lover hanging on his arm.

We passed through the gate to sounds of revelry. Somebody bellowed "I Am the Walrus" and heaved water balloons from the hayloft window. Firecrackers blasted near the lake. Naked figures were jumping over a bonfire. "You boys'll burn your balls up two octaves if you don't watch out," yelled a chaperon, and I recognized Mr. Brune. Within the black trees that separated the pastures from the house, the swimming pool glowed like blue Jell-O. Drunk students fell off the porch and thrashed around in the shrubbery.

When we roared back toward Dallas in the growing light I knew it was our last night together. Parking in the driveway Mark clutched me tightly against him and then guided us toward the backdoor leading through the kitchen to his room. He was nearly sober. I was utterly so. The air cracked between us; it kept dividing and dispersing and flowing toward far directions, and as he kissed me and whispered again that he loved me I felt parts of my body drift into limbo. The bedsheets turned to water, to vapor, melting away. After we made love I told him what I'd done.

BO WAS STANDING in the kitchen measuring coffee when I limped through on my way to Perky's room. She watched me without a word. Arranged on her face lay that same tranquility which I now, at last, recognized as sadness. I stopped, turned, Mark's rejection still roiling like thunder through my brain.

"I'm sorry," I said.

Slowly Bo tipped her head to one side. Slowly, sadly, she shook it. "It's worried me, how much you two have invested in each other," she answered. "You're so young."

I breathed in and out, once, twice, three times. Through the long stretch of room I saw her receding into cool distance, far too removed for me to ever reach out and bring her near again. For a second I stood there. Then turning once more I walked to Perky's room and began packing my bag.

FOR THREE DAYS Mark didn't come out of his room. Each time I called from Bernice, Bo told me, with perfect courtesy, that Mark wouldn't talk to me, he wouldn't talk with anybody, he wasn't eating or drinking anything except water from his bathroom. There was no chance to apologize.

In July, to my surprise, he wrote me in California and said he'd see me when he got back from Wales. I could meet his plane if I wanted to. But then, one day before he was due to land at DFW, Miriam, the confidante who had sat beside me through Advanced Placement English and detention study hall and read my poetry and joined SDS, the buddy with whom I was to share an apartment when college started, confessed to me that she'd been going out with him the whole two months I'd stayed in Los Angeles. And that she too was actually scheduled to meet his plane, and perhaps I'd misunderstood, made a mistake. Misread Mark's letter. His word.

"He told me you two were finished," she said.

"Does Bo know this?" was all I could think of in my agony to say.

"Well—yes," said Miriam. "She does."

Then she stared down into her paper cup, pressed her lips together, and sighed. "But she's got nothing to do with it. In fact—look, I'm sorry to tell you this, Lulu, I know how much you like her, but she's kind of become my mentor."

SOMETIMES, TREATIE, IT's felt like no thing has cohered since.

1974: The Budgeteer

I don't trust that any more than I trust a mother-in-law's love.
——SEAN PENN

When I got married halfway through my sophomore spring in college I was on the rebound.

I suppose it won't hurt to tell this now, Treatie, but I cringe when I recall how glibly I married my first husband while feeling deeply and permanently in love with someone else. Ted didn't realize it at the time, of course; it would never have entered his noggin that throughout the months of our passionate interludes I was deep down distracted, my heart flapping like torn cardboard.

During our freshman fall semester Ted and I had met in a philosophy seminar, and drunk coffee in the Student Union and fooled around somewhat, as was my wont. The truth was that throughout that freshman year I docked at many an island down many a fjord, a ready explorer of foreign ports; by May, Miriam was suggesting that I might consider keeping a tally. But it was simple. The one I'd really fallen for wasn't yet available and I've never liked wasting valuable educational opportunities. The whole University soccer team was out there roaming at large like a mobile atlas of Central and South America—it seemed wonderful how so many countries just happened to be contained under one set of jerseys. Other continents lurked in the science and business departments, alongside the hippies reeking of patchouli and fraternity boys in their Weejuns, their ironed Levis and Tony Lamas. Engineering students from Biafra, herpetologists from Bombay, film majors from New Hampshire: Love's geography is a riveting subject while you're studying it. My voyages through its rivers and seas and even the stagnant swamps could turn this little travelogue into an encyclopedia.

But by sophomore year I'd had my heart seriously broken.

Here's what I read in my Medieval Literature class from a treatise on courtly love.

The Ten Symptoms of Unrequited Love:

1. Blushing
2. Trembling
3. Swooning
4. Inability to eat
5. Constant Preoccupation with the Unattainable Beloved
6. Sleeplessness and/or Bad Dreams
7. Palpitations
8. Vomiting

Lulu, I said to myself: let that be a lesson to you.

So when Ted and I remet at the Student Union hamburger grill in September we took one look at each other, went out on two dates, and decided in a trice that what the hell, we may as well set up house.

TREATIE: SEX IS not a tool to get liberated with. Back then we didn't yet know this, us staunch foot soldiers of the sexual revolution, although of course the older generation had drilled us zealously all the way through boot camp. Here's what they yelled: sex is a sin unless you're married! Here's what I say: sex is a powder keg. I don't believe I stated this very clearly or at all on that day you told me you'd already lost your innocence but I should have, I should have howled it at the moon and blazoned it on the sky; this history demonstrates it now as ineluctably as an algebra equation. Sex will blow you and everybody to Kingdom Come if you're not careful. It'll shred children, maim lives, disintegrate homes, and I'm not just talking the obvious diseases. Only very deft, sure operatives should be licensed to handle it. And then only in arranged marriages.

And for me the fuse mechanism tripped into place the instant I slept with anybody.

Thus the following fall, when my parents found out Ted and I were living together, all hell broke loose.

"DON'T WORRY! I won't let you support a morality you don't agree with. I'm moving out!" I yelled at my father at the start of Christmas vacation.

"You're not moving out. I'm throwing you out!" he said.

"Didn't you *know* your father would be upset when he found out what you were doing? Didn't you *know?*" cried my mother in her emergency voice.

"Why don't you come down to Bay City with me and have a little holiday and meet my parents?" said Ted.

Which is how, under twinkling lights and spruce boughs in an apartment scented with fruitcake, I met The Budgeteer.

IF THE PROVERB is true that a man marries his mother, then either I'm Proteus or I know a tankerload of adopted male orphans. Actually, you know, I've come to apprehend that the proverb is only partly true: a man merely marries an *aspect* of his mother, some facet of her whole being that he recognizes on an obscure level in another woman. But even so, what chord could I possibly have strummed in your father?

Setting down our backpacks before the front door with the brass knocker engraved *The Vonicks — Hans and Hazel* in curly Gothic letters, Ted said, "Our name used to be Von Eyck. My grandfather changed it during World War I when the people up in Vermont where he'd immigrated to mistook him for a German."

"He wasn't German?"

"No, Dutch."

"What did they do?" I felt nervous and very sweaty. Although we'd arrived on December 21 the Gulf city steamed like a fricassee pot.

"They pelted him with dinner rolls and rotten tomatoes."

"*New Englanders* did that?"

"I guess they thought he looked undernourished. It beat rocks."

"Hi there!" The door opened suddenly, and a woman with gilded hair set in stiff bouffant waves stood beaming inside a crisp cotton shirtwaist dress. From her earlobes dangled enameled Christmas wreath earrings with doves perched on top. "Ted! Long time no see." She spoke so matter-of-factly that I figured she must be a family friend. "Come right in, I believe everything's almost ready to eat."

Ted crooked his customary ironic smile and patted her shoulder hello. "This is Lulu."

"Hi," I said. The shoulder looked sturdy.

"Well, hi, Lulu. Come right in. I'm Ted's Mom Hazel." She sounded Northern. The words she spoke were barbed on the ends with consonants. A blonde, I thought bravely. Stepping aside, she propped the door wide open with a body that seemed as square and compact as a milk carton pinched in the middle. Her grin was without nuance or variance, full of nice big white teeth. "How was the weather on the trip down?"

"Okay. A little icy out of Huntsville, but of course things heated up once we got nearer to here," said Ted.

"I'm glad to meet you," I said, and held out a clammy hand.

"That's great. You can put your suitcase in the spare room. Dinner's nearly on the table. I've cooked a real genuine Switzer-Deutsch meal tonight straight out of Switzerland, like you always love, Ted—sauerkraut, spaetzle —those are little tiny potato dumplings—" she said brightly to me, "sauerbraten, Wiener schnitzel, and two different desserts—apfelkuchen and Black Forest torte with whipped cream on top. Hans, the kids are here!" She pronounced his name like the appendage. As she bustled us through the living room into the hallway her energy already daunted me, crackling with frankness as it was. In my draggled Indian cotton dress with my hair frizzing like tumbleweed in the humidity I felt unbearably sloppy.

"I have to go check the spaetzle, I don't want it to boil over," she said, and sprinted back to the kitchen.

"Is she German?" I whispered to Ted.

"No. She's Nebraskan. Why?"

"Well—I mean, isn't all that food—"

"Hi, hi, hi!" said Mr. Vonick, ambling out of the master bedroom at the rear. He stuck his hand out for Ted to shake.

"Hey, Dad."

"You made it. Good weather on the road down? How's your mileage?"

"Not great. I've probably done about two miles per gallon during exam week. My percolater's running a little sluggish though. That's filling up with Maryland Club; I do better on Maxwell House."

"Haw haw!" Mr. Vonick barked. His hooked, ironic smile, I noticed, was an uncanny mirror of his son's.

"No, seriously—the old bug's getting about twenty-two per in the city, and better on the highway. Which isn't too bad since they say we have a gas shortage on the way."

"I see. No, that's not too bad," Mr. Vonick nodded. "We've been stockpiling a little. Just some extra cans stowed out in the boatshed at the marina."

"This is Lulu, by the way."

Mr. Vonick turned languidly and thrust his hand out toward me. "Hi, there, how are you?" It felt large and square and dry. He had a Yankee accent also, but not so curled around the edges.

"Fine, thanks. Nice to meet you."

His grin widened with a salesman's reflex while his eyes scanned me over as if sighting down a pool cue.

"Haven't you two washed up yet? Dinner's going to get cold," warned Mrs. Vonick breezily from the living room. "Hans, you quit holding them up."

"Allow me to untie your ropes and go put away my forty-five," murmured Mr. Vonick confidentially through the side of his mouth, and sidled off down the hall.

I turned to Ted. Throughout the year and a half that people had now been confusing us as brother and sister and exclaiming over how alike we looked—auburn shoulder-length hair, brown eyes, olive coloring, thin faces, cheekbone angles——I'd felt other likenesses beneath the skin much more disturbing. Ours was a kinship I'd recognized by gut. Peering at the debonair nineteen-year-old whom I'd known on campus as a clever poet, my philosophy classmate, a boy so deft in gentle sarcasm that you could call him a postmodernist ahead of his time, the Thomas Pynchon fan, I saw I was now in alien territory.

"They don't like me, do they?" I whispered. "Do they?" He smiled down into my face, shut the guest-room door, and kissed me.

"How's the food at that student cafeteria?" asked Hazel. I glanced furtively to Ted: Had he or had he not told them that we were now living together? If they were still in the dark, how would they react once dawn broke? And most especially, did Hazel realize I was cooking a lot of his meals?

"I could starve if I hadn't been willing to lower my standards to rock bottom," he said and piled more sauerbraten on his plate. "You've just kept my expectations too high, Mom."

"Oh, pish tosh," laughed Hazel.

"Your Christmas decorations are really nice." The fake Christmas tree looked 14 karat in all-gold balls and gold tinsel. Fake pine boughs garnished the crystal chandelier, as well as the front door lintel, the colonial maple table, and the small wet bar. Each branch burned with tiny red lights blinking like forest animal eyes. On the coffee table, next to a kidney-shaped ashtray with three little cigarette rests, sat a gingerbread house iced in white, with two little figures standing on the sugar-cube yard, one wearing a marshmallow skirt, and *The Vonicks* scrawled in red icing above the door.

"Thank you. I always do enjoy decorating the house. Yesterday I put that mug tree together to hang my Peanuts mug collection on. Every year the girls at the office give me a new mug for Christmas and this year the girl that drew my name gave me the tree instead which I had to assemble, which was a lot of fun since Hans is usually the wood handyman around here." She pointed at the wet bar where sure enough the painted mug tree stood tagged in mistletoe. "I only have three more little branches to fill. It's kind of a hobby."

"Ah," I nodded. "What kind of office do you work in?"

"I manage the secretarial pool for an insurance firm. Bay City Fire and Life."

"Hazel is the nerve center," said Hans, once again in that faintly derisive tone that was beginning to sound habitual, as if even the simplest acknowledgment needed clarifying.

"Nerve center!" Hazel scoffed.

"That's only what the vice president calls her." He winked.

"Oh, pooh. You're not going to start quoting him, he's always so full of baloney."

"Down at good old Bay City Liar and Strife," he said. "The nerve center for fifty thousand hurricane policies. Run by one head tornado."

"Now, don't listen to him," she turned gaily to me.

"We could start calling you N. C.," said Ted. "Or Twister."

"Oh, shush. Have some more Wiener schniztel and cucumbers." Swiftly she reached over to mop up the juice that Ted was dripping on his green-and-red plaid placemat.

"So, Lulu, what's your major?" asked Hans.

"The Classics," I said.

"Which classics are those?"

"Um, well, you know, Greek and Roman literature. I was a psychology major the first semester of freshman year. Then I changed to English Lit. for a little while. This fall I've been doing Philosophy, but I'm switching to Classical Studies in January."

"Oh, well, my, that's quite a run, isn't it?" said Hazel.

"Around a mighty big block," said Hans.

"Our older son Brian, he was always totally sure of what he was going to do. He went straight into his Accounting major his very first semester at Texas A & M and whipped right on through and got his Master's in Business and then got hired by a good firm and set up his office, but Ted's sister Val just fiddled around and fiddled around, didn't she, Hans? and didn't get herself straightened out until freshman summer school into her P.E. major when we told her she had to decide on something for good or else we wouldn't pay her tuition." She tidied the remains of the sauerkraut into a hill in the center of the bowl, trimming the stragglers with the spoon's edge.

"I guess I'm just curious," I said.

"Well, that's a good thing. I'm real curious myself." She lifted her eyes from the sauerkraut and smiled.

"I WANT TO go Christmas shopping tomorrow morning for my parents," Ted said when he was saying good night in the guest room before going on to his own bed.

"What're you going to buy them?"

"Some cheese."

I paused nonplussed. "Do you have any special cheese in mind?"

"I figured we could go to the supermarket delicatessen and pick out an unusual kind. You can help."

"Your mom seems really nice." She seemed like the most literal person I'd ever met. I was still puzzling out just how the literalness wound up rendering her so opaque.

"Um—are you two very close?"

"Close?"

"I mean, do you two have much, um, contact between each other?"

"Well, you already know I report in to her every Sunday on the phone."

"No, I mean—like, you didn't hug or kiss when we got here." I paused delicately, searchingly.

He pondered. "She doesn't do stuff like that."

"She doesn't? What does she do, then?"

"I don't know."

"You must have some clue. She's your mother."

He frowned, thinking back. "Once when we were little, I remember my sister Val got upset and accused Mom of not loving us. Mom just told her to hush and said she'd rather show it by baking cookies or cherry pie."

"Oh, so then, I guess that dinner was a giant 'I'm very glad to see you, Ted.'"

"It will be once she finishes doing all the laundry and mending I brought down and presses my shirts and under-wear," he said lightly.

IT WAS ON Christmas Eve after we'd eaten an early dinner with Ted's extended family that Ted and I decided to go see a movie. *The Go-Between* was showing at a neighborhood mall. The theater turned out to be nearly empty; one soli-tary old man sat in the back row honking and wringing his nostrils with a fruity squelch from the very first strains of the theme music to the closing bars. By then Ted and I were both crying, too. We held hands. We didn't get up until the credits had finished rolling and the old man left.

Out in the parking lot as he unlocked the Beetle, Ted said, "I know what we might could do about this argument you're having with your parents."

"What?"

"Get married."

". . . *Married?*" A small galvanic tremor like the spurt from an electric fence shot through me.

"Well, yeah, sure," he said. "Why not? It's a practical so-lution."

I stared. His face looked blue and cadaverous under the mercury vapor streetlight; his eyes were dark, enigmatic, plummy with silver gleams. I still felt steeped in a marsh of tears. Transferred grief clogged my throat. My sinuses flooded again. I said, "Okay."

"Great." He leaned over, pulling me into his arms. I heard the VW keys tinkle onto the asphalt. And through the astonishment, through the craziness and unreality and sweet alliance I felt as he kissed me, I thought, Well, I'm never going to fall in love again the way I did before. So I may as well settle for friendship.

WE TIED THE knot that spring. The whole Brune family attended the afternoon wedding, with Perky in orange and green Ungaro and Bo in a navy and white Oscar de la Renta, a creamy rose in her chignon. The groom's mother wore long pastel-yellow flower-sprigged polyester—uncreasable no matter what happens, she said. Most of the guests milled around my parents' gardens and front lawn looking oddly overdressed, waiting for the ceremony to begin. It was a morning wedding. Miriam was to serve the punch at the reception. Mark even came up to my room after I'd already climbed into my gown. He helped button me up while the bridesmaids and friends hung out guzzling champagne they'd smuggled upstairs, inhaling lines of coke from my hand mirror, cracking bad jokes, and making polite excuses when my mother knocked in a panic because we were running so late. "Lulu, honey?" she called softly, piteously. "Can't I please come in?"

"Hard to believe you're doing this," Mark murmured. "Boy, Lulu. I sure hope you'll be happy."

It was a very different scene from my sister Dyllis's wedding eight years earlier. Believe me.

THE SECOND HALF of our short honeymoon we spent in Galveston and then Bay City. There, Hazel and I started really getting to know one another.

"I'll tell you a great little gimmick. When you measure detergent into the washing machine it's much better to cut the amount they recommend by half. That way you don't wind up with clothes all yellow and stiff from too much since they're always trying to get you to use it up fast and buy more."

"Okay," I said, carelessly dashing soap powder straight from the box into the tub as usual until I saw her wince.

"What kind of detergent does your mother use?" she forged on.

"Um—well. Tide?" I had no idea.

"That's an okay brand. It all depends on what's on special though. If you whiz through the specials you can check them against a handy little list you can carry around in your purse—which ones work best on grass stains, which ones work in cold water, which is a good grease solvent, which eats up chocolate sauce. I have a list I'll give you if you want. How about fabric softener? For that I always stick to the same one." She hefted the bottle to show me.

"I think Mom uses that one, too." As far as I knew fabric softener was a concept strictly from a TV commercial.

"You'll probably want to see what blends best with

Austin's city water supply. I believe it's hard if I remember right. Lots of minerals? Or am I confusing it in my silly old head with San Antonio when we went there that time on vacation and I had to readjust for the difference?"

"Oh, soft, I think," I said earnestly.

"Wait. What are you—are you putting Ted's jeans in with his underwear?"

I glanced at the boxer shorts in my hand, scarlet lips on a black background. Then I peeked into the tub, already slathered in suds. "Well—um. They're both darks," I weakly observed.

"That T-shirt isn't."

I looked down. "No. It's not." Like a criminal I tightened my clutch on Ted's spanking new, white Fruit-of-the-Loom.

"Well, anyhow, thank goodness we caught it in time. *That* might have turned into a real disaster!" She chuckled.

"But all those jeans in there are old. Faded."

Reaching over she carefully removed it from my hand. "You never know when something's finally going to decide to bleed."

Then she hoisted up the laundry basket and cheerfully began to sort through the lace and silk lingerie of my trousseau lying all jumbled in nuptial union with Ted's lumberjack shirts, while I stood awestruck, watching the decisive thrust of true common sense.

"I THINK THAT we should all maybe sit down and thrash through how you're going to control your finances now," said Hazel during a Sunday check-up call. "Really we needed to before the wedding, but we didn't like butting in, except I haven't heard how much Lulu's parents are helping out if they're not just matching us like we discussed or how you're managing your household accounts or anything, so we thought maybe you could stand a little advice."

"Hers, she means," said Hans on the extension.

"Well, I do enjoy working with numbers. It's easy when you get the hang of them and balancing your checkbook every day can give tons of satisfaction, and you know I've always said the best times of our marriage were when Hans and I were just starting out and we had to watch every penny, which just wound up bringing us so much closer together." From the proximity of the shared receiver I could feel Ted's lips mouthing the words in unison on my ear: so much closer!

"What is this, *American Bandstand*?" I whispered. Our breaths mingled erotically over the mouthpiece.

"Old story," he mouthed back and sucked my lower lip gently in between his teeth.

"We lived in a very small very cheap apartment for one thing," Hazel went on. "Remember that, Hans? It was so cute and we decorated it on a shoestring——"

"With double knots," Hans said distantly.

"——and we cooked good cheap meals like Vienna sausage pigs-in-a-blanket and Spam hash, which really isn't so bad if you broil pineapple slices on top——I can give you some great recipes, Lulu——and that was our little nest, which you might want to think about since you're paying such a high rent for that house close to campus and I realize it must shave into your monthly allowance something terrible, unless Lulu's parents are maybe contributing in ways we don't already know about."

Ted looked at me. "No, they're not," I answered.

"Well, I hear there's a really good setup with married student housing out near the lake——"

I made a face. Ted stuck out his tongue. It grazed my chin and then wound sinuously upward.

"——very low rent. So, would you like any help on anything?"

She knew, I thought.

Ted raised his brows. Vigorously I shook my head. He nodded.

"Mom, thanks very much. I think we'll have to call you back after we've thought about it."

"*Ted!*" I whispered.

"Well, if you're sure," she said.

Hazel knew that I had no more notion of how to manage money her way than I did how to build a nuclear missile. She could probably smell it.

"Good-bye," we said. "Talk to you next week." We hung up the phone, giggling like lunatics, and then ran into the bedroom, where I preferred not to recall what I then regarded as his diplomatic compromise.

"ONE REAL LIFESAVER in an emergency is to keep a loaf of plain bread in your freezer. It'll make a great ice pack that won't sit too heavy on a sprain," said Hazel. "Oh, and by the way, always remember that if you and Ted ever do have babies you don't need to buy a big clunky sterilizer that uses up a lot of extra electricity because you can sterilize bottles perfectly well in the dishwasher. Now I know that that's a long time off, but it's just a little tip to have handy when the time comes."

"Thanks." We pushed our carts down the supermarket aisle in what I thought of as the bridal shuffle, the stroll wives were taking at that moment all over America in an endless, mundane reenactment of their day of destiny. "What made you think of that?" I asked.

"Looking at those Playtex nursers." She pointed to the display. "Brian and Lynn tried them out and couldn't get them to work worth a durn. The best thing they turned out to be was disposable."

I studied the plastic liners. They looked like space-age socks. "Weird to think that babies could drink out of those."

"Oh, it's a real good idea. A colicky baby with air bubbles can leave you a wreck, they're the death of many a good night's sleep. Make sure you vacuum all your upholstery real well also in case the colic's an allergic reaction to dust mites since they don't know what really causes it." She paused to read a label. "Ted had asthma."

"He told me." The tiny kitchenette in our married students' barracks flashed through my mind, with its prewar pig-iron sink. Dishwasher?

"He used to wheeze and turn blue every time I had the girls over for bridge."

I tried to picture Ted turning blue. Did people really vacuum furniture? Did my mother, when I wasn't looking?

"What did you do?"

"Oh, I rushed him to the hospital, of course. Later on I figured out that if I held bridge parties during school hours he'd come home fine. I always did everything for him, though, like spread up his bed and polish his shoes, just to make sure nothing would tip him into an attack. But I pretty much did that for all the kids until they went away to college."

"What about breast-feeding?" I asked.

"You mean . . . nursing?"

She turned to me with lightning incredulity.

"Yes. It gives the baby more immunities to allergies and stuff."

"Oh, well. If that kind of faddish stuff is what you'd want to go in for." Craning over to peruse the ingredients on a can of formula she fingered a pair of rubber pants and then wheeled ahead. "I like things clean and modern myself," she added.

"Natural childbirth sounds interesting," I ventured.

"Well, heck, isn't all childbirth natural?"

"I mean, Lamaze classes. No anesthetic. Like people are starting to do lately. And maybe—giving birth at home."

"At home!" She braked her cart, astonished. "How in the world could somebody have a baby at home?"

I paused, groping. "Well, the husband helps out, coaching with the breathing. And you have everything ready for when the contractions begin—"

"Oh my heavens, I would rather have died than let Hans watch our children getting born! He would have been totally hopeless and probably would have fainted dead away. Besides, no one can have a baby at home."

"Why?"

"Because doctors don't make house calls anymore."

Firmly she rolled the cart forward and selected a translucent tablet of toilet freshener cached in its little wire frame.

I watched her. Years of brazen rebellion with my own parents, a record of mutiny in the Winfield dorm, plus three formal appearances before the headmaster, and in the presence of this woman I found myself cowed. "There could—can be other ways," I said.

"Oh, well. It doesn't matter anyhow, it's so far in the future."

"I guess."

She smiled, but already I felt myself climbing on to that wild bucking horse that was going to carry me through the next three years.

"How about we pick up some cinnamon rolls for breakfast in the morning? You two don't come to visit that often, which was why it was good I had the frozen bread ready for lunch. We can have something besides eggs once in a while," she said, and really I could see that she meant well—she was warm-hearted, she was nurturing, and her literalness might simply be not only a necessary self-defense, but her sole means of winning in a trick-ridden, complex world.

"Hazel?"

"Yes."

"I'm six weeks pregnant."

And that was how, Treatie, I told your grandmother you were on your way.

I SHOULDN'T HAVE done it. I knew the instant I saw her stunned face I should have waited until nighttime when we could have announced it together. We'd driven down to Bay City especially for this. It was unfair, a swipe on your father. As she stood there speechless with that frozen look in her blue eyes, I thought, Uh-oh.

It took a whole half minute for her to crank up again. The opacity by that time was complete.

"Well, goodness," she said evenly, "you're going to have to replan your schedules, aren't you?"

I nodded.

"School semesters, Ted's job on the side as a teacher's assistant, your job in that clothing shop—"

"That's no problem," I reassured her hastily. "I only got it because I'd never had a paying job before. You know, for independence."

"—your degree calendars," she plowed on. "How you'll juggle your budget. I guess it's too late to apply for a medical-insurance clause that will cover this."

"I don't know."

"Yes, I can see that. That you don't, I mean." She didn't say it bitterly. She didn't even say it with reproof. Her bright pragmatism rang faultless.

"But of course, it *is* too late. So we'll just have to see what-all we can work out. Maybe between your parents and us Vonicks we can loan you both a lump sum for the hospital and the prenatal bills, and then meanwhile—" She stopped. "My goodness!" She looked shaken. "I'm going to have another grandchild!"

"Yes," I said.

The jarred effect changed slowly, like a light fanning down her features, bathing them in a stronger glow. Already your determination to get conceived and born was a powerful force, first defeating the obstacles we'd planted in your path, now rerouting all our futures.

"Well!" she said at last. "The first thing I'll do is buy you two a dehumidifier. I know a great store to get a discount."

I'LL TELL YOU now, Treatie: I hadn't intended to get pregnant with you. We'd used birth control, in fact a double precaution, hedging our bets. We were both too young, halfway through college. Only twenty. We had long lives in front of us.

How could I have guessed how much I'd love it?

"I thought you-all wanted to buy a sailboat and go cruise around the Greek Islands when you finish earning your BA's," Hazel said while we loaded the car.

"We do," I replied, closing the trunk on the bags of groceries. I slid onto the sticky vinyl seat. My bare thighs under my cutoffs smacked together with a sucking sound. Heat waves quivered above the asphalt in silvery mirages.

"How do you possibly imagine or hope to fulfill a dream like that if you have a toddler by then?"

"We could take him with us," I said.

"Oh, pish tosh!"

So of course that was what we planned to do.

You were born in the middle of an ice storm.

Stalactites hung from the trees. Crystals coated the lawns and roofs like sugar grains. All the streets looked black but glistened with a treacherous rind that made tires skid out of control. Everyone had been warned to stay indoors; already seven major pileups had stopped traffic on I-35, and more were expected as the morning progressed. The center of the state was a mess.

Yet after breakfast, when I opened the front door of our apartment, the sunlight struck my face and birdsong sliced the brilliant air. The rest of the city seemed to lie empty, silenced by a transfiguration.

"I'll see you late this afternoon," said Ted as he kissed me good-bye. "Unless you want to go ice-skating."

"Did the Germans give the Hindenburg sled runners?"

He patted my huge stomach and fished out his keys. "If you need anything, phone my mom."

I laughed.

You were two weeks late, Treatie. My doctor had already planned to induce labor the next day. I was packed and ready. As the morning wore on I thought about what an ironic turn it would be if you decided to go ahead and come on your own, considering that I sat stranded four miles from the hospital, your father had taken the car to school, and taxis were out of service until the thaw. So when I felt the first contraction as I struggled up from the bath I recognized it as of course inevitable: you were in fact a true male Vonick.

Which must have been why, when I reached for the phone at the third cramp, I automatically started dialing Bay City instead of Bernice.

"Hi, Hazel," I said when she answered.

"Well hi there! How's the weather?"

"Oh, sharp. It looks like your Christmas decorations." This year she'd gone in for a snow theme and flocked everything white.

"Do you know what time it is? This is peak hour for phone rates," she said. "I'm glad to hear from you but you might would rather call back this evening after five and save yourselves some money."

"I think we'll be busy then."

"Oh, you-all have plans? Considering your condition shouldn't you maybe be staying home until the doctor starts you up tomor—"

"I'm in labor," I said.

"Oh." She went quiet. "Oh, well, then. In that case, I guess the long distance is okay."

"Okay," I said. I felt peaceful. Elated. I felt filled with a growing sense of anticipation.

"How are you?" she asked.

"I'm okay."

"How far along is the labor?"

"I don't know. It's okay." I felt brainless.

"What does Ted say? Can he time it on his watch?"

"He's not here."

"Oh. He's not? Oh my goodness, he's out? In this weather? The insurance I picked out for him won't cover a thing if he gets into a freak accident, it doesn't provide for acts of God. Where's he gone?"

"He's registering for spring semester classes."

"He's out of touch?" she asked.

"Yes."

"Oh, I see. My. Well. It'll be all right. You've already phoned the doctor, I'm sure, haven't you, and explained the situation so he'll be sending the ambulance and so forth. How many pains have you had so far?"

"Three, I think. Maybe four."

"Are they bad?"

"They're okay. They're kind of interesting, to tell you the truth." Unique, I thought. They were unique. I hadn't known anything quite like them before—the seizure in the small of the back, the iron band around the pelvic girdle, tightening, tightening, squeezing, loosening, melting away. The light-headedness. They intrigued me.

"Well, that's good. At least you're not in real discomfort." She sounded doubtful.

"Not exactly," I agreed.

"Okay then, now what are you supposed to do? In this newfangled natural childbirth Lamaze thing you and Ted have been practicing?"

"I'm supposed to breathe in rhythm. The first stage

goes like thi—" But suddenly I was gripped by a contrac-tion so fierce that it paralyzed me.

"Just slow? Or real quiet? I didn't hear you, can you do it again?"

"Ahh—ah—*ah*—"

"Oh, well, my goodness, that sounds just like my old labors. Maybe this Lamaze business isn't so different from what I did after all."

"—*Aiee!*" I yelled.

". . . Lulu?" Her voice came dimly. She sounded like she spoke from a grotto submerged under a deep lagoon. "Are you all right?"

"No."

"You're not."

"I think it's starting now," I gasped.

"It already did, didn't it?"

"Hard, I mean."

"Oh. So that wasn't part of your breathing classes?"

"Nuh," I whispered. For the first time I felt a glove of cold sweat on my forehead.

"Okay, then here's what you have to do. Quick, before the next one comes you show me how it sounds, the way Ted has been training to coach you. Make the breathing. Breathe."

"Okay." Fear had arrived; it was here now, but it floated below the peace and immediacy of the moment. Never has a moment felt so inescapable.

"Ha-aah. Ha-*aah!*" I said.

"Ha-aah," said Hazel. "I've got it. Now listen to me. . . ."

The next contraction waved over on its steely tide.

"Are you listening, Lulu?"

"Yuhh—"

"Breathe. Ha-ah . . . uh-*ha-aah* . . ." And she saw me through the next seven contractions, as I began to build toward the third and final stage of labor, transition.

At last she said, "Okay. Listen. The ambulance should have gotten there by now. It's time to call the doctor back and see when it's going to show up."

"Nuhh," I said.

"Lulu? I said I think you need to hang up now and ask the doctor if he can hurry the ambulance up. Maybe it's gotten involved in some kind of tailspin on all that i—"

"No. I can't." The swell was mounting. I could feel the tension grab down my spine, through the armpits and breasts, my solar plexus.

"Lulu, you have to. The doctor's got to come get you himself if there's been any kind of trouble on the roa—"

"I can't hang up," I gasped. "Stay there. Please stay there, please."

"Ha-ah," she said, encouragingly, "ha-aahhhh."

"I didn't phone the doctor," I said when it was over.

"What?" She sounded blank.

"I just picked up the phone and called you for some reason. I didn't think to call him. Ted was going to do that when the time came." The next wave was just gathering to break.

"Oh my Lord. Hang up. Hang up and call *now*. Call him. Or better yet, tell me his number."

"I can't," I whispered, "I can't hang up," and realized

then that the receiver was clutched so tightly in my hand that white ridged my knuckles. "Don't hang up," I cried, and the wave broke.

"Ha-aah—ha-ah—" she said.

"Now we've got to change to Ha! ha! *puh!*" I said when I could speak again.

"Okay. Get ready. Now start: Ha! ha! *puh!* Ha, ha, *puh!*" Without missing a beat, without another word of ambulance, she swanned smoothly straight into the home stretch.

"I'm going to cuss," I said after a while. "God*damm*it! God*dammit!*"

"That's okay. Ha, ha, PUH!"

"God hell dammit! *Hell!*" I screamed.

"Ha, ha—"

"Hi," said Ted, opening the front door. "I forgot my wallet. Can you believe it?"

"*PUH!*" I yelled in triumph.

"Ted! Come to the phone, quick," cried Hazel through the earpiece all the way from Bay City. "Take the phone!"

"Oh, wow. You're in labor," said Ted.

"Get me to the hospital," I panted like a dog.

"Ted—" called Hazel.

"Okay. Who's on the phone?"

"Your mother."

"Oh. Hi, Mom." He wrested the receiver from my fingers and spoke directly into it. "We're a little busy here right now. Can I call you back later? Okay, thanks. Bye." And only then did his face begin to blench.

We did make it to the hospital in time, after all. You were born twenty minutes later.

YOUR VERY FIRST portrait was snapped by your grandmother in our living room on her brand-new Polaroid camera.

You were six days old. She'd kept the camera packed in its unopened box until she and Hans drove up from Houston to our apartment, despite the curiosity that must have been goading her like a mosquito trapped alongside her in a shower stall. Aiming the virgin lens at her new grandson filled her blue eyes with an unearthly light. "I've always wanted one of these gadgets," she chuckled. Then the flash burst upon you like a distillation of all our joy, and together we watched, transfixed, as the slip whirred from the camera's lip, and then slowly, slowly, second by second, the first imprint of your little arms and legs bloomed against the watery opal surface. The picture was in black and white. "Oh, look, he looks just like Winston Churchill," said Hazel. "Now I *think* you're supposed to cock this little lever here, or maybe that's the timer for when you run around to get in the photo yourself—" She held the camera at this angle and that, pursuing its secrets with her eyes. She wiggled a knob. A beeper buzzed. You, the baby, juddered from your sleep and placidly began to mew.

"Oh. Wait," said Hazel, setting the camera on the couch and hopping up. "I brought this."

Bustling to the door she scooped up a large cloth bag

with presents poking from its mouth, wrapped in silver, pink, and blue. Her arm shot into the depths and swished around, rustling, clanking. "Here it is," she smiled and held out a package.

"But——" I stared in dismay at the glass bottle still attached to its cardboard placard, the row of rubber nipples under their plastic dome.

"All ready to go. I brought the formula. You can just pour it straight from the can these days, you don't even have to mix it, and we can warm it in a jiffy in a pot of water on the stove and then I'll show you how to check the temperature on your elbow's inside."

"But I'm br—I'm nursing him." Anger climbed through my nervous system, converting directly from the dismay like starch transmuting to sugar. "I thought Ted already told you." Swiveling, I cradled you close and glared at Ted.

"Oh, he told me," said Hazel blithely, "don't worry, he'll always do what you tell him to. He's been real good that way his whole life. I didn't have *near* the trouble with him that I had with Val—of course middle children are almost always the worst, real tough and disobedient when they feel like it, so I guess she was typical."

You contracted and stretched in my arms. Your eyelids puckered.

The truth of what she'd said about Ted suddenly struck home and sank acridly through my mind. It was her will, her drive, that provided him with whatever spine he had.

"My goodness, he's so big for his age, isn't he? Ten pounds and nine ounces at birth. He must already be eating a lot; that's what happens when they're late, they get huge appetites. Ted told us about that man at the hospital nursery window when he was looking at Tristan through the glass who said, 'Just look at *that* baby. He must be a good three months old. Do you suppose he's one of those you read about in the newspaper whose mother sneaked out the hospital and abandoned him to the county?' Of course Ted put him in his place real quick, didn't you, Ted?" She laughed with familial pride. "I'll go get this ready—"

"No!" I yelled. The overridden rage broke free. "*I am breast-feeding him!*"

Hazel stopped. Her arms fell to her sides, her dangling hands full of equipment.

"But—I know," she said, bewildered. "That's the best thing, I've already been reading up on it."

Ted stood still halfway across the room. He looked chiseled in wood, like a cigar-store Indian. His gaze slewed toward a neutral ground.

"All the immunities they've discovered he gets from breast milk, and the closeness with the mother—it's the latest scientific findings," she turned to Hans to explain. The hurt I felt I perceived in her eye stung me to frenzy.

"We don't *need* bottles!" I wailed.

"Of course you don't," she said reasonably. "But I do."

"*What for?*"

"How else can I get to feed my grandbaby and love him?" she said, and her air of helpless imploring wrung me like General Lee's comportment at Appomattox.

IT TURNED OUT that you were not a colicky baby.

One month after birth you slept through the night for the first time, and you continued to do so every night for the next thirteen years. You grew like an angel, stocky and happy, luminous with curiosity; you observed the world around you with the benignity of a Buddha. It wasn't long before I had to give you cereal and mashed banana alongside my milk just to fill you up. Our apartment's terrarium atmosphere lulled us both with its closed peace, enhanced no doubt by the air-conditioning. You hardly ever cried. You had a fine sense of humor.

One morning when you were three weeks old I was feeding you breakfast when you suddenly pulled away from my breast and looked me in the eye.

"What is it?" I said. "Are you not hungry?"

The look kept on. You didn't smile or frown; you just gazed.

"Taking a little break?" I asked, kissing the top of your head and rocking the chair gently. Your biscuity smell filled the air, your downy hair brushed my lips. But your eye followed mine. Slowly I stopped. There was a force in your look so calm and direct, so purposeful, that it overwhelmed all other thoughts and preoccupations. It was the most important thing in the world, and the room drew down toward its center.

Here's what you need to know, you said.

I am I, you said to me. I am separate from you.

We are together. Absolute. But we're not the same.

"Yes," I whispered, "yes," and met your liquid eyes, and held you tightly against my heart.

MY PARENTS CONSIDERED you the best thing I'd ever achieved.

For the next few months your Vonick grandparents didn't try to come to Austin to visit, which was just as well. Occasionally we drove to Bay City, lumbering toward the Gulf in our creaky little VW with your infant seat strapped in the backseat. Everybody commented on your good disposition. Even when you were hungry you just made a few burbling noises.

That morning of your annunciation we seemed to have settled something, and I generally swam through my dreamlike maternity to meet your needs before you had to voice them. I could hardly remember what it had been like to attend classes. I cooked meat loaf and spaghetti, and took up desultory oil painting. Sometimes I caught myself looking in the mirror at the doughy body left over from my stunningly grandiose pregnancy—your birth weight had only accounted for one-eighth of my total weight gain—and wondered who that stranger could be and what connection she bore to my former life, but such twinges got smothered in the slumberous passage of the spring days.

In Bay City things always seemed brisker. Your Grandmother Hazel praised your smartness; your Grandfather Hans admired your strength. While still in the hospital nursery you'd flipped right over all by yourself, but the nurses called it a fluke—I suppose they forgot the gyrations babies tumble through in the womb. At one month, though, you'd raise your head and upper torso from the mattress and prop yourself up on both elbows and watch us all quizzically from between the playpen bars.

"That's because he was late," said Hazel, when we visited at the end of your second month. "He's got a head start."

"That's because he's a genius," said Ted, not immodestly so much as in tongue-in-cheek endorsement.

"You can tell what a go-getter he'll be by the grip on his rattle. Look at that," said Hans, trying to prise your fingers off the stem one by one.

"He's too smart for you," chuckled Hazel. "See? As fast as you move on to the next one he just snaps the one you already pulled loose back into place."

You grinned and started laughing, mesmerized by her white gleaming teeth. When she bent close you waved your opening fist toward her mouth, wiggled your fingers, and pushed against the incisors like somebody trying to play the piano.

My old wariness swooped back into life when I unlatched her childproof cleaning closet and surveyed the army of compounds ranked inside. I was looking for some Ajax. "This one's a great disinfectant," she said, handing me a bottle. "Take it home and try it out. Real effective against germs, especially diaper areas like changing tables, and the spray nozzle has a good mist reach."

"I don't use a changing table," I said.

"Well, his crib instead. Only don't let him gnaw on the parts you scour when he starts teething."

I felt defeat branch through my body. Housekeeping

skills were just one more big blank space on my résumé. But slatternly as I was, I faced a greater challenge than the best education could have prepared me for. The University Married Student Housing barracks had a cockroach community that went back to the Depression. Long lines of family, not just ancestral trees but whole forests, had lived and died between those fiberboard walls. The local roach was known to have stopped clocks, eaten through rubber hosing inside washing machines, and disabled telephones. No amount of monthly extermination ever dented the population, since they were now immune to all known poisons. Not only that, they grew to be the size of jets, with wingspans like electric fans—the Boeing 747s of the bug world.

But other fatigues also clenched me: the rust stains on all the porcelain, the grit that seemed to drift out of the moldings like shaken salt. They affected my motivation toward the things I could have done something about. Inertia took over. Nowadays there was no question that Ted was living in dubious conditions; I wondered if he'd complained to Hazel about the bathroom sink freckled with dead gnats. The splashes of ketchup encrusting the kitchen linoleum. The scurf of dust on all surfaces, even vertical ones. The gray piles of jockey briefs that hardly ever made it to the washer. He never did—to me. Whenever I came to Houston and saw Hazel's spotless appointments— her shining chrome toilet-paper dispenser unblemished by fingerprints, her smudge-free kitchen cupboards—I knew I was standing on sterile ground. My cast-iron inheritance of Christian guilt fell open then like a pirate's chest, its heavy treasure weighing me down. Immediately I took all your baby blankets, bundled them into Hazel's Maytag, and doused them in Pine-Sol.

IT WAS DURING your tenth month that things started to go wrong.

I suppose the hormones only last so long—the ones that tranquilize new mothers and help them avoid facing their larger mistakes. I'd been gliding ahead reasonably well, tending you, living with your daddy, imagining life was going to be fuller in the future than it had been so far. An invisible wall of experience now lay between me and my friends. They were all still standing in a certain spot in their lives—the jumping-off place occupied by young students encumbered by only a backpack, ready to zoom away in interesting directions, ready to take wing to Europe or Indonesia or graduate school in San Francisco or the Peace Corps in Mozambique, unburdened as yet by the intimate responsibility of parenthood. Whereas I stood still in a still center.

When you cut your first teeth I was just beginning to grasp this. By the time you started biting on my nipples the full meaning of it had sprung. I began having dreams at night of boarding jets and flying high above the International Date Line, of lounging around a palm tree in a hotel somewhere on the French Riviera. Your restlessness matched mine; it wasn't long before you'd pull away after nursing for only a couple of minutes and climb down from my lap to go crawl around, exploring the grotty corners of the bedroom. You had this way of plucking the stuffing out of your disposable Pampers and leaving it like a trail of feathers in your wake. The whole apartment would be littered white at the end of the afternoon. When we went to Bay City, Hazel tried to stop you by taping the diapers tight as a corset so you couldn't reach inside, but you were too smart for her, too; you waited until the diapers got nice and soggy. How you loved that feel of fluffy cotton rubbed between your fingers. I'd never told her what else you loved the feel of, scooped from the Pampers to use as fresco finger paint on your crib headboard; it seemed better to just assure her that the disinfectant she'd given me was 100 percent effective.

Ted still took it for granted that we would be off to Greece the minute we finished our degrees. It made me wonder how real this now was for him: surely he could see the bog of our reality closing in. His mother could. She no longer needed to say anything, offer any advice. She'd known very well how cheerfully life would engulf us. The only way to fight it was with a matching cheerfulness, as she'd shown by example, plugging full steam ahead and ignoring all setbacks. But this complacency went right against my grain. The worst part was how tired I had grown of hearing Ted's voice—that continuous, measured, carefully sardonic inflection, that light drone commenting on whatever came up during the long day: a new critique, a professor's wit, your vomit, my French class, the gas bill. Even our lovemaking had long ago developed a similar mechanical dispassion. Nothing could be taken seriously. Not even sexual heat. Life seemed not to have touched him deeply anywhere.

It must have been this very quality of your father's easy-going compliance that had initially attracted me, but his equable nature repelled me now. He'd been raised to please, and compensated with light mockery. "You sound just like Hans!" I shrieked at him during an argument.

"Well, that's interesting," he answered.

"*Interesting!*" I roared in outrage. "I am *not* your mother!" I yelled, "Stand up for yourself! Stop expecting me to take care of you. *I am not Hazel!*"

"No, you don't even look like her," he agreed, "she's older," and then he coolly added, "You must be getting your period, or why else would you be this upset?"

"HANS USED TO always say, 'Are you starting your period?' whenever I got mad at him," Hazel confided to me surprisingly one day during a shopping trek through the Houston Galleria. The remark came from out of the blue. I hadn't told her about our fight. "Now that I've gone through the Change he can't do it anymore. It used to make me want to commit murder."

"It's genetic," I concluded, and the next time Ted said it to me I opened our single kitchen drawer and got out the butcher knife.

He got into the VW and drove away.

My dreams of cobblestone streets and Venetian bridges washed by moonlight waxed more and more intense. One morning, after waking up from the Bridge of Sighs, I went to the local seafood store and bought squid and brought it home and fried it, just to taste that memory from when my parents had taken me to Venice. Ted took one look and refused to touch it. "Tentacles!" he said. You crawled over to the low coffee table where we ate our meals, grabbed up a fistful, and avidly started trying to munch.

The real encumbrance was not you, but him.

The day came when my flesh rebelled. A devil entered me. I took a step.

It wasn't a good step, Treatie. It was impulsive and harmful. I had an affair. Although it was borne of a kind of loneliness, I won't make any excuses for it; at that point it felt like a break to freedom, a realm of live possibility in the midst of old, dead ones. Suffice it to say that your father proved to me just how far his dispassion extended in every direction, even unto a lack of jealousy.

The next affair was his. The fabric, already badly torn, began to rot.

By that time you were toddling all over the place. I pushed Ted away, furious, and complained about everything from his body odor to his weak and lazy ways. Now we seemed bound only in the routines of our old promises and the guttering flame of our old friendship. He did everything I told him to, just as Hazel had warned me he would. It felt intolerable. If I told him I wanted to buy a particular book when our bank account stood at subzero he'd go out and do it. We'd gotten married for convenience, I thought now; we'd cinched it to clean up a mess.

It seemed best to end things before the friendship had to withstand any more damage. It seemed best for you.

I was so stupid that it never occurred to me he was obeying me out of love.

WHEN THE DIVORCE came through your father dropped out of the Masters program he'd entered and went to work for an international fishing company in Galveston. The judge had insisted a sum be set for child support, although I requested that it not be; for the moment Ted had no money, and in the years to come I wanted all his contributions to flow from his own sense of responsibility toward his son, an act of love constantly renewed, a voluntary participant in your life.

I was young.

The judge awarded the absolute minimum possible at the time, to be paid on a monthly basis.

"I'll start handling it for him," Hazel told me after a couple of years' drought. "I'll pay you the support. Now that he's getting remarried and transferred to Sweden, it'll be more practical for me to get my signature okayed on his checking account and make sure you finally start getting a check every month. Besides, you know how much I love keeping up with figures."

Only then, Treatie, did I begin to see your grandmother fully, and apprehend the magnitude of her heart.

1977: The Scourge of the Nazis

A synonym for marriage in Chinese is "taking a daughter-in-law."
—MAXINE HONG KINGSTON

We fled Austin in the arms of a biologist from Palo Alto, California.

I SUPPOSE, TREATIE, that in the past I've fallen in love easily. In fact you could say my capacity for attachment is reflected by my sheer wealth of mothers-in-law—so many different women, so many experiences, so much to adjust to. Education never ends, although marriage certainly does. I could trace the footsteps of my many Mr. Rights through the galleries of professions I've married into, or the houses we've lived in, or the museum of hair colors that have fallen out on the pillow next to mine.

But this is not the story of a marriage, or not entirely. It is not the story of towheaded Declan, the longest, skinniest baby ever born in Amarillo, Texas. It is not the story of his rise in a high-tech field, his cabin in the woods, nor the way he eagerly took both you and me, a new wife and stepchild, into his loving care. It is the story of a witch.

DECLAN MILLER WAS lean but not taut.

When one saw him crossing the room at a corporate banquet, weaving his way between the tables, he made a soul-warming sight: wiry yet frail, sinuous yet clumsy, West Texan yet provincial. He had the kind of happy vagueness that reminds one of legendary physicists. And if there happened to be a glass of red wine clutched in his hand, as there was the time when he was standing directly above the company president's wife in her white-sequined Valentino gown, laughing his frank, childlike laugh while he gestured more and more wildly through a joke he was telling—well, that's as far as I wish to go.

Yet his shrewd business sense also moved him to found a small empire. And it was the paradox of his goofy talk and bizarre brilliance that won me over, after Ted and I finally hollered uncle.

We met each other when Declan was visiting a friend in Austin. I know you were too young then to remember, Treatie, and I haven't ever talked much about those early days with you since. Declan had just transferred from a job in Atlanta to the Bay Area where he was due to start work as the new "innovator-type guy" at a biological engineering firm. His boyhood friend happened to be our next-door neighbor. When I saw Declan walk through the door I could hardly believe it: apparently his jeans had shrunk several inches to reveal his bony ankles, perhaps back when he was in grade school. His crimson T-shirt, appliquéd with a big blue butterfly, had also shrunk and now reached only to the bottom of his narrow rib cage. On his feet he wore perished rubber thongs. But it was the acrylic mohair cardigan, a sort of cowpat brown, that entranced my eye. The month was August. The weather was one hundred and five in the shade. In the town of Austin, one of the more sartorially offhanded capitals of the world, he stood out.

"My mom tried to throw it away once," he said shyly when I asked him how long he'd had it. "Back when I was in the tenth grade. She's a nurse, and I guess she thought it looked a little dirty. But I fished it out of the trash."

I couldn't help looking at his long, long, long hair, pale as dandelion silk, tied back with a twistee wire from a bread-loaf bag.

"Aren't you hot?"

He shrugged. "I don't notice heat much. My body temp runs real low. Ninety-six point nine, usually. Besides," he grinned and held up his bottle, "I have a beer."

The next morning he wandered over again alone at breakfast time. The jeans showed accidental bleach spills in unlikely places, for instance right along the fly. Thanks to Hazel even I had better laundry skills than this. I offered him French toast but he said he'd just have some Cheerios. "Did you know that Cheerios are just about the perfect diet? Growing up in Amarillo I discovered that real early on. You can pretty much eat them three times a day and live on them. If you have to. So long as you use milk. Supplement them with a few vitamins. Wash them down with some apricot nectar for the C."

"I'm out of all juice," I said.

"Oh, that's okay."

"Hey. What color did that sweater used to be? When it started out in life?"

"I can't remember. Maybe . . . maroon?"

"Hairy maroon?"

"You like this sweater, don't you?" he smiled.

"Are you an only child?" There was something bright and untarnished about his face that made me suspect he'd grown up free of wear and tear, i.e., siblings.

"Almost," he said, and thought a moment. "Just about," he said cheerily.

I looked at him.

"I do have a brother," he reflected.

"Older or younger?"

"Younger."

"By how much?"

"About an hour."

"My God. You're a twin?"

"Kind of."

He smiled again and scooped a big spoonful of Cheerios into the middle of it. "He's actually a month younger than me."

"How is that possible?"

"The doctor reckoned he got conceived one month after I did. So when we were born, he was one month premature. I was on time," he said modestly around the flecks of cereal and milk droplets spattering out his mouth.

"I never heard of such a thing."

"Apparently it happens. He had to stay in an incubator. My mother says that's why. She's a nurse." He shrugged. "It happens with puppies, sometimes ones from the same litter even getting conceived by different fathers."

"Yeah, so you said. I mean about your mother being a nurse."

"She's pretty cool," he nodded.

"Where's she from?" I pictured a strong, big-hipped Panhandle woman with brawny arms and a warm, brisk tolerance for her boy's maundering ways—probably of farmer stock.

"New York."

"Oh, really?" I transferred the good no-nonsense nurse somewhere upstate, like Schenectady. "Where does she live now? Still in Amarillo?"

"Heck no. She and Dad live up in the mountains of New Mexico now. She got out of Amarillo just as fast as she could. She hated being stuck anywhere in one place, especially one place in Texas."

"How fast was as fast as she could?" I asked, feeling something stir within me.

"Oh, about twenty-six years," he said, and that's when my mind turned a corner.

I DIDN'T ACTUALLY meet Filalia Miller until seven months after the day Declan escorted us out of Austin, out of Texas altogether, far away to a suburb near Palo Alto.

"Declan and I are going to live together," I told my parents before we left. "Strictly live together. Get to know each other over a long time. See what we think of each other, see if we're compatible. And make it a nice, slow process."

"Hmph," said my father, "why buy the cow when you're already getting the milk?" and turned away.

He was no different once we were installed in the tract house that Declan had bought when he'd first moved to California and furnished with wooden fruit crates and his waterbed.

"If you ever want to have any kind of relationship at all with your father in the future, you won't *do this*," my mother hissed over the phone during a long-distance call she'd dialed in secret. "It just makes him blow a gasket. He is absolutely livid. It upsets him more than you can possibly—"

"Mother. I do *not* have to fall into this narrow-minded trap."

"He's *extremely* upset."

"Everything upsets Dad! He disapproves of anything he doesn't decide to do himself. These days everybody with a grain of sense lives together first."

"This will be the end. I'm warning you."

"Look—we're not even in Texas any longer. Nobody you-all know can ever see us living in sin. This is California! Standards are changing. I will *not* follow some old, outmoded belief system if it's not right for me. If Dad can't see it our way, then that's just too bad."

"He'll wash his hands of you," she said.

"Then so be it. If he loves me so little that he'd do that, then c'est la vie." I hung up.

"You want to take a little vacation down in L.A. for Memorial Day?" asked Declan a couple of weeks later. "Go see some friends? Have some fun? Hang out at Disneyland and the beach?"

"Marry me," I said.

YOU WERE SOON to turn three years old. We decided to go to New Mexico for Thanksgiving, as it would be a good idea to finally meet the in-laws and vice versa and try out my new name, Lulu Penfield Vonick Miller, among other Millers to see how it fit in. I hadn't even spoken with them over the phone yet. Declan's twin brother Alvin was the only family member I'd met so far. Every time Declan talked with his parents, which was seldom, he relayed little messages of greeting. But the one time he offered the phone to me I became suddenly limp-armed with terror and couldn't take it; I just shook my head no. We figured that introductions might go better in person. Declan and Alvin had bought a cabin near his parents' house, and he wanted to check on it and make sure the pipes hadn't frozen.

"Why aren't we staying there? In the cabin?" I asked.

"Oh, well, I generally like to stay with the folks. Stick close when I go visit. Be handy, kind of."

"They expect you to, huh?"

"Well, not really. I like it there. You know, I think you're really going to enjoy my mom. She's kind of a free spirit."

Besides, he said: Alvin was going to follow in a couple of days and stay in the cabin. He was kind of depressed lately and might want privacy, so it would be better for us to stay with their parents. Besides, this way we could show up without having to worry about heating up the cabin or messing with the electricity or turning the water on or anything the minute we got there. In case he was too tired to do those chores. Since what he wanted most was to get started right now and drive straight through without stopping. Because there was nothing Declan loved better than to sally forth through the night into windswept, desert-type country at ninety miles an hour. He was most at home on the range.

A drowsy, catlike expression came over him as soon as we left the cities behind and started speeding toward the badlands of Nevada. At the same time he seemed enlivened. "Hey, I know what. Let's listen to Jimi Hendrix!" You'd at last fallen asleep in your carseat around eleven P.M., somewhere outside Reno, but he plugged the cassette into the stereo full blast for "Purple Haze." Then he started to sing along off-key. Once we hit the Arizona state line he appeared to become even ganglier, the breeze ripping through his strandy locks, his eyes turned inward like the eyes of an ecstatic somnambulist. The window of his rattling old 1959 Ford pickup stayed cranked down through the miles all the way to Four Corners, despite a sharp breath of mountain winter to come. He wore only the mohair cardigan over a T-shirt. It seemed cold didn't bother him, either.

So that first trip we made it to Angel Fire in well under twenty-four hours, churning through the five-foot-deep drifts across the Rockies and ignoring the caffeine-and-marijuana-glazed redness in Declan's eyes. We didn't stop once at a motel. Motels were for sissies.

"*Hey, y'all,*" he hollered at top pitch and honked the horn as we drove up to the sprawling two-story log cabin.

All around lay forest: silence, hard sunlight, the sweet chill scent of aspen, cedar woodsmoke, and piñon. Back in Farmington we'd stopped at a service station so Declan could have the snow tires put on. But the driveway in front of us looked manicured, the powdery quick shoved back to the edges and glossed with white ice. He braked the truck and honked again, leaning on it. You woke up. It was ten o'clock in the morning.

"Look, Tristan. Look at all the white land," marveled Declan.

"What is it?" you asked. His excitement was infectious.

Tenderly he unhooked the straps on your carseat and lifted you out. He clasped you in his arms. "It's water. Frozen water," he whispered. "Turned into little tiny stars that fall from the sky and smush together. Come on, I'll take you out to see. You can taste it."

"Are we here?" you said, blinking in awe as the glitter struck.

"Yes. We sure are. We're here!"

"Let me tie his hood, at least," I said.

"Aw, he doesn't need it. It's not really that cold. Come see for yourself." And he clambered from the truck, picked you up, set you down, and held your hand to guide your crunching steps across the drive to the snowbank under the trees.

His eyes shone in exhilaration.

"Hello!" a voice seemed to tinkle out of nowhere against the air.

"Well, hey there!" called Declan back.

"Are you playing in the snow?"

"We thought we might."

"We could make some snow ice cream for supper." The voice came from somewhere around the side of the house. I turned. "We've got vanilla and maple syrup."

"There you are. How you doing?" said Declan.

"Fine. Or we could use butterscotch flavoring."

"That sounds good. This little guy'll sure like it."

"It's been a long time since I made any," she said, and she scrambled clear of the shadow under the icicle eaves. The hood of her red parka was lined with rabbit fur; her cheeks and nose were red also. She stood about four feet, ten inches tall.

"Where's Dad?" he asked, stooping down low to give her a big kiss and hug. "This here's Tristan."

"Oh, isn't he cute?" she said, reaching out and caressing your cheek.

"Lulu, come on over and meet my mom."

"She is, too." She looked me over as I walked up.

"Hi," I said.

"Hi!" She bounced up to peck me on the cheek, and I bent and met her halfway. She had a winey smell, mixed with L'Air du Temps and a trace of menthol, that was surprisingly pleasant. "You don't look quite like your pictures."

"I don't?"

"In your pictures you look like an Indian. Do you have Indian blood?"

"No. I don't think so."

"Are you sure? Cherokee or Sioux? Or maybe it's Mexican Indian mixed with Spanish."

"No." I shook my head. A cloud puffed out as I exhaled.

"Mama, look!" you cried and pointed. "Smoke!"

"That's air and water. Like fog," Declan said in your ear.

"Fog. Water fog," you said gravely.

"He's smart!" said Filalia.

"Yes," I admitted, liking her already.

"You could be Italian. I knew an Italian girl during the war who looked a lot like you." She cocked her head and put her finger to her mouth. "Or Lebanese."

"It's all English, Irish, and Scottish," I apologized, having gone through this inquisition before. "All the way back. On both sides."

"I'm picking up the vibes of something else, though. Let me see." She closed her eyes. A low hum came from her chest, up through her throat, out her nose. You watched her carefully, holding on to Declan's hand. "There's something else there," she said, her eyes opening again. "But I can't pin it down out here. It's too cold. How would you like some hot chocolate?" she turned and asked you.

"Okay," you said.

"Where's Dad?" said Declan again.

"He's in Santa Fe, picking up your wedding present. He'll be back tonight. Let's go inside to the fire."

"Cool," said Declan.

"Come on, Treatie." I picked you up, and together we all entered the log cabin, a structure that turned out to be the size of a small ocean liner.

Out in the main hall we passed under two rows of heads. Most of them were bucks, although a couple of elk flanked the living-room portal and somebody's old moose dominated the right-hand row. "Trees," you noted, peering up at the bare branches above each glass-eyed stare.

"Right. Antlers!" called Filalia over her shoulder. She led us past a rattlesnake coiled on a plaque, a mountain lion, and a large rainbow trout nailed high on the wall that you leaned clear of my arms to touch. "What's that?" Filalia asked.

"That's a fish," you said.

"A fish out of water," she retorted. "He can't swim or eat. He has to stay right there, but he doesn't care anymore."

"No," you agreed.

"What's that?" She pointed to the flames that filled one end of the huge living room, roaring and twisting in the stone fireplace of ox-roasting proportions.

"Fire," you said, your eyes widening.

"You bet it is. Don't get too close."

"Okay."

"Now come have some nice cocoa. Lulu, Declan, would you like some? Or would you rather have hot buttered rum?"

"Oh—cocoa for me, thanks," I said.

"Coffee, Mom," said Declan.

She unzipped her parka, threw it across the carved back of the Victorian sofa, and got down to business over the counter. I could see her rosy mouth pursing and smiling above the saucepan and the measuring spoons and the Waterford crystal tumbler. There was in her face something I'd read about in novels and poems but could only now fully appreciate, with the same sense of revelation you feel when tasting an exotic fruit that you never expected to encounter: a button nose. It shone below her curls, and in that climate its color was truly becoming.

I wondered how she felt about divorcées.

"Mom, I think I might have to go take a nap," said Declan, suddenly slumping down onto another sofa, this one of tooled leather.

"Oh, baby. Are you beat?"

"Yeah, I kind of am."

"Well, go back to your room and climb into bed. The sheets are already on it."

"Okeydokey." He struggled to his feet and shambled on down the hall.

"He's a good boy," she said.

"He sure is," I said.

"Do you believe in reincarnation?" She held a gallon bottle of rum above the counter and assessed it critically in the window light.

"I, ah, I haven't ever thought about it very much, to tell you the truth. But I guess it's an interesting idea. I did study it a little in a college class."

"Well, I'll fill you in on something you should know: in one of his past lives Declan was a monk."

"Really?"

"It's true," her head bobbed solemnly up and down as she filled a tall glass with rum, placed it and the bottle beside two mugs on a tray, and carefully carried them back to the sofa. "All the peasants who lived around the countryside just loved him. They wanted him to get sainted by the pope. This was in England during the Middle Ages."

"I had no idea."

"But the pope wouldn't do it; he was too jealous. When Declan was born I named him the same name he'd had back then. Here, baby," she said, leaning over to hand you a steaming mug of cocoa. "I added a dash of cold milk so it won't burn your tongue."

"That's very thoughtful," I said.

"Do you like this mug?" she asked you. "It used to be your Uncle Alvin's when he was a little tiny boy. He loved those crazy bears standing on their heads. He was always much littler than Declan."

You sipped from the mug's edge, then grasped the sides, took a big slug, and branded your upper lip with a mustache.

"And much more mischievous. He's the one who used to get them both in trouble. He'd say, 'I'll hold the stepladder while you climb up and reach the cookie jar,' and then he'd run away and leave Declan there red-handed when he heard me coming."

"But how did you—I mean—well, um. How could you tell it was Alvin who thought that trick up?" I asked.

"I wasn't stupid." She rolled her eyes and hoisted her glass of hot buttered rum sans butter.

"Oh."

"Look! He's finished that mug already. Do you want some more, baby?"

"Yes," you said.

"Yes, *please*," I said.

"Please." You gave her the mug, carefully inspecting the bears in their funny hats.

"That's good that you're already teaching him manners."

"I figure it's pretty essential."

"You said it. Anyway, I named Alvin after his reincarnation, too. He was a fool."

Somehow this didn't come as a surprise, well-acquainted with Declan's twin brother as I now was. "I guess maybe some things don't change from one life to another."

She threw back her head and cackled. "No—*you* know! A fool. The court jester to the king."

"Oh!" I watched her, bemused. "You wouldn't happen to know to which king, would you?"

"I can't remember his name. It started with *A,* I think. Or *R.* Maybe Richard the Lion-hearted." She took another swig of her drink and stood up to prepare more cocoa. Her glass already looked just about polished off. "He wore one of those caps with bells ting-a-linging on the ends," she turned and explained to you. "But then he got beheaded."

"What for?" I asked.

Blithely she reached for the rum bottle. "For screwing the wrong girl."

"Oh!" I stroked your head, stealthily covering your ears as she moved off toward the kitchen.

"You better watch out about that, Tristan. About getting caught out in the wrong place at the wrong time. Listen to your Granny Filalia," she sang and shook her finger playfully from the counter. "It can get very dangerous!"

"Jangious," you said.

"Parts of your body sliced into piec—"

"Ah—where did you find this out?" I interrupted quickly.

"From a dream, of course."

"A dream," I said.

"These things come to me in dreams," said Filalia.

AFTER INHALING THE second mug of cocoa you'd drifted off to sleep in my arms, a last chocolaty burp percussing from your mouth.

"I've known for many, many years that I had the gift of sight," Filalia explained now. "When I was a teenager in high school I used to dream what would happen to my friends—who they'd marry, who would wind up rich or poor, or running a bakery, or who'd land in prison. Most of my friends were guys," she added offhandedly. "Sometimes they offered to pay me. But I'd rather tell people their fates for free."

"Is this some kind of skill you inherited?" I asked.

"Who knows?" She shrugged. "I sure don't."

"Oh."

"So when I had the dream about the boys I thought,

Well, it's a good thing they're getting born to me. Because I can understand. Did you know, that was the only time I ever got pregnant? Because I was always so careful with everybody except Leroy." She looked at me expectantly.

"Ah-*haa!*" I said. There was something seductive about all this open-hearted candor. She's *refreshing,* I thought, charmed.

"He's their daddy. So I could assure him they were definitely his. And I knew I wasn't telling a lie. No matter how many parties we went to beforehand," she added roguishly.

". . . In Amarillo?" I asked, suddenly scarcely daring to cleave the air.

She nodded. Then she nodded more hectically. Two spots of color bloomed high on her cheeks. "Sure! That was his hometown. That's where he took me after the war, where we'd met each other."

"That was in the army?"

"He'd gotten wounded and I was his nurse over in France. But I'll tell you what: the dreams I had while I was pregnant sure came thick and fast. I dreamed all about Declan in his monastery, and Alvin and his girlfriend from up in the castle, and his little cap. Whew!" She fell into a fit of coughing.

"Filalia? . . . How is it, do you think, that you have this gift? I mean, to be able to dream about people's pasts as well as the future?"

"You mean like the one I've had about you?"

I paused. I closed my mouth. I took a deep breath. "Um—you've had one about—"

She smiled. "Because I'm a witch."

I SHOOK DECLAN to wake him up. A dry snow had begun to fall, beating with a sandy hiss against the thermal window-panes. The curtains were drawn wide, and the light looked very different from an hour before when we'd arrived: thinner, cloudier, like a glass of ouzo diluted with water.

"Why didn't you tell me your mother was a witch?" I demanded.

"What?" He jerked a little, like a gigged frog. "Oh . . ."

"Why didn't you tell me she could read past lives? Or tell the future?" I was practically jumping on the bed.

"My mom's a lot of things," he said, dazed.

"What else does she do? Besides dream?"

"Don't worry about it," he sighed, and turned over, trying to reentrench himself. The prospect of having a Salem refugee as a mother-in-law, no matter how delusionary, exalted me: it was an un-looked-for prize, a boon dropped from heaven. It was dense with possibility.

"*Tell* me."

"I don't know. She does voodoo sometimes."

"Voodoo? Like rooster sacrifices? Blood predictions? *Drums and dancing?* What?"

"Nah. She's got a doll." He sighed again.

"A doll."

He nodded, face down into the pillow.

"You don't mean for pins and stuff! Do you?"

"Only when there's some snobby person bugging her. She hates snobs."

"Has she *used* it?"

"Oh, man. I don't know."

"Yes you do!"

"Well . . . there was this lady back in Amarillo, real stuck-up. She thought she was God's gift on a gold platter. Better than everybody else in the neighborhood. My mother always called her Miss Priss. And she *was* pretty bad." He yawned; he could barely keep his eyes open. Then, suddenly, he laughed. "Her son was one of the biggest dope dealers in the Panhandle, but she didn't know that. It was kind of funny. But shoot, I don't care about that stuff. People can think what they want to about themselves, it doesn't change anything in the bigger world. When you—"

"I know," I said quickly, and shoved him hard. "What did she *do* to this woman?"

"Well, she—I don't think she did anything, really. But the fact is, the lady ended up with a permanent back spasm. Lumbar. She just couldn't get rid of it. Horrible pain. She's still confined to a wheelchair the last I heard, she's pumped up on codeine, a full-scale addict. It's probably just some vertebrae erosion affecting the psoas—"

"My God!" I said. "Declan!"

He shrugged and smiled.

"You're pulling my leg," I accused, and swatted him.

"No, I'm not."

"Did she tell you she'd had a dream about me?"

He mulled for a moment. "I think she kind of mentioned it once, a long time ago," he said.

"How long ago? Why didn't you tell me?" Sometimes his slow delivery sounded so passive I wanted to shake him.

"I don't know. It didn't seem real important."

"What was it?"

"Heck. She'll tell you herself. If she remembers to," he said, and while I was lying beside him, pondering the imports of this new white evanescent world and our connections in it, he began gently to snore.

"HELLO!" YELLED A voice from the headhunter hall. "Any strangers here?"

"That's Leroy," said Filalia. She was showing me the back parlor suite, which was decorated like an 1880s Western bordello, complete with red velvet drapes, gaslights, red cut-velvet wallpaper, and a big antique brass bed that looked shaky enough to have been an authentic artifact of the trade. You'd tried to climb onto it but I stopped you when the flimsy frame started to moan, at which point Filalia cracked a bawdy joke and you moved on to fish around inside the brass spittoon.

"You're home early," she called down the corridor. "It's not even five yet."

"The weather cleared up after Taos."

"Well, us girls are back here in the whorehouse."

"Okay. I'm coming."

"He's got your wedding present," she whispered, crinkling her eyes. "Wait'll you see it."

"Shouldn't we get Declan?"

"Oh, sure. *Declan!*" she hollered. You stopped, your eyes wide, and crawled under the bed quick as a rabbit.

"I don't think he heard you," said Leroy in mild sarcasm.

He stood in the doorway holding a huge kite-shaped framework that looked like a rawhide cannibal feasting platter—at least, one hoped rawhide.

"You call him, then," she said sweetly.

But Declan was already right behind Leroy. "Are you getting a job as one of those walking billboards, Dad?"

"Oh, goody!" cried Filalia, clapping her hands as she caught a closer look. "Isn't it beautiful?"

"This here's a little something from your mother, for you and your new wife," said Leroy, bringing it into the room. He set it down and whumped his gloved hands together: a short man, stumpy almost, with a big shock of brown hair and a weathered red face, a good match to Filalia's *rondelet* petiteness.

Declan introduced us. Leroy hunkered over and smiled at you hiding under the bed. Then he squatted down and held out his hairy-backed hand. "How you doing, podner?"

You blinked up at him. You took the hand and waggled it.

"That your little fort down there?" he asked.

You nestled backward, your eyes gleaming in the shadows.

"Good enough," he said.

"What do you think? Look at this! Are you surprised?" cried Filalia.

"Wow." Declan stood back and eyed the kite that Leroy was balancing upright. "It sure is one hunk of something," he said. "What is that? Skin?"

Filalia turned to me. "What do you think, Lulu?"

"It's, um, amazing," I said. I bent over it, scrutinizing the colored drawings scrawled down the spine. Two jagged lines, one sun with zigzag rays, several eye-type symbols, several unidentified quadrupeds with long tails.

"Okay, better tell them what it is," said Leroy.

"It's a spirit shield! A medicine man's shield. There's a modern-day artist who makes them. He lives on the highway near the turn-off to Los Alamos, close to the old cliff dwellings at Puye. He's named—" she pondered a second, tapping her front tooth, "—Weeping Willow Marvin."

"Has he been making them long?" I asked.

"Ever since he returned to his ancestral land from Chicago last year. Back in Chicago he ran a bar."

"He must be a fast learner," said Declan.

"The spirits tell him what to draw for each individual person. I told him I thought you were probably Indian, Lulu."

"Oh. Well. Wow," I said, admiring the shield.

"Wow," echoed Declan, stroking it lightly with his fingertips.

"This is very special," I said, turning to her. I gave her a hug. Under my arms she felt no bigger than a Patty Play Pal. "And very thoughtful. Thank you."

"It'll bless you both. And you too, cute little droopy-drawers," she bent and called under the bed. "See the feathers? I told him to use red and blue ones because I thought they were prettier, but he told me they had to be traditional. Indian feathers. He said he'd be sure and get eagle."

"Now, that's illegal, Filalia," reproved Leroy. "That's an endangered bird."

"Oh, don't be so stuffy. Oh! Illegal!" She pealed with laughter. "Leroy, go make us some cocktails and I'll start cooking dinner. Lulu can help if she wants."

"Sure," I said.

"What's for dinner?" Leroy unbuttoned his enormous black Polar parka and loosened his white wool scarf. In the coat he looked like a stuffed panda. Underneath he wore a blue jean jacket, Levis, and a bronze-buckled belt stamped with a Lone Star, and looked like a good old typical West Texas farmer, which he wasn't. He'd made his living owning a shoe store before he'd sold up and retired.

"Venison. I'm using stroganoff mix and thawing out some French fries and green beans almondine."

"Sounds good!" He whapped his gloves against his thigh to knock off the last of the ice crust. "We had a real good deer season this year," he added to Declan.

"You can rest easy, knowing your marriage has full protection from all those outside tamperers who might want to screw it up." Filalia turned to face Declan and me, giving the shield a final pat. "And if they try their spells you just tell me about it."

Following her back up the corridor I thought about all those outside tamperers and how strongly they might pit their wills against this pint-sized enemy. Despite her tiny body, she'd make a tough cookie to crack, that was for sure. Nonetheless, I couldn't help wondering: knowing my previous record, and with all the goodwill in the world, would that shield so much as keep off the rain when it came to the real forces of danger? What was going to protect our union from my goading restlessness, the enemy within?

THE NEXT FEW days took on a pleasant rhythm of sleeping, waking, tramping through the snow to search for bird tracks or to pick up the mail, then back into the house for breakfast. Afterward we might take the jeep sight-seeing into Red River or even Taos. Then we'd jump on the sled with you and go tearing down one of the nearby slopes. Afternoons stretched into white naps; early evenings usually found Declan and me talking about maybe skiing the next day. By the following morning we were already repeating the same steps as the day before.

"THIS IS MY magic voodoo doll," Filalia said, reaching to the top closet shelf and hauling down a Raggedy Ann bristling with pinheads.

"Remind me not to make you mad," I said, examining the familiar red yarn hair, the ruffled pinafore hiding the painted red heart. "Do you know——I had one of these when I was five years old."

"You won't. We're going to be like sisters. Declan told me when you two first got together how much I'd like you. He said we had a lot in common." Her oversized black satin dress was sliding off one shoulder and she had to grab it, hitch it back, and anchor it with a spider-headed brooch. Before she'd made her big entrance from the bathroom I hadn't known what to expect. The Hallmark Halloween quality of this garb was a relief, despite my lingering wistfulness to have a real witch in the family. She couldn't possibly have harmed a human with Raggedy Ann, not that she was likely to want to anyway; and the dress just dated from a long-ago costume party. "Any girl my boys love, I love, too. Except that Rita," she added.

"Who's Rita?"

"Oh, she was Alvin's old girlfriend. Haven't you heard about her yet?"

"I don't think Alvin's ever mentioned her name," I said. Neither had Declan.

"Well, don't worry. He got rid of her. With a little help, that is," she added zestfully. "Easy come, easy go."

"Was it very long ago? He doesn't seem to go out with women much, and I've sometimes wond—"

"Oh, he claims it broke his heart, dumping her. But that's just horseshit. She was bad news, I tell you. Here, Tristan, look at this little guy, isn't he funny?" She took down a shoebox marked *Miller's Shoe Palace,* reached inside, and a black ball bounced on an elastic string in front of your face like a yo-yo. It took a second before I realized it was a shrunken head. It took one more before I realized it was rubber. "She kept him so unhappy. Always telling him he didn't measure up to her dreams or he wasn't romantic enough or refined enough or this or that enough. I've never forgiven her. Look, Tristan, here comes his little friend." A writhing black scorpion as long as a hot dog whirled down the air toward your eyes; you shrieked and batted it away. Quickly I picked you up and held you close.

"I'm sorry, baby. Did that scare you? Here, we'll put him back to bed in his little house." She gathered the toys, slipped them into the shoebox, picked up her ever-present tumbler full of California Pale Dry Sherry, and took a big slug. "Yep. Cooked her bacon."

ALVIN SHOWED UP the next day.

Unlike Declan he liked to take his time and sleep at least one night on the road, preferably in a good motel or at least one with Jacuzzi and cable. His itinerant work situation never seemed to trim his lifestyle much; he took the occasional job in the pharmaceutical industry, usually lasting until a tantrum or a prank got him fired. Declan was the frugal one.

When Alvin pulled up in front of the house he was driving a brand-new Chevrolet pickup, custom painted metallic cherry red. Next to Declan's old Ford it looked like a diva from the Met.

"You're not allowed in here if you're going to give me any grief about my drinking," called Filalia from the front porch. Alvin shook his head.

"Shoot! All I want is Thanksgiving dinner. You think you could spare that to your own son, at least?"

"Just make sure you remember. I don't want to hear any sherry jokes this trip."

"Naw, no jokes. I promise."

"We're not having turkey," she said. "We're having a goose that Daddy shot. Lulu's been roasting it all morning. Yesterday she fried chicken! Just how Leroy always liked it growing up. She's the new chef around here now."

"Thank God for that. Otherwise we'd just have to bust out the Rice Krispies family pack," jibed Alvin, and crunched up the porch steps to give her a stiff-shouldered hug.

"Where'd you get that truck?" called Declan. When we'd left the Bay Area Alvin had been still driving a '71 two-ton Dodge.

"Stole it." He smacked Declan's bicep with his fist. "Hey. Hiya, Lulu."

"Hi." Each time Alvin kissed me hello it was always a little too long, a little too centered on the lips.

"Hey, look, Smartass is here," said Leroy, climbing the steps with his arms full of firewood. "How you doing there, son?"

"Good, Daddy. I just got a new job."

"Well. Good."

"Hey, did you know that already, Declan?" asked Filalia. Declan smiled sunnily.

"It's a clinic slot over at Stanford, working for a neural research outfit," said Alvin.

"That sounds interesting. They pay you good?" Leroy asked.

"I'm making out," he said, and winked one eye and then the other at me as he followed his father inside.

• • •

THAT NIGHT DECLAN finally explained to me about Alvin's single status and told the story of Rita.

Alvin had had a girlfriend in high school that he'd been crazy about, in his own frenetic way. "That was Rita?" I asked.

"No. Her name was Sharon," he said. "But then she began sneaking out with the Tigers' tight end behind Alvin's back. And then soon after that she broke up with him and went with the football guy full-time out in the open. That was when she started calling Alvin a nerd."

"Was he hurt?"

"He kind of shut up for a while—you know."

"Yeah." I remembered Mark, locked in his room.

"But shoot, I always got called a nerd. It's no big deal. Especially not from those kinds of people."

Looking at his unbound, lustrous spider-web pale locks I reflected upon Alvin's ear-length dishwater bob and buck teeth. They both wore aviator glasses, short-sightedness being their only similarity. "You don't fit the bill," I said, stroking his chest.

"Sure I do. Anyhow, when Mom started harping on about it—she thought she could cheer him up by kind of making fun of him—he just laughed it off."

"Making fun how?"

"You know, kind of poking fun. 'Alvin's dirty-leg old girlfriend wears jockstraps.' Stuff like that."

"Oh, no."

He shrugged. "That's just Mom. You can't take her seriously. I think she was still seeing us as little kids. You know, kind of like kindergarten. Alvin always got crushes on girls in kindergarten and grade school. He sent a lot of valentines and gave away a lot of candy."

"What about later? In college?"

"He had more girlfriends, I guess. But he always ran off from them before he could start caring too much."

"Anyhow," I pulled back my hand for a minute, "who's Rita?"

"She was the girl Alvin finally really fell in love with. He met her in Georgia year before last. She moved out to San Francisco with him when he went looking for a job."

"Did she really dump him? Your mom said it was the other way around."

"Nah, he dumped her."

"Is he still in love with her?"

"Well, it's hard to say. She got pregnant."

"*Really?*"

He nodded. "When she told him the situation Alvin freaked out. You know, panicked."

"So he *dumped her?*"

"No. He wanted to keep on living with her. He just said, 'The sooner you get rid of it the sooner we can relax and have some fun together again.'"

"That's the coldest thing I've ever heard," I snapped.

"It was the better thing to do. She was only after money. That's why she got pregnant in the first place."

"How can you say that? How can you *possibly know* that? How can you be so unfair?" I sat bolt upright. "*What money?*"

"You know. Child support. Ongoing life-through-the-years type money."

"You've got to be kidding." Already mired deep in my own child-support predicaments, I felt a sudden urge to hit him.

"Well, he's always found good jobs. There are plenty out there in his field. And Daddy and Mom have a little money. She knew that."

"Don't you realize that it takes two to make a baby? And that children *cost* money? They're not some woman's free *meal ticket*? What's *wrong* with you?"

He shrugged. "She shouldn't have acted so manipulative, then. Mom told me at the time she could see straight through her, and she's a woman."

"She said that in front of Alvin?"

"No. Of course not. But why would she say it if she didn't smell a rat? Rita looked pretty obvious."

"My God." I lay back and pulled the quilt up to my chin, deeply upset. "So she had to get rid of the baby."

"Well. Possibly."

"Or else face raising it on her own." Then I woke up and realized what he'd just said. "Declan!"

"What?"

"Don't tell me Rita's still pregnant?"

"Yeah," he said. "I think so," he said. "Maybe. I'm kind of not too sure, last I heard."

"Oh, no!"

He turned sideways and curled his long body into something more compact.

I sat up, leaning on my elbow. "Declan—what would you do if I got pregnant?"

He just looked at me uncomprehendingly and smiled.

LATE THAT AFTERNOON Filalia finally told me her Lulu dream.

We'd finished Thanksgiving dinner about two. Alvin belched while he rubbed his stomach. "Best Thanksgiving goose I ever ate."

"The only one you ever ate," said Declan.

"Yep. Biggest, too."

"Believe I'm going to go take me a little snooze," said Leroy, rising from the carver's chair.

I'd already put you to bed. Claustrophobia was setting in; the powder drifts outside seemed to meld with the air of the house, dampening my brain. Nothing focused very well, neither silverware nor faces. Dozily the two brothers sprawled side by side across the table.

"We'd all better take a snooze," Alvin said, stretching. But this time I couldn't force myself to drop dead in the middle of the day.

"I'm going for a walk," I announced. "Declan. You want to come with me?"

"I don't know if I can move," he said.

"I'll come," said Filalia, and to my surprise she jumped up from her seat, no more unsteady on her pins than any windup toy, and went off to fetch her parka.

"There you go," said Alvin. "Women. They're the ones with all the energy." He smirked piratically at me, daring me to read through his words to the darker innuendo. Unlike my frank experiences among the Brunes and the Vonicks, the Miller brothers seemed closer to home territory: there frequently was a darker innuendo.

OUT IN THE snow Filalia shook off her lassitude, stepping briskly down the road. "It's nice to get out in this! The first snowfall always reminds me of France, the winter I was there during the war."

"It reminds me of the day Treatie was born," I said. "But of course more so."

"I'm glad you've already had a child," she said.

Her remark took me by surprise: because I had practice? because I'd proven my fertility? my mothering instincts? stock value? "Why?"

"Well, you've probably got that maternal urge all satisfied now. You can feel free to go on to other jobs without getting too clucky."

I glanced at her sideways. "Were you? Free, I mean?"

"No. I never did go back to working as a nurse after the boys came." She threw up her hands. "I had twins! Are you kidding? They kept me busy enough for three jobs. At least at first. Later not so much. I'll tell you a secret," she tilted toward me and cupped a hand around her mouth to funnel her whisper. "I'm not all that great with little kids." She straightened. "Besides, back then I liked to party too much. You can't have fun if you're watching the clock for a hospital schedule."

"No, I guess not."

"Amarillo was pretty boring. But it wasn't long before Leroy and I made a few friends who knew how to have a good time." She paused and slewed her eyes sideways at me. "If the wives didn't get too mad, that is."

A pine bough overhead abruptly dipped and dropped a bale of snow on the track beside us. I didn't know what to say. "How long did you nurse during the war?"

"Two years. I met Leroy when he was a patient in the leg wound ward. We liked each other and he proposed, so I said yes. But before that I'd had some pretty crazy times. The nurses would meet the entertainers that toured around with the USO shows. Some of them were really famous. One time I lit off to Spain for the weekend with a piano player and we hit all the bars and cantinas in Barcelona! It was a blast. I got in trouble but they needed nurses too bad to quibble much."

"Was it hard?"

"Sometimes. Operating got pretty gory."

"I can only imagine what it must be like, nursing next to a battlefield."

She shrugged. "One reason I go into Taos a lot is because the adobe architecture reminds me of that weekend in Spain. That and the Old West, of course. By the way, that's part of the dream I had about you. The Old West, like Taos in the old days. You were an Indian once, did you know that? You and that Rita both, as a matter of fact."

"Both of us?" Suddenly I felt a yearning for a blast of wind.

She nodded her head up and down inside the red hood.

"Not from the same tribe, but winding up at the same place at the same time as Declan and Alvin. It's all karma."

"Where was this same place?"

"Little Big Horn."

"You mean—like with *Custer?*"

"You and Rita were together. She was one of the Sioux squaws who pulled the boots off the cavalry soldiers and robbed their corpses. She even did it to Declan after Alvin killed him. She scalped him along with some other soldiers. But that was just part of the victory celebrations."

Declan. Scalped!

"Just goes to show you, doesn't it? But you'd been a captive from somewhere else far away, and you wouldn't help. Do you have any memory of it at all?"

"No." Violently I shook my head.

"While all the others were busy over Custer you climbed up the hillside on the opposite shore of the river. And there," she paused in the middle of the white, silent road, and closed her eyes to visualize it, "you turned into a hawk and flew away!"

"My Lord," I said. "Really?"

"Just flew right away. Just rose up over the hills and vanished into the blue." Her eyes opened. She blinked, irises shining and brimming with tears in the cold. "So you see? It's karma that you and Declan found each other and got married."

"Do you think that's why he fell in love with me?" I asked. In a pig's eye, I thought.

"It's possible. Just like it's karma that that old Rita

would strip a dead man of everything he had on him, even his hair."

Quickly I steered the conversation back to the earlier topic. "Why did you say that about my maternal urge?"

She stopped, shrugged, wheeled around, and started toward the log cabin. "Oh, you know. Because of that crazy notion Declan has that he's genetically unfit to reproduce. So I figured it was a good thing you'd already gotten it out of the way. It's funny, isn't it? That he's a modern genetic engineer, and he thinks that?" She shrugged again. "After I made the mistake of telling him about my grandfather and my uncles who were all born with six fingers on each hand, and my aunt who had a baby with no esophagus, and about Leroy's first cousin that they had to keep locked up back in Arkansas, he just took it the whole hog."

I stopped, watching her toil on through the packed crust. The peaked red hood swayed like a cardinal's crest, strong as blood against the snow. Each footstep sank six inches, leaving a small oval pit floored with a rubber tread-mark. It wasn't until I felt the dry chill reaching down my gullet that I realized my jaw was still hanging open.

THAT EVENING AS we sat around the living-room fireplace Alvin and Filalia had an argument. Even to my fresh ears its booms and nags sounded routine, an old script dusted off for another season's run. Declan and Alvin never fought, which I thought was surprising between brothers. It seemed that Declan, like Mark Brune, didn't know how.

But Alvin was a different story.

"What are you talking about? You're always so blitzed by this time of night you wouldn't know a steam locomotive from a caboose," he yelled.

"Aw, quit railing at her," said Leroy with a twinkle, and Declan grinned.

"I am not blitzed! I may get a little high, but I can see just as much as *you* can a steam locomotive. And you're in my house, so stop telling me what to do. In my own damn house. Go off to your pissant little cabin and behave yourself." Filalia fluffed around in her easy chair, threw back her head, and sniffed.

"It's better than staying here in the Bates Motel," growled Alvin. A feral leer stretched his lips across his teeth.

"I should have known you'd start up just as soon as you came. Your same old stories. Yap, yappety yap."

"Respect your mother, now," warned Leroy.

"Dad—just look at that bruise on her arm! It's as big as Lake Texoma. You know perfectly well she got it bumping into something when she was tanked. Remember that black eye in Amarillo where she hit the clothes dryer? I'll bet she's got three or four purple ones on her legs right now from crashing into furniture corners."

"I bruise easy," said Filalia airily.

"Because you're a lush and you don't eat right!"

"Oh, go to bed."

"Declan and I never wanted you to meet our friends. Did you know that?"

"Bullshit!"

"Bullshit my *ass!* We dreaded it every single day. We were always too embarrassed!"

"I wasn't," said Declan mildly.

"Yes you were! Remember when she swiped that lid off of Buford Grady?"

"Oh, yeah. That was kind of funny."

"Yeah! Remember that?" hollered Alvin at his mother.

"Buford sure did feel bad," Declan smiled nostalgically.

"Toughen up and don't embarrass so easy," retorted Filalia.

Leroy went over to the woodbox and stacked more logs on the fire.

"You should have seen Buford's face," Declan murmured to me. "He'd worked and saved up for three months for that lid. We were smoking the first joint from it in our rec room. Then Mom came downstairs and started sniffing. 'What's that I smell?' Old Buford turned white as a sheet, and then she grabbed him by his shirt and told him she was calling the police and turning him in unless he handed the entire thing over to her."

"I know what's wrong with you," accused Filalia.

"I sincerely doubt it!" Alvin snapped.

Declan leaned toward me. "Mom said, 'I've got to go test this out clinically. I'm a nurse.' And she carried it off and he never saw it again," he added in a whisper. "Some evenings Buford would come over to our house and there would be a smoky smell wafting down from the upstairs hall, and he'd just look so sad."

"You're still mad because of Rita," she pronounced, and suddenly Alvin went pale and fell silent.

"You boys clean up the kitchen for your mother," said Leroy. "Go on, now."

"That's okay. I'll do it," I said gratefully, starting to rise.

"Clean it up for Lulu, too. She did all the cooking." He gestured for me to sit back down.

"Yes, sir," said Declan. But Alvin just tensed there in his chair with his lips barely open, his eyes blank under the huge, shaggy brown brows that were his alone among all the family.

WE WENT BACK to California two days after Thanksgiving. Declan was in the middle of an important project and couldn't take any more vacations for a while. I was looking for a better job and having no luck. Whatever had I imagined myself doing with majors in philosophy and the classics, besides reading Ovid and arguing about the linear perception of time? I worked in a jewelry store; my boss was a compulsive gambler. My fellow clerk was an elderly gay man from South Dakota who looked like Mark Twain and smelled like bourbon. The merchandise looked like it came from a Cracker Jack box. The most you could say was that it was hockable. To get to work I drove on the freeway to an exit four towns away. Each afternoon I returned home to the suburban sixties tract house exactly like all the other sixties tract houses up and down the block for an area covering ten square blocks that led to another neighboring suburb with a different style and floor plan of repeated tract houses; then I changed clothes, picked you up from nursery school, went to the supermarket, and drove back home to Fresno Street. Fresno Street was a couple of blocks off El Camino Real, the old august, romantic Spanish King's Highway that ran all the way down the Peninsula and was now the streambed for a flood of MacDonalds and dry cleaners. The way I recognized our house was that some former owner had painted the front door red and black, just to be different. Also our next-door neighbor had put in "Hawaiian" landscaping: a flower bed full of volcanic rocks and three Polynesian tikis. Landmarks could change your life in a place like that. The neighbors themselves we hardly ever met; people came and went as fast as poker cards. It was nothing like Bernice, Texas, where families occupied the same rooms for decades and sometimes a whole century. Silicon Valley had just started to grow and burst its seams; we happened to be living smack-dab in the center of the place that was changing the neural system of the whole planet. The fact that homes were rising in value twenty percent a year didn't perk me up much. Waving to the unknown teenagers across the street I unloaded the grocery bags. They stood in their driveway and watched, flicking the ash off their roll-your-owns. Two or three nights a week Alvin would come over for dinner. Afterward he and Declan would sit around smoking pot and devising strategies for Alvin to get another job. Alvin would insult Declan in a new and inventive way, he would smile amiably and give Alvin a little tease about long-ago girlfriends. If it was Sunday they'd go outside and vacuum their trucks. Sometimes if Declan got home from work before nine or ten P.M. we went to the movies.

I felt faceless.

In that first year of our marriage I experimented with cooking: tempura, eel. I learned wine-tasting from Napa wineries. Occasionally we threw ourselves away on a visit to some friends of Declan's at a commune in the Santa Cruz mountains, or went crazy once every three or four months eating dim sum on a Sunday morning with Miriam, who was now finishing her psychology Master's in San Francisco. Miriam introduced us to various people she knew, including a couple of painters, a clutch of therapists, and a journalist named Dan Hambleman. Declan failed to find these people very intriguing, though, and I made jaunts up to the city by myself as I began to crave more nonscientific conversation. But not often. Mainly we stayed in, because by the time Declan came home from the lab he'd feel so exhausted, buzzy with the day's tasks, and stoned from the "cocktail" he'd smoked on the drive home, that he'd eat dinner and fall into bed with no more than a sigh. I'd sit up in my study and write until two A.M., developing the plots for the mystery novels I hoped to write (*Murder in Madagascar, Hamburg Homicide, The Acapulco Assassin*), with the worldly footless sleuth (much brighter than that pathetic servant girl in *High Tea and Cyanide*) who would someday solve them.

Then I'd go to bed and dream of handsome, sensitive men with purposeful gleams in their eyes.

We had stopped making love sometime in the fall. When I thought about it I realized that it was right after Thanksgiving and our inaugural trip to New Mexico, but that didn't answer anything for me. Declan seemed to have become supremely disinterested in sex. I wondered if he was impotent. Occasionally I'd initiate things just to find out, and at those times he responded healthily enough— but only if I climbed on top and did all the work. Even then I felt like I was raping him.

The trouble was, he seemed to prefer that.

I will never show this journal to you, Treatie. I know that now.

Winter passed in its edgeless Bay Area way. Spring came. I went from feeling dispirited to feeling I was stuck in a frictionless schedule to feeling despair. You, on the other hand, blossomed.

"I look out the window, and what do I see? Popcorn popping on the apricot tree," you sang happily with the other kids in your nursery school chorus. "It wasn't really so, but it seemed to be. Popcorn popping on the apricot tree." Ah, Northern California. Fruit orchards or their ghostly remnants lining the bays of the foothills, at least before the next electronics firm swallowed up the land. Fields and clouds of trees in flower. It was like what Saroyan had once written about. Or at least I could almost see how it had once possibly been when Saroyan had once written about it. Almost, before it slipped forever over the edge of that old world and fell into the chaotic void of this one. "Look, Mom!" You pointed out the car window at a lone prune tree in full bloom as we stood stalled on the asphalt river amid factories and shopping centers in the rush-hour traffic. "Popcorn!" I reached over, rumpled your hair, and kissed you with tears in my eyes.

IT WAS HIGH summer when we finally returned to Angel Fire. The sagebrush glowed a silvery green, the color of Declan's hair after a few hours in a chlorinated pool. The scents of the mountains seemed even stronger than they had during the snow. Days stretched long and hot and dry with their cobalt skies and bright clean light; the aspen leaves shivered like rippling water. At night cool air flowed down from the Rockies, cloaking us. I took deep gulps of it.

"I bought you an early birthday present," said Filalia after she greeted us on the front porch.

"What's that?" I glanced at her two hands, cupped around some hidden object like they were a box. She was always generous, almost to the point of embarrassment.

"A concho belt!"

She opened her hands wide. I took the length of leather threaded with little stamped silver medallions. "Oh, Filalia. It's beautiful. So delicate!"

"It matches mine," she said, and touched the one strung around her waist. "It's Navajo. Hey, I heard something really funny the other day. Did you know that a Navajo man isn't allowed to speak to or look at his mother-in-law or even live close by? The tribe believes that any contact between them can make him sick! He could go insane or blind, or get bad diarrhea or halitosis or something."

"Sounds like what they used to tell kids about masturbation."

"Hair on his palms!" she said. "It's no joke, though. Good thing you're not a man, Lulu. In some Navajo families the mother-in-law has to wear a bell around her neck to warn the son-in-law she's coming. Can you imagine me with a little silver bell hanging from my cat collar?"

"I wish we could live here," I said, suddenly wistful.

"Maybe you could talk Declan into doing consulting work by computer long distance."

"No chance. Not in a million years."

"Why not? You could live in the cabin."

I thought of the cabin, the chimera floating beyond the hem of the woods. It was part adobe, part log and beam, the kiva fireplace molded by loving hands long ago — an extension of the wall behind it, an organic bulge, the living warm heart of hearth. Three acres of the property faced Forest Service land. The house had two little bedrooms plus a tiny study, plus a small shed out back that seemed to me eminently convertible, plus a deed upon which both twins' names lay inscribed but for which Declan had made the down payment and now paid three-fourths of the monthly mortgage. From the back you could walk straight through the aspens up a mountain. From the front window you could see Wheeler Peak.

"He won't budge," I sighed. "He likes his work too much right now. For that he needs a lab. According to him, we live on the cutting edge of scientific progress and he wants to be part of it."

"I always respected Leroy's job, too. But it sure kept me in Amarillo a lot longer than I'd ever intended," Filalia said.

"Yeah. I guess that's what we pick when we marry, isn't it?"

"Work on him."

CAN WE STAY in the cabin this time?" I'd already asked Declan as we'd crossed into the Rockies on our way there.

"Nah. I kind of promised Mom and Daddy we'd hang out with them awhile."

"It's only half a mile from their property. We can walk it, easy."

"We'll go there and spend a day. Take a little picnic maybe."

I leaned over to the driver's seat. "There're things I want to do with you in there," I whispered intensely in his ear, and then licked it with the tip of my tongue. "In the night. In the wee hours. Just. Us. Two." I ran my hand up his thigh.

His eyes half-closed as he whipped around a mountain curve. "Well, Alvin's showing up day after tomorrow. He's planning on staying in it, I think."

"*What?*"

I pulled back.

"He's still kind of depressed. He called me right before we left home."

"Why didn't you *tell* me?" I moaned. "Alvin. Alvin! Always Alvin! *Damn* it!"

"Are you mad, Mom?" you asked.

"Yes!——but not at you, Treatie."

"Alvin?"

"That's right. I'm afraid that's true." I turned on Declan again. "Can't we go anywhere without him trailing along behind us? Can't we even take the shortest, tiniest little vacation alone? *Why* is Alvin doing this?"

"He's not doing anything." Declan looked surprised. "He's just depressed.

"*What is it this time?*" He was always depressed, when he wasn't jubilant or manic.

"He just got word that Rita had the baby."

"Oh my God." I slumped back.

"He's real unhappy."

"Well——what's he planning on doing about it? Is he finally going to go to her? Like he should have six months ago?"

He shook his head. "She also married some guy yesterday back in Georgia."

"Oh," I said, and stared at the road, silenced.

"WE'RE THINKING ABOUT coming up to California in the fall to visit you-all," said Filalia over dinner.

"Really? Cool. You've never visited me before," said Declan.

"I guess it's about overdue, then," said Leroy.

"You always lived like a bachelor before. It was better for you to come home and see us," said Filalia. "Besides, you're the oldest."

"Well, that hasn't changed."

"The bachelor pad has. Now that you're married we

should visit you and see your house. That's what's right. Do you still sleep on that sloshy waterbed? He had that bed in college," she added to me.

"I know," I said.

"Yep," he said, and smiled. I hated the waterbed with a scornful hate, but Declan wasn't aware of that.

"I always figured you got up to plenty of mischief on that thing," she said wickedly and rolled her eyes.

"Oh, not too much," said Declan.

"I'll bet so. After all, you're my son, aren't you?"

"That's true."

"And Leroy's!"

"Oh, wow. Look at the time! I've got to get Treatie down for his nap. He's been awake half the night traveling."

"Bye-bye, Tristan." Filalia ducked her chin tight, tipped up her eyes, and waggled her fingers. "Bye-bye, sweetie pie. See you later in the afternoon."

"Bye-bye, Filay-la," you said, and held my hand as we walked down the hall.

"**Am I supposed** to clean your cabin for your brother again this trip?" I asked nastily. We leaned back on a bed of moss by a stream and stared up at the sky through willow branches. Mountain asters and daisies bloomed in the meadow behind us; a rainbow trout slithered behind some boulders against the opposite shore.

"You don't like Alvin much, do you?" Declan said.

"He's irresponsible and immature and mean, and what he did to Rita was horrific."

"What about how she got pregnant when she'd claimed to be taking precautions?"

"Declan. Remember? It takes two to make a baby?"

"Yeah, well. There might have been just a teensy little question about just which two made this one."

I looked at him. "Are you implying—Rita was seeing someone else?"

He plucked a long piece of grass, shook his head, chewed the pale root end, and shrugged. The fan of bright hair spread over his shoulders and glistened in the sunlight like spiderweb.

"Were there grounds to think that?"

"Not for sure," he admitted.

"Then—couldn't he just trust her?"

Declan looked at me and made a quick, wry face.

"How can you claim to love someone you don't trust?" I asked.

"Men live with women they don't trust all the time. You just have to accept that when you accept the person, and love her anyway."

I stared at him, frowning. He looked very clean and in-nocent as he spoke. Guileless.

"Besides," he added, "it's been done before." He watched a grasshopper crawl along his jeans leg and then carefully lifted it off and tucked it inside some tall grass. "Mom thought so, too. Except she didn't say it to Alvin at the time. She only told me."

"Did she."

"But she did repeat it out loud later to Alvin, when he

told her about the split-up. After all, don't forget, Mom's a woman. She knows those kinds of tricks."

"*What* kind of tricks?"

"Oh, never mind."

"What did Alvin say?"

"That it was bad enough the first time he'd heard it."

"You mean—he'd heard it before she offered him her opinion?" Suddenly a horrible thought struck me. I sat up and grabbed his arm. "Declan. Did you tell Alvin what your mother had said? About the baby maybe not being his?"

"Well. He's my brother."

I gaped. "Oh, no. Declan! How could you? How could you repeat something so *destructive?*"

"He's my brother. I have to take care of him."

"But it wasn't your business!"

"Of course it was. Shoot—I'd want him to do the same for me if it ever came up."

"Poor Alvin," I whispered as the curtain fell away and the full picture gleamed out in all its awful clarity. "Poor Alvin."

"What are you talking about?" Declan scoffed gently. "He's not poor. It's turned out fine. He won't have to lift a finger."

"HEY, TAKE A gander at this," said Filalia a couple of mornings later, poring through an old photo album of black-and-white snapshots. "Can you believe Leroy in his uniform?"

We were sitting in the breakfast room, sipping Bloody Marys, while Filalia rummaged through a stack of books and loose papers for Declan's and Alvin's baby pictures.

"Is that you in yours?" I asked.

"Sure is. Look at my cap!" The figure shading the sun from her eyes stood in front of the Eiffel Tower. Above her arched hand sat a jaunty little white pillbox. "We weren't supposed to wear them like that. It was strictly against army regulations. But I always enjoyed breaking a few rules, and I'd crimp down the side corners after they got starched."

"What years were you in France?" I asked.

"Oh, after D-Day. Before then I was in North Africa and Italy." She tilted her head, studying the picture. "Even though I had a lot of fun I always made sure I did my job."

"You mean in the operating room." I wondered how often she'd had to hand instruments to a surgeon while throbbing with a hangover.

"No, I mean like cleaning up loose ends." Smiling, she wrapped one of her curls around her finger. "You know, like the odd German prisoner convalescing in my ward."

"Oh, you had German soldiers in the hospital?"

"Of course. It was a field hospital. Whenever they took wounded prisoners we got them."

"I guess I hadn't realized that's the way it works."

"It turned out convenient," she said.

"What do you mean?"

"Well. For instance. Have you ever heard of air bubbles in a hypodermic?"

I stared into her eyes. I couldn't look away. They peered up, mercurial and blank with light.

The cold flowing through my legs made me feel sick. It was hard to stand. "I need to go use the bathroom," I said. "Excuse me."

"Oh, come on. You're not a sissy, are you?" She pursed her lips as I backed away from the sofa. "You kids just have it too soft these days. You haven't had to face the stuff we did."

Right as I reached the door I suddenly turned around again. "Have you heard the news about Rita, by any chance?"

"You mean that she's found another sucker? I heard that." She reached over to the end table by the sofa and poured herself a topped-off glass of sherry from the gallon flagon sitting there.

"No. I mean that you're now a grandmother."

"Oh, balls." Comically she shook her head. "Grandmother! You didn't buy *that* story, did you? My Alvin, knocking a girl up?"

"Do you think you're maybe too hard on her?" I tried one last time.

"Nah. I'm not hard on anybody. Girls have to do what girls have to do." She smiled again, tilting her head up toward me, and drank half the glass straight down in one gulp. "You know that."

DECLAN GOT AN offer from a firm in Spain. An English company had opened a top-secret research lab on the island of Minorca, and they wanted him to come live there.

"Oh, Declan! I can hardly believe it." We were due to go out to dinner with the company's representatives that night for dinner.

"It's pretty interesting, I guess," he said.

"It's fantastic! All day I've been so excited I could hardly think. I've been looking at the Atlas—come into the study, I'll show you the layout of the Mediterra—"

"Naw, that's okay."

"It'd be a good thing to look at the island before the reps get here to pick us up. That way you can have some idea of what they'll be offering in terms of location, houses and all, so you can be more specific in what you ask for."

"Well, I don't know that I'll be *asking* for anything," he said diffidently.

"Do we have to take company housing? Or could we live in a little village in the mountains?" I asked.

"Well, I kind of don't think I'll be able to accept company housing," he said. He sat back and lighted a joint.

Anticipation quickened in my brain like champagne. "That's okay by me. That's great! I've got a book with some pictures—"

"Accept the job, I mean," he said.

"*What?*"

He ducked his head and took a long toke.

"You're kidding."

"Well, sort of. Not exactly." He drew another toke, sipping off the end of the smoke like a person sipping from a cordial glass. "Not really."

"But—why? What are you talking about? You'll have the chance to do the most advanced genetics research in the world! They're paying you a fortune!"

"Yep. They said they would." He nodded.

"Five times your *present salary!*"

"Uh-huh."

"How can you talk this way? Declan—you're their whiz kid, you'd be their top scientist!" I gathered my breath.

"I think I really would rather not leave America right now," he replied. "I'd kind of prefer to stay here."

"*Why?* We can come back! We'll come back! Later!" I was getting frantic. I could almost touch it. I could almost smell European soil. I could feel the passport in my hand, feel the tug as it got wrenched away, feel my fingertips brush it right before it disappeared into the darkness.

He filled his lungs with smoke, held it there a minute, and then expelled it with a long, slow, practiced *ahh-whummpf.*

"I kind of think I need to stay closer to the folks. Do my own thing. Spain's a real long ways away," he added.

"Your *parents* are why you won't go?"

"Well—family."

"Alvin! *Alvin's* the reason! That—*chipmunk!*"

He looked at me. "Hey. Don't forget Alvin's my younger brother."

And after all, he was the one with the job offer to accept or reject as he chose. The power, the rights were all his.

TWO MONTHS LATER I missed a period.

It seemed surprising, since I was taking the Pill with fanatical regularity. But there was no point in brooding too much on it until one Tuesday morning when I woke up sick as a housecat on a ferry.

"Declan," I said that night, "I want to explain something."

"Okay," he said. "You sure look happy. I hope it's not that you've gone and bought us a mink bath mat on my credit card."

"Don't be ridiculous," I said, and climbed onto his armchair and curled into his passive lap. "I'm not approved for signing your credit cards." A certain level-headed quality that had always attracted me beyond his goofiness now filled me with sweet exaltation: he would definitely prove good genetic material. His tenderness with you, his stepson, insured attributes even more important for the years to come. Gently I wrapped my arms around him and kissed his forehead, his cheek. "You know—ever since you threw out the Minorca job I've been having a little trouble coming to terms with your decision—"

"Well, I've kind of noticed that," he said.

"You have? How?"

"Oh, something about the number of times a week you drive up to San Francisco to see your friends, even though Miriam's already moved back to Texas. And at night when you're thrashing around and pacing all over the living room smoking cigarettes until four in the morning. It kind of clued me in that you might be upset about more than just Alvin eating up all your birthday fudge."

"Yeah," I admitted. "Although I think that was just a symptom. But I'm over it now. It's turned out to be the best thing in the long run. I just want you to know."

"Is that all you were going to say? Heck, think nothing of it."

"That's not quite all."

"What's the rest?" He slid his hand softly up and down my arm.

"I'm pregnant," I said.

His hand stopped and went slack.

"So it's good that we're still in the States. Instead of living on an island far away from our parents and everything."

"I thought you were on the Pill," he murmured in bemusement.

"I've never missed a single day. But I went in and got a test at the doctor's this afternoon. It's certain."

For a moment he sat silent.

"I'd like to think history's repeating itself," I said. "The doctor said that even though the Pill made my body believe it's already pregnant I ovulated anyhow. You know, like your mother did with you and Alvin."

"Wow," he said finally, his voice unnaturally dry. "Are you really sure?"

"Yes," I whispered.

"Well, then. Who's going to phone the abortion clinic —you or me?"

And for the first time I met the rigid steel that was to turn Declan into a billion-dollar genetic engineering tycoon by the age of thirty-seven.

WHAT CAN I say?

Three months after the operation my parents invited my cousin and me to the U.K. on a little family junket. England and Scotland, three weeks. Five days in the Highlands. Two days in Wales. Four in the Cotswolds. One afternoon alone at the Tate Gallery, sitting on a bench in front of a Bonnard—Bonnard, the painter whose picture in Bo's copy of *The Magus* now at last had a living image— feeling the presence behind my back as someone else sat down.

That's all it took.

Filalia and Leroy kept their promise and came out to visit a few weeks after I got home. On their first night Filalia cornered me in the ladies' room of the restaurant where we were eating dinner. "You look different," she accused.

"Do I?"

"Yeah."

"Uh. Hm."

"How come?"

"I've got to get out of here," I blurted.

"The bathroom?" She glanced around at the stalls.

"California."

"Oh." She went quiet. "For good?"

I meant to answer, No. Of course not. Just for a while.

I don't know. For a little while, to see what I've missed. To not have to look at your mistrustful son. Whom you have created. "Yes."

She unscrewed her lipstick and leaned toward the mirror. "To leave Declan."

I nodded. Lying at that moment was impossible.

"You got any money?" she asked after a pause. She dabbed her thin lips with raspberry pink.

"A little monthly income that I inherited from my grandmother. That'll see me through the basics for the next few years. At least until I can start getting my mystery novels published. And I can get a job in London as a secretarial temp. And I'm going to sell my jewelry. I've got all these antique pieces I've been picking up here and there since I started working in the trade. Some of them are fairly valuable. Rubies, emeralds, sapphires."

"What about Tristan?" I couldn't tell what she was thinking. My own feelings had grown too ineluctable, their momentum now a torrent; they hid everything else from my eyes.

"His father's living in Europe. He hasn't even seen him in two years, not since Ted and his new wife moved to Sweden. Treatie can spend a little time with them while I travel, and then when I know where I'm settling I'll fetch him."

She looked unreadable. "Have you told Declan?"

"He's got an idea." He'd seen the letters with their foreign postmarks lying on my desk. He'd seen the grass burns healing on my lower back. He hadn't said a word.

"How does he feel?"

"I don't know." My mouth was dry. "Not particularly bothered." He seemed oblivious: no changes in routine. Alvin for dinner. Work, come home. Never mention the thing between us. Nor respond if I brought it up, weeping, or crying out, or railing with anger. Not a word, ever.

She smacked her lips together, watching her own face in the mirror, and carefully recapped the lipstick. "Well, you know what? I'd love some new jewelry," she said. "Leroy's overdue to buy me an anniversary present, and since it's our thirtieth it had better be good. How's about you show me what you've got in the morning?"

THESE DAYS SO many structures have broken down that no one thinks about them much anymore. Marriage, family, government. You know how it is, Treatie. You were there when it started devolving. You saw the seeds.

When something no longer works you can just leave it. That's what American civilization with its cheap airfares and superhighways has taught us over the last twenty years. When the boredom and disconnection go on too long, hit the road. When something hurts too much, when the pain rends too deep, then it's over. Leave it and try something else. The country's a big one, full of many landscapes. And there are so many other countries out there waiting for sojourners to arrive.

Or as Filalia had once observed: easy come, easy go.

1980: Crucible

That's the way married people are supposed to be. Why, my mother and father fought like cats and dogs for forty years. I wouldn't take two cents for a dame without a temper.
——HUMPHREY BOGART in *High Sierra*

"Are you English?" I asked him.
"No. I'm a New Zealander," he said.

I'VE THOUGHT ABOUT the mother-in-law, daughter-in-law structure quite a bit in my life, Treatie, and all the forms it takes around the world. There are Polynesian extended families whose members live under one roof almost as a multicelled organism, with parents or parents-in-law as the deciding brains. There are the infamous mothers-in-law in India who snatch the new bride's dowry (gold jewelry, refrigerators, TV, silk saris) from her hard-sweating family, and then murder her off using some handy household tool—with the son's assistance—and burn her dismembered body in the kitchen stove.

But the old Chinese custom is the one I've always feared most in my heart. Before the Revolution, a bride was handed over to her husband's family without so much as a glimpse backward, which effectively stripped her of all previous identity except that conferred by the new mother-in-law. What a thought. Imagine never seeing your parents again, forfeiting your brothers and sisters and all other relatives like they'd ceased to exist. Imagine becoming a slave to your arranged husband and his mother, performing all the domestic chores, looking after your mother-in-law's every little whim. Imagine living in a household where you have not one single ally.

Far worse than the housework was how carefully daughters-in-law got watched for signs of conception, and blamed and punished—*by the mother-in-law*—if no son arrived quickly. Often they became the household scapegoat. All they could do was silently pray for revenge, the only one likely: that they too would give birth to a boy who, someday when he grew old enough, would contract *his* life to some other innocent little girl's and haul her into the home to fetch rosewater and bathe her new mother-in-law's feet.

Cyclic consolation is all very well for some, I suppose, but I sure wouldn't want to depend on it. But if there's one point in my life when I first learned about the dynamics of revenge, it was when I met Geoffrey.

I'D WATCHED HIM out of the corner of my eye, his reflection swimming across the glassed etchings and bronze rails as he followed me from hall to hall throughout the gallery, without any indication whatsoever that he realized there was another human being within five hundred yards.

You're extremely noticeable, I wanted to say; don't imagine you're not. But I didn't dare.

"I'm a New Zealander," he said.

"So does that make you a tourist?"

"I've been traveling a bit." He shrugged. "I'm living here for the interim."

"The interim between what?" His presence felt so complete that it made me nervous. He seemed swathed in radiation. I'd sensed the pull on my back the instant he sat down on the same bench I was sitting on; without turning around I'd known, out of all the crowd in the Tate Gallery that Friday afternoon, who it was.

"Before whatever comes next, I suppose." He smiled shyly.

"Oh."

"Have you looked at the Turners yet?"

"Yes," I said. You know I have, I thought. You were there.

"Right. How about the Blakes?"

"Yes. The Blakes also."

"Reasonable, eh? What do you reckon?"

He seemed boyish. He seemed bashful and eager, with his thick yellow hair brushed straight back off his brow and his up-slanted green eyes sparkling like Errol Flynn's, his pale, clear, unfreckled skin above a well-pressed khaki collar. Self-effacement colored his voice even when he asked a blunt question. The strange thing was, I'd actually first caught sight of him three days before in Trafalgar Square, as the offices of Whitehall disgorged their workers and people hurried toward tube stations. May light had shawled Landseer's lions and husked the London stones in gold. He'd been standing in a bus queue; for some reason my eyes had snapped onto him like magnets. "What an unusual looking man," I'd murmured to my cousin Mary, who stood beside me smoking a cigarette and glowering at the traffic. She glanced without noticing, bored by Stubbs and sick and tired of the Italian pre-Renaissance and not giving a damn what I was looking at. An unmistakable man, I thought as my neural system gave a subtle tremor; anyway, I'd really spoken to myself.

And here he sat.

"To tell the truth I've waited a lifetime to finally see some Blakes. Well, ten years, at least. Real ones, I mean. In person," I answered now. "Especially watercolors. I mean—well, I studied him a lot in college."

"Ah." Unmistakably he suppressed a smile, which made him look mischievous.

"He's kind of my hero."

"Hm." His mouth corners twitched. "Hero, eh?"

"Well—what about you? Or do you not have any heroes?" Despite the miracle of coincidence in a city of millions, which had struck me as all of a piece with seeing the Blakes and therefore requiring my most intense and earnest attention, I wondered why I felt so edgy.

"His draftsmanship's pretty amazing, really. Considering."

"But it's his vision!" I didn't stop to ask: considering what? "It's his vision that—" How could I put it? Moved me? Haunted me? Gave me a glimpse of truth, of the ineffable? Could I say these things to someone who'd happened to sit down on the same museum bench? They composed the last shreds of metaphysics I hung on to as I hurtled compulsively through life——more an inkling than a belief system. He hunched there behind me, listening with his feet flat on the ground, his legs cocked out to straddle space, chin notched on his fist. "It's his vision that I wanted to see. The paintings are so much stronger and more delicate than reproductions. In books. Realer."

"Naturally." He eyed me quizzically. The air around crackled with a dim yet audible static that seemed possibly to come from the light fixtures but that I knew was really generated by the surface of my skin. Into the midst of it Mary strolled up. She took one hard look, raised her eyebrows, started to sit down on the bench, then changed her mind. With relief I watched her slouch off into the next room to prowl through the collection of Spencers.

"Reproductions can look real sometimes," I defended.

"No. Never."

"Yes, they can. I mean——well, for instance, when they're etchings or lithographs. Or woodblocks, maybe."

"If you were an artist you wouldn't say that."

"Oh. Well. Are you an artist?"

"Printmaker." His gaze swiveled off toward the middle distance.

"Like——etchings and lithographs?"

He nodded diffidently. "Woodblocks. Painting. Monotypes."

"I see."

"Yes. Seeing——that's the point, isn't it? It's more a question of using the eyes. The old eyes," he nodded wisely to himself, narrowing his blue ones.

"What do you paint?" I asked.

He merely looked at me sideways and smiled.

"Well." I turned primly to face the incandescent bathroom in front of me. "*This* painting is just about perfect."

"Now there's a big word."

"Well, it's something else I've waited quite a long time to see."

Indulgently he squinted at it. "Bonnard's all right. A bit decorative. But 'perfect' is rather like taking a tank after rabbits, don't you reckon?"

"*Decorative?*" The tiled wall with its squares of Riviera light, its solid, soft shape floating in opalescent water—long legs, blue-shadowed rib cage beneath the breasts, the pink underbelly of the tub that cradled her body like Venus inside the shell, her musing face rising clear—was the world I'd dreamed of entering since the first time I'd seen it on Bo's kitchen table.

"Gutless."

"But it's so intimate."

He threw his head back, dismissing intimacy. Then he gestured toward the next painting. "Look at that. See? Bowls of milk beside French windows. Pleasant, seductive, tidy little middle-class setup. But his darkness never gets truly dark, does it? It's all pretty. Petty. Bourgeois! He wouldn't know what darkness is."

"No." Dubiously I stared at the shadows with their mosaic of glowing color and evanescent detail. But on the other hand, if he hadn't known darkness, how could he have known so much about light?

"He never did tackle anything you could sink your teeth into, old Pierre."

Mary trudged back to the doorway, meaningfully catching my eye, held up her wristwatch, and jerked her thumb toward the main entrance. I tried signaling her back: one more minute. Her brows hiked even higher and she disappeared into the gallery. We were scheduled to meet my parents for dinner after everything closed; they were spending the day at an antiques show.

"Well, I think we're going now," I said. "It's been nice talking to you."

"Going? Where to?"

"The British Museum."

"How come?"

"Because—we want to. Except that we have to find it. We don't know where the tube station is. That's the reason I asked you if you were English. I figured you might know."

"Ah. I see. And who's 'we'?"

"My cousin Mary and me."

He searched around the hall. Sitting spine to spine this way I could mark his scent from a few inches and feel his body heat through my T-shirt. "She's that dark-haired woman in orange who just went back in the next room," I said.

He swung back to his natural position and craned toward the doorway. "She seems busy enough."

I couldn't see from that angle. "What's she doing?"

"At the moment she's looking down her nose at the nude portrait of Stanley Spencer and his wife Patricia, lying next to their nice big red joint of mutton."

"Oh," I said faintly.

"And licking her lips."

"Maybe she's hungry."

"*Ha!*" He gave a shout of laughter.

"She's a contracts lawyer. She's had five whole days of nothing but museums," I added, as if that explained everything.

He turned again, and suddenly as a falling brick, dropped backward across the bench so close his breath grazed my cheek. "But aren't Americans the most puritanical people in the world?"

"What are you talking about?" I forced myself not to pull back.

He smiled, staring into my eyes.

"No," I said above my suddenly pounding heart rate. "We're not, actually! What a stupid generalization."

His smile turned sunny, brimming amusement. "You all take yourselves so seriously."

"Hey," barked Mary, clumping up to my side of the bench and ramming her watch at me: four o'clock. "You ready?"

"Yeah. Sure." Trying to collect myself I sloped casually sideways. "Ah—how are we going to find the B.M.?"

"How should I know? You said you'd ask directions at the main desk."

"Oh, yeah! I did. The first guard didn't know where it

was. The second guard was Indian. He said he didn't, either." My voice sounded unnaturally shrill.

"What did his being Indian have to do with it?" asked the New Zealander.

"Nothing. Except he didn't speak English very well."

"Typical," muttered Mary, but I knew she didn't mean the guard. She scowled at the New Zealander in deep suspicion and tightened her bleached-knuckle grip on the strap of her shoulder bag. "Well, we might as well forget the B.M. Let's just go back to the hotel."

I felt movement. The New Zealander was picking up his guidebook and rising to his feet.

"Okay," I said, giving up.

"Hey. Listen. I have an *A to Zed*." The New Zealander came around to our side of the bench and held the book out to her, offering me his other hand at the same moment as if helping me rise was the most automatic courtesy in the world. "We can look it up."

"Excuse me," said Mary stiffly. "Do we know you?"

"Not yet."

"Come on, Lulu. Let's go."

"But you might," he added.

"Is he—were you planning on him coming with *us?*" she wheeled on me. I sat grinning like a mummy with anxiety, trying to ignore the hand.

"Maybe." He smiled winsomely. "If you don't mind."

"Who are you, anyhow? What's your name?" asked Mary, her glare now accusing me of introduction failure.

"Geoffrey Rutherford," he replied.

A prickle lifted the hairs on my neck.

"Nice to meet you." I stood up. "This is my cousin Mary Sue Penfield Cole from Tyler, Texas."

"Pleasure."

I heard the word and weighed its implications.

"My name's—I'm Lulu Miller—*Penfield*," I said, clearly and firmly.

Mary, her eyes wide, let out a hiss of indignant reproof.

I REALLY WONDER, Treatie, just how far away you have to be to smell pheromones. Certainly I've proven that one can pick up their unmistakable track from many, many yards off, say two-thirds of a football field, and under obtuse circumstances, for instance six hundred people jamming a major thoroughfare (each one, mind you, secreting his or her own personal molecular strand, the warp and weft of six hundred sex lives undeterred by deodorant), in the midst of which that sole person releases the one irresistible whiff that wends through the crowd, climbs a two-story flight of steps, crosses a porch the size of a cruise-ship deck, reaches the brain, slips like a noose around desire, and yanks the hapless victim toward her DNA destination. No doubt if we were cats or Doberman Pinschers we'd take the distance for granted. I'm sure some researcher in Sweden has nailed the exact trajectory to a micromillimeter—not counting the airline miles it took to set them into the right vectors in the first place. But I'd like to see the numbers.

For this reason I'm convinced that a chemical connec-

tion exists between the mother of the pheromone transmitter and the receiver.

Whatever the case, it no longer strikes me as surprising
that I saw Geoff, a wayfarer born half a world away, and
knew him instantly, and what's more kept crisscrossing
paths with him until we finally clanged together. The force
was bigger than both of us.

Of all the art galleries in all the cities in all the world,
he had to walk into mine.

IN THE END we couldn't find the right station so we took a
bus.

Perched on the top floor of a double decker, jouncing
through the city beneath a hazy spring sky, we saw the
dome of Saint Paul's flecked with pigeons, and right away
spotted several memorably quaint pub signs. Thundering
through Fleet Street in the gold late-afternoon light, we
breathed exhaust and listened to brakes squeal while
Geoffrey stared glittery-eyed as an amphetamine addict
toward every fresh sight. "Look at that!" he'd cry, pointing
out a blue punk hairdo or a Wren chapel as the bus trun-
dled down the blocks. "Brilliant!" It was all new to all of
us, except that while Mary sat surly as a char on her way
to clean a basement, he grinned like Robin Hood.

"According to your map, this is our stop," muttered
Mary at last as the ticket conductor came by.

"Is it?" He leapt up and ran down the staircase. Out on
the street he flipped open the *A to Z* and turned it first one
way, then another, peering at the maze of blocks.

"This is the one, isn't it?" I asked.

"I'm not sure. What direction is left?"

"Left after what?" asked Mary.

I watched him hold up one hand and experimentally touch the fingertips together, then do the same with the other, as if testing the wind. "You mean—like left or right?" I asked. Mary snorted. Then, whirling around, she stalked off toward the end of the block and back.

"We go that way, I *think*," he said, pointing in the opposite direction.

"*Why* did you ever pick him up?" snarled Mary in my ear.

"He's the guy I pointed out to you in Trafalgar Square the other day. Remember?"

"No."

"He's interesting," I insisted while we lagged behind on the sidewalk. I meant intoxicating.

"Cute," she said. "Handsome, maybe. But interesting— definitely not."

My foot stopped in midpace. How could she even add the maybe?

"Hey, come take a look at this!" he yelled from several yards ahead, "Hurry, he's getting away. *Quickly!*" I raced up to the patch of tiny park where he stood, so attracted to his accent that I nearly collided with a passerby on the path.

"What?" I said, hunting around the side grass for a lizard or a griffin. "Who?"

"Isn't he bloody marvelous?" He pointed to the man I'd just avoided, a sober-faced dewlapped professional in a pin-striped suit, striped tie, and bowler, carrying a rolled umbrella under one arm with a newspaper clamped against it.

"Brilliant! Do you realize what he is? A real, live British civil servant! A natural specimen! Can you believe it? The *hat*—did you catch the hat? And the brollie, the paper—*that's* perfect, my sweetness-and-light, *that's* what perfect is. My God, now *I've* waited a lifetime to see that." He stood in the middle of the sidewalk, gazing raptly at the man's retreating back.

"Oh Lord," murmured Mary. "A nut case."

"Not necessarily," I whispered.

"Really? What is he then?" she snapped. "That you introduced yourself to with your *maiden name?*"

I flushed. "An artist," I answered.

ONCE WE DISCOVERED the British Museum was locked for the day, Geoff said, "Let's go find a pub."

"They don't open for another hour," said Mary.

"How about this tea shop?" I suggested. I guided us through the door; it was all I could do to keep up with his comments, and I was dying to sit down. His shirt collar lay open. As we pulled out our chairs I noticed just below his throat, below the tender hollow of his clavicle, a sprig of golden hair.

"Tea. Lots of it," ordered Mary. The waitress wrote it down, gave Geoff a speculative once-over, and trotted off.

"So how long have you lived in London?" I asked weakly.

"About a fortnight," he said.

"Oh. Well, um . . . where were you before that?"

"Greece."

"*Greece?*" I squeaked, and cleared my throat.

"Greece and Turkey. What's the matter?" He turned those green eyes on me.

"I've been wanting to get to Greece my whole life."

"Have you?"

"It's the second big thing besides—like the Blakes. The other big goal."

"Ah," he said. "Well. I'll tell you something. The time to go is spring. Did you know that on the island of Rhodos, when the poppies seep up through the earth, it looks like the grass and rocks are bleeding?"

"No," I said after some thought, "I didn't."

"Stippled in blood. Gold and scarlet. With the cobalt of the sea sliding beyond punctured with light."

"It sounds beautiful."

"The air hangs absolutely clear, thin—weightless. The shadows carve the earth blue-black. Like a scythe. Nothing can compare to the light of Greece. But what's even more amazing is Cappodocia."

"Why?"

"There the rocks stand around like—like human limbs, deformed ones, whole fields and mountainsides of them. Amputees. The human wreckage of a war or something. The colors will knock your eyes out. Pink and rose, orange, and the sky above them floats in a wash, true cerulean, straight out of a tube. And in the towns—God stone the crows! you wouldn't believe the carpets. Bloody Turks know how to weave, my Christ they do. All these rich Giotto colors glowing from the doorways of dark interiors, tiny copper coffeepots on braziers sizzling through the afternoon, the old fellow waiting inside to haggle, not a female on the street after sundown so you go to a café for a feast that staggers on for five bloody hours, nothing but men everywhere. Then you all stand up to dance, and the *music*—not to compare it to bouzouki music in Greece, now *that* would rip your heart out in two seconds—"

"Oh," I murmured. It hit me then, with full, specific consciousness. This was the sexiest, most charismatic man I'd ever met.

"—then you crawl off drunk as a skunk to the baths and get pounded on a marble tabletop. By the massage fellow, I mean. *Ha!*" He crowed with laughter.

Mary sloshed the tea into her cup and took another sip.

WHEN WE PARTED at Oxford Circus across from our hotel he wrote down his phone number. "Ring me when you get back from Scotland. If you feel like it," he said, bashful once again. Despite his recent travels I got the impression that he hadn't really had very much experience with girls; he looked so young, art-studentish, and once the conversation veered away from the worldly into the personal he appeared to grow touchingly self-conscious and unsure of what to say next. A smoky look brushed his eye when I asked him where he was staying; his mumble, "Hammersmith," seemed distracted. Then he frowned so hard into a boutique display that I assumed the window dressing offended him. "Look at that rubbish!" he cried, thrusting a hand toward a mannequin dripping in peach lace. "What a color. Chunder! Whatever happened to Carnaby Street?" He swung back toward the street, pressing his lips together. They were full, chiseled.

"So, I'll phone you," I agreed.

His face brightened. "We could find that pub!" he said. "Don't you reckon the pubs here are worth it? Draft Guinness, can you believe? And *warm, flat beer!* my Christ, what a sacrilege. Weasel's piss! I'll meet you if you like."

"We'll be coming back to this same hotel. Two weeks from now," I said. "Our last night in London before we fly out."

"Will your cousin come along, do you think?" He stared across the street where Mary was already clopping toward the lobby doors in disgust.

"I don't know. Possibly." Maybe I can lose her, I thought. Mother and Dad would be calling it an early night. Maybe she won't feel so duty-bound to socialize after two weeks traipsing through stately homes and cathedrals. "She might want to spend the evening sorting and packing."

"She's got quite an intriguing mouth. Have you noticed that? Begs for paint. With those smudgy black eyes and those cheekbones." He frowned as the hotel foyer door closed behind her. "Well. We'll see you, then," he said, and flashed the shy, quirky smile once more. Then he waved and stood watching as I picked my way through the traffic of Oxford Street. In the creaky old lift, I felt his eyes all the way up to the fourth floor.

THAT FINAL EVENING in England as Mary and I walked through the twinkling dusk of Picadilly, she announced, "You know he's just some guy on the make."

"What makes you say that?"

We dodged a pair of West Indian prostitutes in pink and yellow hot pants and turned down Regent's Arcade. London was much warmer than Edinburgh had been; the U.K. was experiencing a heat wave, and most of it seemed concentrated in Soho. I had been sweating ever since leaving the Cotswolds that afternoon although I was trying hard to act nonchalant. Mary paused before a jeweler's window full of antique gold and rose-cut diamonds. "Look how he picked you up."

"He didn't pick me up! I tapped him on the shoulder."

"*What?*"

"After we'd been sitting on that bench awhile—I asked him if he was English," I said ingenuously.

"He's a total stranger! From some obscure tiny little country down at the bottom of the world. You have no way of knowing who his family is. You can't find out if he's just lying about himself or if he's some complete psycho. For heaven's sake, Lulu, where's your brain? He could be a serial killer, or a gigolo. Don't you have any sense whatsoever?"

"Mary—"

"Besides, he only wants one thing."

"What?" So far, I'd received no definite carnal signals from him, and wondered if she'd noticed something I'd missed.

"Money."

"*Money?*" I recoiled. "Don't be silly. What money?"

"He doesn't know that. We're Americans."

"It's his first trip abroad. He's just enthusiastic. Naive."

"You've been romantic like this your whole damn life." Stupid, she meant. "Not to mention married, remember? Not even telling him your real last name is—"

"Why are you making such a big deal? People meet all the time when they travel. It's part of the journey, it doesn't mean anything."

"Oh, yeah. Sure," she said darkly.

"It's only a drink, okay? If you don't want to come, go back to the hotel. He's very young and lonely. He just wants some friendly company." I remembered the cool older woman's voice who'd answered when I'd dialed his number an hour earlier, and the tone of formal surprise she'd used to summon him through the distant house. "Geoffrey? Excuse me, please! Some person wants you on the telephone." And then the muffled admonition. "Please use the one in the drawing room, *if* you don't mind."

"And I *also* guarantee he doesn't have a penny."

The virile innocence—a power he seemed truly un-aware he possessed—returned to me charged with the Tate's secular hush. "Who cares?"

• • •

HE WAS WAITING at the King's Head when we got there. "Hullo," he cried, leaping up. "You found it! What would you like to drink?" I ordered a single-malt whiskey. Mary asked for lemonade.

"So what did you see on your journey?"

We told him about Scotland and Wales while he sipped a stout. Once in a while he would laugh at something we said, "*Ha!*"——that burst of raw delight I'd heard the first day——"*shaggy cattle! Bluebells!*"——then he'd counter it with a vivid morning spent in the Plaka or the ruins at Gnossos. It seemed hard to imagine what land he came from, impossible to picture that he might have parents, or family, much less friends, and as I sat there listening I thought: this person is pure.

An hour into the travelogue Mary suddenly stood up and said she was going home to pack. "Are you ready, Lulu?" she asked.

"Oh——well——I hadn't——" Halfheartedly I shoved back my chair.

"Do you need to?" asked Geoff, turning to each of us in childlike disappointment. "It's still early."

"Yes," said Mary.

I avoided her eye. "I think——I'll see you back in the room later," I said. "Our last night and all."

She raised both brows. Her eyes looked black as wells. "If that's what you'd really rather do," she retorted, turning and headed toward the door.

"She seems a bit annoyed," said Geoff, gazing after her curiously.

"She's a lawyer. She can't help it."

"Pity." He looked regretful. "I would have liked to get to know her better."

A couple of drinks later we left the pub.

We wandered the blocks down Oxford Street toward Hyde Park. I couldn't help wondering if he was ever going to touch me, even brush against me accidentally, but his shy courtliness seemed so neutral that the suspense merely served to heighten my thrall. I finally got the answer when he grabbed my arm as we crossed the street in the path of an oncoming cab. "Watch it!" he cried, but the rough, electric authority of his hand dazed me too much to apologize; each finger seemed to brand my biceps with fire. For a few seconds after the danger was past he didn't let go. Then he took my hand. Silently we walked on toward the park, aware of each other's every bone. At last he stopped, standing within a few yards of Marble Arch. He stroked my hair and then stroked my cheek and kissed me. The hour was late, almost midnight; traffic had died, the park lay empty except for the occasional whisper and rustle in bushes that sounded deceptively close.

"I have a son," I said breathlessly. I felt it was time to offer some token of private life.

"Really? How old?"

"Five."

"Well, that's a turn-up. I have a daughter. I haven't gotten to see her in six years," and then he proceeded to open my mouth with his.

By the time we fell to the ground under an oak and began unbuttoning each other's clothes I'd lost sense of everything but surrender. Not until several hours later, when we scrambled up and got dressed by the street-lit shadow of Marble Arch, did I feel the deep scores clawed across my spine by tree roots and the wiry park grass. Even after he walked me to the hotel, kissing me good-night ("Write to me. Don't ever cut your hair. Send me a picture of a cable car.") and leaving me to knock and bang until the night porter finally stumbled up to unlock the doors, even after I shuffled into my bed and lay there stunned, vital, breathing carefully and lyrically in the darkness, I failed to note just how mangled were the nerves in those gashes. It took a voice pared thin as a watch crystal, floating above the other bed, to flick that pulse into life.

"While you were out Geoffrey's girlfriend called."

I lay frozen.

"That was about an hour ago now. At two-thirty in the morning."

"What?" I whispered.

"First she phoned your Mom and Dad's room," Mary said precisely. "Your dad has already come here twice, looking for you. Then after she'd waked them up she phoned this one. It seems that she insisted he give her this number as a contact before he went out—just in case."

She waited until it grew plain I wouldn't answer.

"She was worried that he'd had some accident. He hardly knows the city at all and he tends to get lost very easily. Apparently he did that quite often while they were in Greece together."

"You must be mistaken," I mumbled at last. "It must have been the people he's staying with. He doesn't have a girlfriend."

"She was very upset. She'd gotten a telegram right before he went out that her mother has just died in Australia." You fool, she seemed to say, as the darkness bucketed, and my flesh began to twang, and I heard my father's outraged voice in the corridor calling my name as his fist pounded, pounded on our door.

I WROTE THE first letter the morning I got home.

Declan took you out for a barbecue sandwich so I could recover from forty-eight sleepless hours, but furtive as a trap-door spider I snuck out a box of perfumed notepaper the instant the front door closed. "Dear Geoff," I wrote, "you never mentioned a relationship. Who was the woman who phoned in the night?" Tearing it up I started again. "My father is ready to lynch me. By the way, whose mother died?" After I tore that up, "How are the grass burns on your knees? What you said about the poems of Cavafy lingers in my mind, along with the taste of your upper lip. I'm a little confused by the girl calling herself Raeleen, however." The letter evolved, each sheet in turn taking its place on the pile of confetti reeking of Shalimar. "I miss you, I kiss you, you're all I think about. I smell you on my shirt. No one has *ever* made love to me like that. I want you right this minute"—a page that in no time was cinders smoking over the toilet bowl. But it was the most truthful, the nub of my obsession. By the time you and Declan got back from lunch I'd reduced to shreds all of my old high school stationery plus the embossed monogram thank-you cards from my first wedding. Declan settled you down for a nap and went back to work.

I picked up the phone.

My throat held a lump the size of Mount Rushmore. My hands shook. First I listened to the double ring jangling half a world away; next I listened to his brooding explanations of a long-failed love affair and the last-ditch attempt to salvage it through travel. Soon I found myself sympathizing, then feeling horrified. The poor girl's mother had just dropped dead of a cerebral hemorrhage. Raeleen was already on a plane to Australia for the funeral. They'd sadly agreed that it was over forever. Applying Novocain to my conscience, I protested when he somberly suggested maybe it would be better if we kept our fancies free, even though he'd been savoring my memory since the moment he'd kissed me good-bye.

By the time we hung up I was already sorting through dates to book a flight.

You WENT TO your father's for four months, Treatie. I know how well you remember them. Because it was the first long visit you'd had with him since right after your second birthday, I had to numb myself so I wouldn't gnaw my arms off trying to let you go. Instead I put the other need first.

"I'm off to Greece," I told my parents when they asked if I'd fallen off my rocker. "I've wanted to go there since the age of twelve, and now I'm going. Other people do this kind of thing every day." Indeed, I couldn't wait to reach Greece. The islands, the isolated coastlines—all the idylls Geoff had described, sitting in that humid English tearoom, shimmered before my imagination as they had since childhood. But first I needed to stop in England, spend a little time in the country; recap Oxford, ramble once more through the V. & A.; maybe consult a seasoned traveler who'd really steeped himself in the Aegean and knew the ropes.

Everybody could see my craziness but me.

We arranged to meet on the National Gallery porch. He sauntered up the steps looking less Irish than Nordic, Ireland however turning out to be the original source of those tilted eyes, that golden mane, that brash set to the shoulders, the solid-packed torso that tapered to a fine waist, the reckless insouciance and stoic pathos. We took the tube to a kebab café for dinner. The next fourteen hours we spent on a cot in the basement lumber room of the house where he was staying, in Hammersmith, our heads slamming against old suitcases and peeling picture frames as Geoff's prowess over and over revealed its Herculean scale. By morning I was hallucinatory and could hardly walk. Over marmite and toast I met the house's other inmates: two teenagers whose mother had just run off to Ibiza for a holiday pick-me-up with her clandestine lover. The son was a high school dropout looking for work; his sister had a fashionable lisp, top-rank A-levels, and a crush on Elvis Costello—suitably churlish middle-class London youths. Geoff had met the mother and her official boyfriend, a film director, on location in Greece. Now he was living there as a long-term handyman house-guest.

Over the next few weeks Geoff and I went to the theater, the cinema, a German retrospective at the Hayward, curry restaurants in Chelsea, and Harrods Food Halls; we went rowing on the Serpentine and attended free lunchtime concerts at St. Martin's-in-the-Fields. He had the gift of making me see and hear and notice things I never had before. I would amble around a gallery puzzling over the midnight *acidie* of George Grosz until Geoff joined me, animating the matte planes and harsh black outlines of Max Beckmann's self-portraits with his passion. "You have a brain!" he would cry. "Use it. Celebrate it!"

Since my arrival, I'd noticed, he'd become a bit less bashful and more direct.

But I wasn't insulted. I found him bracing. Weekends we spent at the director's Surrey house, where Geoff raked leaves and pickled pine doors and whistled Bob Dylan tunes as he split kindling for the Aga. Scarlet Virginia creeper cloaked the brick walls while the air turned crisp and sharp as a Cox's Pippin. Wood smoke flavored the autumn evenings above the ruined Norman church tower. About five days after landing at Gatwick I'd rented a bedsit in Putney in the home of an ex-Penthouse Pet whose claim to fame was a once-a-year liaison in the Canary Islands with a famous rock star. The Pet referred to Geoff as the Don Juan Creature because she, like Mary, had picked up something I hadn't: Geoff was so experienced with girls that he would eventually boast to me (under the lubrication of a two-liter flagon of Chianti) that he'd had more women than I'd had hot breakfasts. But that news was yet to come. In my blissful ignorance I lay around with him on Saturday mornings listening to Romanian concertos and George Steiner interviews on the BBC and making torrid, profound love, all the time congratulating us both on finally having found our real soulmates. Afterward we'd wander down to the pub where I'd buy our luncheon pints with the pittance I made typing wills in a solicitor's office.

Family remained an illicit subject between us. We talked about everything else—books, university, music, friends (of whom he had many and wrote letters to by the bale) —but somehow mention of genetic kin was so off-limits as to seem lethal. I knew only why *I* avoided the subject. Fear made my veins burn. The last thing I wanted was for him to hear about my outraged relatives—especially the sexless husband I'd just abandoned.

But the first clue I got that Geoff had come fully equipped with parents was when we stood in a department store basement two weeks before Christmas admiring the toys. I was picking out your Christmas present. My transient life did nothing to quench the pain of your absence, and as I pawed through boxed Queen's Guard sets I could no longer afford, my tears blurring the foil tinsel on the Star Wars display, Geoff appeared brandishing a kaleidoscope. "Leave those Hollywood rip-offs and have a look at a genuine gem," he ordered. Then he jammed it hard against my right eye. The tin circle bit into the flesh and knocked my occipital ridge.

"Ow!" I winced.

"What's the problem? Don't whinge in public. Good Christ—Americans, one tiny accident and they start moaning. Well? Isn't it a beauty?"

I rubbed the eye socket, dumbfounded.

"I want to buy it for Aline." A masklike look crossed his face as he mentioned the child he hadn't seen since she was two. From what I'd already pieced together, she'd been conceived with a woman he'd lived with for several years —an alabaster, copper-haired schoolgirl named Fiona whom he'd seduced when she was sixteen and he was an art student of twenty-one.

"Lend us a couple of pounds and I'll buy this and post it on through my mate Nigel. He's still in touch with Fiona and her bloody Kraut husband. Oh, yes: the wolves prevailed, but I still have the best eye for Aline's gifts," he muttered. Suddenly his voice boiled. "Why the hell do you keep swabbing your eye like somebody just shot it out?"

It was my first clue that he had a temper.

"Here, stop sniveling and let me look through the bloody thing again before I decide for sure," he said disgustedly, seizing the kaleidoscope and holding it against his eye. "Some of the others have different color spectrums."

As I stood there, my socket throbbing, I was visited by an urge. I reached up and tapped against the tube's side.

He jerked it away from his eye. "What the hell are you doing?"

I glanced down. My head began to buzz.

"You bitch!" he stared in astonishment. "That was deliberate!"

"I—I'm sorry," I stammered. Suddenly I felt sick.

A slow crimson bloomed up his face. Wind gusted through his nostrils. "Malice. *Malice!* Pure—bloody-minded— vicious—malice."

"Geoff, I'm sorry. I didn't mean—"

"My God. *You're just like my bloody mother!*" And with that he pitched the kaleidoscope hard at my breast where it jounced off to ricochet against a bubble-blowing-pipe bin. Then he wheeled and strode away, shouldering through the nonplussed onlookers that blocked the aisle, ignoring their whispers, until he melted into the throngs swarming below the escalator.

His mother.

"Geoff!" I cried. "*Geoffrey!*"

Outside on High Street the holiday shoppers closed in like the Red Sea. Far off through the distance under the snow-clouded sky I could see a copper-gold glimmer, but it was rapidly gaining space and in another few seconds would be lost forever. My heart ratcheted. What did he mean, his mother? What blight had he survived, what childhood? Terror raced through me; I saw a hundred pictures: little Geoff cowering in bed, sobbing, little Geoff rubbing his black eye. Somehow I had to catch up and prove I wasn't like that. He'd hit me by accident; he'd said so. What had I done?

"Geoffrey! *Please!*" I begged, air sawing through my throat as at last I struggled to his side on the tube platform. I grabbed his arm. He was about to board a train to Victoria Station.

He jerked the arm away.

"Please! I'm sorry! I didn't mean to hurt you."

His remote, sightless eyes swiveled in my direction. "Leave me alone."

"It was horrible of me to do that. Please!"

"My mother stabbed me in the bloody arm with a kitchen knife when I was ten," he muttered.

"I had no idea! I was just—"

"She's capable of anything. But by God, I didn't think that you were!" He turned. "Leave me. Go!" The underground train screeched to a stop. He got ready to shoulder through the doors.

"Please don't do this! Please! Listen." I wept, dripping snot, the guilt wringing me through the gut.

"You're just the same."

"I'm not! I love you!"

"You don't know what love is." He wouldn't look at me. The doors were about to shut.

"Please. Geoff. I'm so sorry. I'll do anything to make it right!"

And that pretty much set the tone for the next three years.

BY THE TIME we married I'd traveled through England, Switzerland, Germany, France, Spain, Italy, and Texas, but never once set foot in Greece.

You spent part of that year with your father, of course—at least during my English and Northern Continental period, when you went back and forth between us. I came and got you for good right before we left Italy. By then I'd lost count of the number of times when I'd been obliged to convince Geoffrey that we could make it, that I was a woman who loved him unconditionally; I wouldn't screw him around, he could conquer this if only he'd open up to me. Despite all my work, jealousy attacked like a tomahawk in the night. Constantly he pointed out how perfidious I was at heart—look at the way I'd whispered into the Magic Bus driver's ear when we'd stopped at Mt. Blanc for breakfast on our way to Milan. "I was asking where to find a bathroom!" I wailed. Once in a restaurant in Florence, as I gazed at a big iced crystal bowl of strawberries, he jumped up from the table and barreled out through the brass doors into the street. When I finally climbed into bed in our pensione he kept to the far edge of the mattress, his back stonily turned, until he started snoring and flopped over into the middle, ramming his knees into my soft parts while his arms gathered the sole coverlet into a clump. For the next three days he wouldn't speak a word but glared if I so much as suggested what fresco we might visit next.

Eventually I shut up and kept my distance. Patience, I thought. Patience. Not until we were on the bus back to our rented villa (four-hundred-year-old stone walls, overlooking a valley full of chestnut trees, paid for six months in advance with the skimpy dregs of my savings) did he finally reveal why he was so angry. "I saw the way you were staring at that waiter," he said. "You couldn't take your goddamned eyes off him. I know what you wanted." Waiter? It was hopeless telling him what I'd wanted was a bowl of fruit. For another two days he shunned me, dismissing all advances, guzzling chianti, and sleeping in the spare room, by which time I'd planned a means of escape. I couldn't take it anymore. Even I could tell this relationship was insane, his possessiveness actively growing dangerous: there was one poor man in the village whose throat he'd threatened to rip out for offering me a ride as I carried a box full of groceries balanced on my head the five kilometers back up the hill.

Early one morning, before the larks started singing, I crept to the villa's front entry room with my backpack strapped tight. Cautiously I swung the door panels a few inches open on their creaking hinges and sniffed the Tuscan spring. Relief flooded in. Freedom lay just beyond the luminous threshold. I was just taking my first step outside when all at once an earthquake slung me backward, flinging me to the stone floor.

"Where do you think you're going?"

There should have been some warning. Something transcending his stealth. Fear should have drummed through my limbs as I lay there looking up. Instead all I felt was the dissociation of shock—empty, light, and blank.

"Geoff," I said.

"Whore!"

"Wait. Listen," I said.

"What are you up to?"

He bent over, seized my shoulders, and shook me until my teeth rattled. "Pulling a caper like my bloody mother?"

Then he straightened, his fists bunching and unbunching. I gulped. "Is bullshit all you know? Leave me here without even a good-bye, sneak away like some goddamned coward, don't give a fuck, no money, *nothing?*"

"No," I whispered.

"Everything you say is shit. That's all you are! *Love!* Betrayal is your fucking name." Contemptuously he stood above me and spat on the floor, then kicked the pack still strapped to my shoulders like it was a football.

"Stop! I haven't lied to you!" I cried. "I just can't stand any more! I can't stand the crazy things you say!"

"What the fuck do you *expect?*" he roared. "When you claim you love me and then steal out of the house like some *puta* who's just robbed her customer's wallet?"

"I just want a breather. A walk. Just to relax. To calm down."

"Oh, yes? Let's have a look!" He shoved me over, yanked the pack off my back, then tore the zipper apart with his bare hands and dumped the contents on the floor: underwear, jeans, spare dress. My toothbrush sprang against the stone wall. "Walk? Just for a morning?" Snorting now, he pointed trembling to the pile on the floor.

"Whore!" he screamed.

"I can't help what your mother did!" I yelled, struggling fiercely to my feet so I could face him square on. "I didn't do these things to you! I didn't abandon you when you were six months old and come back a year later! I didn't drop you in a nettle patch! I don't lie all the time. I'm not *like that,* I'm somebody else!"

"Prove it!" he cried, and then, tears welling up his eyes, he grabbed me and shook me, and just when I thought I was dead for sure he strained me against his chest, kissed my throat, and ripped the buttons off my dress in desperate, agonized desire.

I went numb.

It became an act of duty to make love with him after these bouts. The alternate spurts of attempted escape and rebuttal of his black beliefs turned into the pattern that bound us together until I finally fetched you from your father's vacation house in the Pyrenees. I brought you back to Italy (because I'd promised, I'd given my solemn oath that I would return, like people do in fairy tales, and I knew what happened to them when they didn't keep it), and three weeks later told Geoff that I'd received a phone call at the local taverna informing me that my mother was seriously ill (all perfectly true, up to a point, as the barkeeper and then the entire village later assured him when he asked) and I had to go back to the States, rejoin my family, my dolce bella mamma. In a flash he became sympathetic, full of tender concern. My mother. Sick. The poor blameless woman who'd written those sweet, anxious, loving cards from that pathetic cowboy town: Bernice, Texas. Of course he understood. Of course he would help me reach her bedside.

Together we took you on the train to Rome. I picked up the money that had been wired from my Texas account to the Bank of Italy, handed him half of it (so he could eat or go to hell, I thought), and bought our plane tickets with what was left.

"Come back as soon as you can, darling. I'll be waiting here every day until you do."

"All right," I said, hurrying toward the Alitalia gate with you in my arms and quivering with anticipation at the prospect of peace. And that was the last I ever saw of the Continent.

YOU AND I spent two months in a rented apartment in Bernice. Then, when I knew for absolute, surefire certain he had moved on to Germany to look at the Grunewalds, I booked us tickets to England so that we could pick up the Attic trail at the spot where I'd gotten diverted, and then together we two could at last find that white house on Naxos and eat olives and feed the chickens in the yard and live happily ever after.

Or I *thought* I knew for absolute, surefire certain.

Your father came over from Sweden to London and met

our plane so that you could spend a few days with him. So I was staying alone at a friend's upstairs flat above her Putney boutique the day Geoffrey found me. He'd become alerted to our defection when he phoned my number and discovered it was disconnected. That launched him on a frantic hunt, for which he drafted the services of his British friends—for he was in fact now back in England—insisting they disguise their identities (never mind their accents) and telephone first my parents, then my brothers and sisters, then other connections. It was your grandmother Hazel Vonick who, all unaware, told him we'd flown to the U.K. From there it didn't take long for him to stalk the list of my London acquaintances, interviewing each of them with the fervor of a religious zealot, until at last, while grilling my friend Daisy, in a living-room corner, half hidden by a sofa, he happened to catch a glimpse of a backpack he recognized.

"*Whose is that?*" he cried, springing up from his chair.

"Mine," Daisy said.

"*Where did you get it?*"

Collecting her cunning, Daisy said, "I bought it on a trip to the States."

"When?" he demanded.

"Oh, I don't know. About, perhaps five or six years ago?" She shrugged.

"Where?"

"Iowa," said deadpan Daisy.

"Oh, yes? And since when are your initials *L.P.V.*?" he pounced as if accusing her of a badly planned murder.

Dragging the pack from its bolt-hole like a gutted carcass he proceeded to stab his forefinger repeatedly at the Magic Marker capitals hand-scrawled on the flap.

"They're not. Don't be silly," said Daisy. Her coolness had always impressed me; a mix of Cockney and Gypsy, she sailed through her days equally prepared for an orgy or a wake (in Daisy's family they were much the same thing). "Those letters are left over from when I toured the South of France last year with the *Viva Piaf!* company. I had to travel back ferry with the rest of the chorus when we ran out of money instead of flying first bloody class, the cheap bastards. Seasick. They stand for Long Passage with Vomit. A joke." She made a sardonic moue. "Fucking management."

"Balls!" Geoff's face had tightened into the Minotaur mask; he swayed above, fists clenched like blackjacks. "Bollocks! Don't you bullshit *me,* my girl. Where's your American friend?"

"Who? Lulu?"

"Christ! No, Barbra Bloody Streisand!"

"I have no idea. Frankly, I haven't seen her since you and she toddled off to your little palazzo. And if you don't cool down, matey, I'll have my brother and his cronies come and scrape you off my doormat like a wad of gum. Fucking lunatic. I mean—look at yourself! Why Lulu would ever want anything to do with you is beyond me. Colonial dickhead." Languidly she plucked a Silk Cut from her Chinese cigarette case and lighted it.

Anguish rinsed his face, filtering through rage. He let out a roar, unclenched both fists, and reached for her.

That did it.

"Knock it off, Geoffrey," I croaked, stepping out from behind the curtained-off bedroom arch where I'd been hiding.

"*What?*" He whirled. The whites of his eyes showed.

"Leave her alone. Don't you dare touch her."

"*Lulu—*"

"Back off."

"I'm not *about* to bloody touch her—"

"Stop phoning my ex-mother-in-law. Stop threatening my friends. Stop upsetting Treatie and hounding my sister Dyllis and everybody in my family." Now I was whipping all my fear into anger.

"What are you bloody *doing* here?"

"Oh, for fuck's sake. He wasn't going to touch me," said Daisy with irritation.

"I'll talk to you. I'll sit down and talk with you. Only —God, please—*behave yourself.*"

"Christ." He started crying. He stood with both fists buckled, legs planted wide, nostrils flaring, mouth in spasm, tears springing down his cheeks. "How could you? How *could* you? Christ!"

"Look," I said.

"Bloody drama," muttered Daisy.

"Geoff, look." His face was tearing my resolve into metal scrap. "It's just too hard. I can't take it anymore."

"Don't you think I know how hard I've been on you?" he wept.

"No. I don't think you do."

"My God—do you think I *want* to make you miserable? Like my bloody mother did me? Don't you understand that yet? The *last* bloody thing I want!" Stricken, ignoring the tears drenching his face and dripping down onto his collar, he thrust forth both hands in supplication. "Can't you grasp how much I love you? how deep it goes? Good Christ, I've staked everything I have, my whole bloody world's wrapped up in you, my work, my thoughts, my hopes. Can you comprehend how hard it is for me to give in to a feeling like that? And then you sneak around and go behind my *back?*"

". . . I'm sorry," I said finally.

He stumbled over to me and crushed me in his embrace.

"My God. I've missed you. I'm so sorry for what I did," he cried, muffled against my neck.

"You've got to *change.*"

"I will. I will. I swear!"

"You've got to treat me right, Geoff. Learn to trust," I insisted.

"I'll cherish you," he mumbled into my hair.

It could have been a Roger Corman movie.

Except that on Daisy's face lay the rank disbelief that I had actually given in. Plus another look: a cold, measuring disdain, the direct result of how I'd just betrayed her deft loyalty and proven her a liar. Since I'd been spinning in place within this very paradox for over a year now, I could hardly summon the courage to so much as flinch at the look's justice.

But it was a look I would come to remember well.

WE WERE MARRIED six days later by special license.

The day dawned tensely. Harsh squawking pigeons huddled outside the cheap Bayswater hotel room like winged rats, waiting for handouts of leftover papadams and takeaway Wimpy chips. Geoff climbed up from the depths of a hangover, running late and already furious that I hadn't yet ordered a minicab to the train. For the previous twenty-four hours I'd scrambled around the sales racks of midprice department stores, feebly searching for an affordable dress that would honor that combination of martyrdom and integrity carrying me to the altar—probably one more suited to human sacrifice than bridal rites. All I'd found was a peach-colored rag imported from India that looked like a tired relic of the Raj—maybe a flag of surrender.

I was busy keeping my word.

"Hard to believe I'm throwing in the towel at last, eh?" joked Geoff to Maurice, one of his artist friends from Sydney. Maurice now lived in Kent. He and his wife were standing as our witnesses. "How many bloody women have tried to drag me to this moment, old salt? I ask you. Could you count them with a bloody abacus? Can you credit it's actually happening?"

"Not really," admitted Maurice, shaking his head. He too had affirmed the stories of Geoff as a woman's man: the pub nights in Manly when barmaids tried to tear his shirt off; the girls who offered to screw him in the alley, the love letters slipped under his door at the art college begging for a rendezvous; the time Geoff's younger brother had taken a long-coveted girl to bed, only to have her moan, "Geoff! Geoff! *Oh, Geoff!*" at the moment of crisis. At which point in the story Maurice and Geoff collapsed in drunken hilarity.

"Ah, well. It's all over now," he sighed. If this was supposed to make me ecstatic that I alone had captured the elusive Don Juan of the Pacific and forced him into a half nelson, somehow it failed to work. All I knew was that, clearly, you do get what you deserve.

As we stood waiting on the curb outside the Registrar's Office, I looked at him and wondered. What had happened to the innocent, zesty boy I'd spotted a year and a half before wandering through the Tate, his hair golden as a setter's under the fluorescent fixtures? How had I gotten myself into this? How could I have misread a first impression so completely?

Who was the woman who had crafted such a piece of work from that first burst of infant personality?

"All you girls, piss off. I'm landed," he said, and straightened the knot in his grin before we climbed the steps into the reception hall. "Returning to the shores of Enzed, grounded at last. This one's tied me fast. Captain Cook, row us home."

And for the first time that day, he kissed me.

MY DARLING TREATIE: how can I ever justify the next few years to you?

I've never been sure just why we human beings crave serial monogamy so. On one hand it's a dead-end street, the outcome of many flawed emotions. Restlessness. Longing. Disappointment. Loneliness. Hope. Lust. Need. What more deserves to be said about the carousel of human arousal, or for that matter the alacrity with which our domestic courts have come to serve it? Most of all it demonstrates our spiritual bankruptcy.

On the other hand, serial marriage is a kind of a path, a continual fumbling toward love and commitment, toward an honorable intimacy. We want that intimacy. We break homes and enrich legal structures to get it. And we keep on seeking until we inevitably come to the truth: that what we're looking for doesn't lie within another person at all.

Unfortunately, at that time little did I yet know.

THREE DAYS AFTER the wedding we caught a flight to Sydney to visit Geoff's younger brother.

Geoff had lived in Australia for several years until the day he wooed and bullied his way to Europe with Raeleen (who, it turned out, had bought his airline ticket). His brother still lived there. The real crunch was, so did his mother: she'd moved across the Tasman when her second marriage folded and now shared a tiny flat with a boyfriend twenty-two years her junior. The fact that this man was four years younger than Geoff seemed to endorse fragments of a portrait I'd already sketched out: a femme fatale, a hedonist, an impulsive shrew, a woman with no brakes. In a very short time I would finally meet this fish-wife.

The night before we left I finally phoned my parents and told them what I'd done and where we were going. They remained incommunicado for the next six months, just a hair longer than my newfound, heartfelt union with Geoff lasted. The cherishing stage had clocked in at about ten minutes. By the time we rushed to Heathrow and boarded our plane Geoff had thrown three tantrums, cursed the cab driver when he refused to exceed the speed limit and withheld his tip, cursed me for having lost our tickets (until he discovered them in the inside pocket of his bag), and insisted I jettison my backpack and shove only my most essential clothing items into his to avoid paying excess baggage costs on his boxes of souvenirs and record albums. That's when I realized how I'd just cast myself and you, Treatie, seven thousand miles into limbo.

SHE OPENED HER door.

"Geoffrey, darling," she said, "how wonderful."

"Hello, Mother," he said.

Her hair gleamed red. This was the first thing. She reached up and pecked Geoff's cheek, her sleek pageboy swinging aside and draping one eye like Veronica Lake's. Her skin glowed like an arum lily, but was threaded with tiny lines. The self-contained way she shook my hand didn't surprise me. What did were the dulcet voice and the sinuous slide of her hips. A little smile played on her mouth, never expanding or diminishing the whole time we were there. Hers had been the sole photograph missing from the family snaps, and now I realized who Geoff most took after.

"I was wondering when you were going to come see me," she said. "Peter told me you were due to arrive sometime this month."

"We got in six days ago," he replied with a practiced wariness. "It was a bloody long trip with a bad twelve-hour stopover in Bangkok. Two whole bloody days afterward we spent sleeping. The rest of the time I've been showing Lulu and the boy all the sights—the Domaine, the Rocks, the Opera House."

After all that sleep I still felt I was in a dream.

"Well. Now you're here, darling." Beckoning us into the narrow living room, she sat down in a small armchair and indicated the love seat. Geoff perched himself on a bar stool. The room's one large window looked out on the harbor. Beyond her copper hair shone sheets of blue.

"Who is this lovely little boy?" she said archly.

I coaxed you out from behind my skirt, even though my instincts warned against it. An image of Hansel and Gretel cringing from the door of the gingerbread house floated by for a second.

"This is Tristan," I said. Touch him and I'll cut out your gizzard, I thought.

"My, aren't you big and bonny." She bent forward a fraction at the waist to study your eyes. "My name is Cassandra."

"Hi," you said. Your hand felt hot and moist in mine. We went and sat down on the love-seat cushions.

"Do you like sweeties, darling?" Rising, she went to the table, opened a green straw purse, and fished around inside, fetching out at length a tube of Polo mints.

"Thank you," you said.

"My, what good manners. What a nice boy you are." Her voice spread like marmalade.

"Yes, he's a very good boy. Aren't you, me old mate?" said Geoff, and patted you with false bravado on the back. "Amazing traveler. Never once complained when we passed through those bloody machine-gun guards in Bangkok. Not even when one of them nicked his computer toy and played with it for half an hour. We weren't sure he was going to give it back, were we, Tristan?"

"Goodness," she said.

"Then the poor wee chap nearly melted in the heat once we got outside. His face bleached white as lye. We had to find an air-conditioned restaurant fast, didn't we, Tristan my lad? before you wound up in a big puddle and drained straight into the klongs. Ha! Equatorial all right. Bloody humidity worse than a steambath. Sky like mother-of-pearl."

"Louise, have you ever been to this part of the world before?" she asked.

"Ah—no. I haven't," I said.

"No doubt you'll find it's quite different from America. Culturally speaking."

"Yes, I'm sure I will."

She sipped her tea and replaced the cup in its saucer, the little smile inflexible, chill with watchfulness.

"At least it's not Texas," said Geoff. "Aussies may be crude, but they're not in the same kettle as the Yanks I've met while traveling overseas."

"Geoffrey," chided his mother with a mild chuckle.

"Don't bloody Geoffrey me, my old dear," he turned on her. "The States is a bloody wasteland, you take my word for it."

"Australians *can* be a bit coarse," she observed to me, but her words seemed coy.

"At least they're fit. Meet up with a tour bus full of Texans and you'll think you're in the middle of a bloody cretin convention. Whole inbred families weighing sixteen stone per member. Big, white, fat larval mounds of flaccid pudding in Bermuda shorts——"

"I haven't traveled beyond the Antipodes," she remarked. "Although I'm hoping to go to Bali."

"Ah. When?" I asked.

"Bloody barbarians," continued Geoff, paying no attention to my discomfort.

"Someday. When I can afford it."

"I admitted Aussies are crude, didn't I? I'm not denying it. Pub nights in the outback can make your bloody hair stand on end," raved Geoff. "I once saw this bloody great goanna go for a man around behind a pub when he'd stepped out to shake hands with the unemployed. There he stood, taking a quiet piss; the next thing you know he's tearing around the corner to the front door, pants down around his ankles, running like a mad kangaroo and tripping over the pants and yelling and clutching himself with both hands while this bloody huge lizard as big as a mastiff runs chasing right behind him trying to nip off his goolies! *Ha!* We nearly pissed ourselves laughing."

She shook her head in reproof, smiling at me.

"What are goolies?" you asked.

"Crown jewels, my boy," he cried, "your bloody whatnots."

"He wasn't brought up to speak this way. Back in New Zealand people show more restraint. Although I haven't been there for years," she said, pouring me another cup. "But they're usually slightly more civilized."

"'The Passionless People,'" Geoff said. "Too bloody right! Bunch of soulless sheep, frightened silly that they're going to stand out from the crowd. Ever hear of the Tall Poppy Syndrome? Cut down the tall poppies the minute they rise above the national mean?" I hadn't seen him so feverish since the first day we'd met. "Why do you think I moved to frigging Sydney, Mother?" he cried.

"Because I was here," she answered.

"Not by a long shot, Mater Dear," he said, leaping up from his seat and pacing through the tiny adjacent kitchen so he could rattle through cupboards and bang the fridge door.

When he returned he carried a box of cookies, which he offered to you. "Gingernut biscuits. Here, Tristan, stuff these in your gob," he said, thrusting it toward your face.

"Geoff's father and I parted for the final time when he was twelve," his mother confided. "I married someone else and Geoff went on living in the old house in that tiny New Zealand rural community with his dad. Male bachelors together. That must be the reason his manners are so rough."

"He's told me about his early years," I said.

Her smile continued placidly. "Of course, when he followed me here after art school I was delighted. But I couldn't let him stay. This flat is far too small, as you can see. But it didn't take him long to find a flat of his own, did it, darling?"

"I didn't ask you to let me stay, Mother. I was here with my two best mates, remember? We were renting our own bloody digs."

"Oh, yes. Nigel and—what was the other one's name? Your other young friend. Of course, I've only ever got to see photographs of the little girl. My granddaughter. I've never met her. She had to stay behind with her mother in Christchurch. Such a gorgeous wee moppet. I'm sure Geoff's told you all about her. A big head of beautiful curls, just like his when he was a baby." Her eyes measured me brightly.

"My mother never deserved to meet Aline," he had told me one night in Italy when he'd finished off a litre of chianti and was waxing gregarious, describing his childhood to me. "My mother regarded herself too refined for my father. She thought she'd sunk down to the bottom of the paddock, all right. She met my father during the war, after he got shot in Tobruk and shipped home to Canterbury. They stuck him in hospital in Christchurch, he was there nearly three years, a boy from the bush who'd never left the district before the day he'd signed up, and she was working as a ward sister. She read him magazine stories until he was nearly well and then bang, that was that. Not love—oh, no, never love, not on my mother's side, she wouldn't know love if it bit her in the jugular. Pregnancy. It tossed them straight into marriage although she'd never admit it, it was too embarrassing to confess she was up the spout with a bastard, an Irish Catholic girl." He drained the dregs from the Chianti bottle. "The result was me," he said. "They went to live in my father's home village. My father never entered Christchurch again unless he had to. For thirty years he worked railway maintenance and spent his weekends fishing or hunting with his dogs. He's honest. Honest and simple, salt of the earth." He paused and delivered a long, meditative belch.

"The first time she left him I was six months old. She'd met another man. My aunts looked after me until she came back a few weeks later. Then when I was nearly two she left again, this time for much longer, several months, I don't know how many. Someone else. Each time my father took her back, and she bore him another infant. So he gave it yet one more go, just one more. For his part, he never looked at any woman but her." He paused again. "She's got no business near any grandchild I might sire."

I watched him uncork a new bottle and tip it back, watched the chianti splash red down his chin.

"Now, my mother, she's the one I take after when it comes to handling the old piss," he'd said. "Oh, yes, by Christ. The old girl loved parties. Throwing them, in particular.

"Every couple of months she'd prepare a big buffet meal: roast beef, ham, curried eggs, rolls with tinned asparagus, beetroot salad and puff pastries, pavlova. Real Kiwi tucker. All the neighbors would be invited. She'd take off her apron and leave the feed laid out on the kitchen table, and she'd go to her bedroom and put on some elegant frock, some posh little item that no other woman in the village owned anything like—chartreuse green taffeta with skirts that rustled, an off-the-shoulder peasant thing printed all over in tiny Eiffel Towers and French postage stamps, a pink chiffon long-sleeved number with ruffles down the whatsit. Very up-market. She wore perfume. High heels, nylons. You could hear her swish when she walked.

"Gallons of booze and beer would start arriving as everybody showed up. The men mostly had on their best clothes—shirts and ties, a few in work singlets. If the women came at all they'd have put on drab Sunday dresses under slubby old cardies with wool pills under the arms. In my father's village half the houses had started out as piano crates. I used to watch them all from the bedroom doorway, watching my mother enjoy her glamour fantasy, swanning among the peasants, too gracious and well-bred to snub any of them. She'd swish in from the mirror where she'd been putting on her lippie to our tiny little front door and open it like Ava Gardner and knock their bloody eyes out.

"One of these party nights my father's best pig dog sneaked into the larder. Old Blue. Mother had been cooking for three bloody days: cream puffs, brace of chooks, a turkey. I think it was their bloody anniversary or some sort. Old Blue must have thought he'd walked into Paradise. When Mother threw open the kitchen door and stood aside for the guests she let out a screech! My flaming Christ, you could have heard her in Dunedin. The table was a massacre. Blue lay there on the floor with his belly swollen like a watermelon, so glassy-eyed he looked stuffed, cream froth all around his mouth. Mother stood there shrieking and waving a meat hammer while the men kicked at him to force him to his feet, but he couldn't budge an inch. He had this one great turkey leg clamped between his teeth, and every time somebody tried to take it away he'd growl low down in his throat. That was all he could do." He laughed over his glass so hard that tears squeezed out of his eyes. Then he stopped.

"My mother was so outraged she left Pa the morning after. Said she couldn't stand the bloody provincials another second."

He set the bottle down.

"When I was six I had a nightmare," he said. "I dreamed she stood at the corner on my way to school. She was wearing a long blue gown like the good fairy in Pinnochio. Her hair was all long and curly, red and gold. But she wasn't good. She was beautiful, and I knew what she was really waiting to do with those long sharp nails tucked in the side folds of her dress. She was going to snatch me and rip me apart and eat me as I ran past. 'Come along, Geoffrey. Come to me, darling. Hurry!' she said. I still dream it sometimes."

I shut my eyes. He recorked the bottle and wiped his lips.

"She never gave a damn about anybody but herself."

"AND THE LITTLE boy," Cassandra added suavely now. She picked up the teapot and poured another cup.

"Um—I'm sorry. What?"

"The wee boy. You know. Geoff's first one. Such a sad thing. Losing a member of the family that way." She sighed.

For a moment I couldn't see her. It was as though she'd flickered into blankness, a pale smudge on the swimming light.

"Little boy," I said, repeating.

"Yes. Geoffrey's first girlfriend Robin was a bit of a moody girl. Oh, well, they were in a very difficult predicament. Geoffrey only had one year of art school behind him. Both of them nineteen. Still—so sad having to give the baby up. Oh, but surely—pardon! Have I said something I shouldn't?" She glanced serenely around the room.

"Oh, no, Mother, never. Not you," said Geoff. His mouth had twisted into a strange shape.

"At least I'll get to see more of *this* little one," she said with an air of shifting to a pleasanter subject. Reaching over she playfully squeezed your knee. You blinked up at her, dazed by so much creamy female charm.

"No chance. Don't worry. We're moving on to New Zealand in a fortnight or so," Geoff said.

"Oh, darling. No! Are you really?"

"Naturally."

"You and Louise—it is Louise, isn't it? Lulu is just a nickname, isn't that right?—you could live right here in Sydney, couldn't you? Just as you've been the past seven or eight years. It would be so **much more** convenient." Her smile looked like a cake decoration rose.

"Convenient for what?"

"Well. The culture! The shops. Galleries and so forth. For your art."

"No bloody way. Godzone for us. For all its flaws it's the safest place on the old globe. Get some bloody sanity," he said fiercely.

"Oh, I see. Are you truly willing to settle in New Zealand?" She cocked her head at me. "Surely not, after being so used to all the mod cons and so forth in the United States."

"Too bloody right she's willing," said Geoff.

"Has he told you what it's like? Although of course I haven't been back there for years."

"It sounds wonderful." I had to speak around a rock in my throat. Wee boy? Adoption?

"Does your father know?" She looked blandly from me to you where you sat cracking your teeth on another gingernut, then back to him. Her mouth primmed artfully with unspoken comments.

"I've written him that I'm coming home, yes. But it'll be ages before we ever see him, since we're going to be at the top of the North Island and he's way down at the bottom of the South."

"Ah. That's good."

"But I haven't yet broken news of the dirty deed," he said.

"He's going to get a tiny shock, then." And that's when I

realized that not once throughout the conversation had she dropped a single hint that she knew we were married.

VIOLENCE HAS ALWAYS been an alien rhetoric in my family. Until Geoff, no one ever raised a hand against me except for the obligatory spankings of childhood. If I thought about violence at all it seemed unimaginable. How could a human being deliberately hit another? Break a nose? Kick a rib cage? Why would they? What could drive this lightning desecration of another's person? Especially a child's? True violence resides in the tongue. So I had always presumed, and it had surely seemed a mortal enough weapon, my own family's whip of choice. The welts it could raise I knew well.

Yet now I stood in the vestibule, looking at a physical expert.

"It's been very nice meeting you, Louise," said Cassandra. "I hope you have a lovely stay in Sydney. And you, too, Tristan. Beautiful, lovely boy." Leaning down she planted a kiss on your cheek. You kissed her back, a loud smack, which should have made us smile.

"I'll phone you before our plane takes off," said Geoff. No one seemed to think it necessary to repeat that we'd be in the city another three whole weeks.

"All right, darling. Safe journey. Tell your father hello."

"Thanks for the tea." He brushed his lips somewhere near her head. "By the way, where's your young fellow? The bloke? What's his name? The boyfriend?"

"Oh," she said lightly. "Not here."

"Ah."

"Actually, we broke it off."

"Oh. When?" Geoff sounded brusque.

"A year or so ago."

Geoff had been gone for fifteen months. "How come?"

"Well, you know, I decided—I felt he was perhaps be-coming just a wee bit dependent."

Apparently only I noticed the cramp in her tone. Geoff said good-bye and steered you and me quickly out the front door, his hands flat on our spines.

NEW ZEALAND IS the most beautiful country on earth.

I know you know this. I first saw it swinging into my vision through the plane window, a cliff of green rising sheer from the blue ocean, dotted with sheep.

Throughout the world many green cliffs litter the horizon, cutting high above waves and mist. There seemed at the time no reason to recognize this one as special. I held you close to the window. "There, Treatie. See?" I whispered. "Home."

Later, as we rode up the East Coast toward the countryside, over the Harbor Bridge and past sliding surf and breakers cresting beaches with white, past tiers of green bush dropping down the hillsides into valleys, the sense deepened. Back in London I'd dropped us into this freefall without any sense of where we'd hit bottom.

Now we had.

I'M TELLING YOU these things, Treatie, to remind you. You were so young the day we two were introduced into the place that you never got a formal context. Afterward you absorbed it all by osmosis, taking your new surroundings for granted the way a child does wherever he finds himself: this is home, a place of wonder.

As soon as we arrived and headed straight north from the Auckland airport I felt the landscape touch me; I *am* home, I thought. Home at last. It seemed so strange. Why should I connect so instantly to this place down at the bottom of the world? Its history captured my imagination; the soil itself seemed to hold time, with old bones and sunken forests and burned villages covered over by tree ferns and thick moss, and before that the primordial purity of natural death. Over dinner that first night at Geoff's friends' house I started learning everything I could. For the next three years I immersed myself in stories and customs taught to me by a Maori kuia from the marae down the road. I devoured every chronicle and history I could find. This was the heart of my new life, the distraction I threw myself toward so as to avoid feeling the other thing: the constant fear.

WE MOVED INTO the little house that you remember, Treatie, a paddock away from the mangroves and the sea.

On mornings when I looked across the bay to Whangarei Heads and saw Mt. Manaia raise its jagged teeth of stones, the song "Bali Hai" trilled absurdly through my head. How embarrassing, I thought, how banal. But this is the South Seas, I would remember. We're in the South Seas! My birthplace and family seemed all the farther because we were marooned on an island. Miles and miles and miles of water rolled between Cape Reinga and Mexico. Antarctica lay much closer than Texas. Every direction carried one straight into vacancy; the North Island seemed so tiny and frail, locked within this vast shifting ocean. Giant kauri trees grew nearby that had been alive twice as long as humans had occupied the country—over two thousand years. Even they looked temporary against the churning waves.

It was enough to send some people crazy.

The house we rented from a dairy farmer had been built at the end of the last century, an old homestead cottage set in an orchard, with borer tracks hieroglyphed in the rimu floor. Our nearest neighbors lived two fields, or paddocks, away. Early, before light, we'd hear the cows lowing as they got herded into the milking barn, and the chug of the farmer's motorcycle while he rounded the end stragglers, chasing them into position for his wife to hitch up the milking machine. The sound of his voice barking orders to his dog faded as the sun came up over the pinkening mangroves. An hour or so later Geoff would amble out to the beach for a swim, practicing the strokes that had made him a champion competitor in high school. Then he'd retreat to his studio, an old shed with a dirt floor in which lay buried a midden of mussell and pipi shells more than two hundred years old. Losing himself in a haze of turp fumes he would paint all day and only emerge in time for a bath. "Where the bloody hell's dinner?" he'd yell and then drift off to sleep in the steaming water with a beer in his hand until I shook him awake to say the food was growing cold. You went to the local country school. Remember? Remember learning to sing "God Defend New Zealand" and "Po Karekareana"? You made friends with a boy two farms away, and spent the afternoons eeling in the stream by the marae. Life seemed exquisite and deadly, a sharp blade constantly being honed.

THE FIRST TIME he hit me I couldn't believe it.

The second time was just on noon. I retreated into shock the way I had the first, and he had to scrub the blood from my sweater and pants with household bleach to keep anyone from noticing the stains. I sat in a chair and shuddered. You were at school. He had as usual ambushed the mailman and opened my letters, including one from Dan Hambleman, my journalist friend in Berkeley who candidly admitted he was very interested in seeing me if I should ever return from New Zealand. I couldn't stop shaking or wipe the blood dripping down my nose. All I could see was red fanning through the air as the crunch sounded. His rigid face loomed above mine. His hands reached out to crush my throat and then withdrew.

"You're not worth hanging for," he said.

Lying on the floor in the entryway where he'd dragged me I stammered a prayer to some unknown listener: "Please. Please make him all right." Faith seemed the only thing ready at hand. My mind had fled, and the gabbling was automatic.

THE THIRD, FOURTH, and fifth time, I began to strike back.

He shackled my wrists with one hand and protected his face, paying me for my audacity the instant he could drop the other elbow and make a fist. I didn't care. Blows meant nothing anymore. Something had snapped. I fought by pure instinct, unwilling to permit this punishment to go on, unwilling to concede that I might deserve it. At the moment his face froze I suddenly recalled the glibness of that farewell scene at his mother's flat; the apparently meaningless exchange murmured in my ear. It rang a chime, like a still glass in the eye of a raging storm. "Safe journey." "Thanks for the tea." The words underlined by her small, knowing smile.

When a friend of Geoffrey's asked me what had happened to my nose I said, "I fell in the bathtub." Later, listening to a radio program on battered women, she learned what I didn't yet know: I'd used one of the two commonest excuses for black eyes and broken blood vessels. Raeleen, she remembered, had been nursing a split lip the one time she'd ever met her; she'd claimed she'd slipped on a diving board and hit the edge of the pool. "That was when the penny dropped," the friend said.

Which is more than it did for me.

AT THE END of the second month in our new house and the third month of our marriage, when I was just starting to return to writing again, I found I was pregnant.

Treatie, what can I say? I'd already known. I'd suspected that I might be before we even left Sydney. In spite of the circumstances, a low-grade smolder of joy began burning inside me, fusing me to the new life I felt growing there.

But then came the moment a few weeks later when I had to explain to Geoff what the doctor had just seen on the ultrasound screen.

"Twins?" repeated Geoff. He shook his head. His face blanched.

"Yes," I said in my brightest voice. "Oh, Geoff! It's so amazing! Two little embryos no bigger than lentils, but you can actually see the hearts beating. Oh, I just wish you'd been there."

"How is that possible?"

"With an ultrasound machine. They have this screen that works like a moving X ray, and the doctor took a transmitter thing and ran it down my stomach—"

"How can you be carrying twins?" he rapped out.

I stared. "Well . . . it's biology," I said slowly and carefully. "A woman drops two eggs. Or one egg splits after it's fertilized and—"

"There are no twins in my family."

The trembling that had begun in the hospital examination room now grew acute. My throat began to close up. It seemed tragically appropriate that our passionate collisions should bear such abundant fruit. I reached for his arm. "Geoffrey—"

"Nor in yours either."

"No—not true! That's not true! We've had multiple births before." The doctor had already asked me, so I'd come prepared. Implications had crashed like a thunderbolt as I lay on the examination table staring at the screen. Instantly I'd started concentrating, working my way back, back through the family tree for what I had to find, what I'd better find. Accidents of nature were not permitted in the screwball rationalism of his universe. "My mother's father! He had twin siblings. They both died when they were born. My father's side had them, too, a girl and a boy, they're still alive right this minute, old, old people. It skips generations, Geoff, it——"

"Bullshit," he said flatly. As he turned away, looking out across the sunlit peninsula, the pohutakawa trees, the lapping tide, I knew it was past time for protests, past the hour of hope.

"Geoffrey, listen. You've said you longed for a child. Now you'll have two! Sons. Daughters. It won't be like what happened with Aline or—or the other one. We'll raise them as New Zealanders, they'll grow up where you can teach them and live with them and love them——" One last attempt, I thought.

"Who's the bloody father?" he snarled.

I'M NOT GOING to relive the next six months here. There's no life in reciting a litany. Daily my belly swelled larger. In a short time it was the size of a jeep. Mostly you kept busy with your friends and school and Cub Scouts, blessedly unaware of the upheaval going on except for a vibration filling the house like static. You seemed reasonably happy. At least, I've spent the last sixteen years hoping and praying that you were.

However, considering what a diplomat you've always made, I suspect you might have known more than you let on.

Some days Geoff accepted his new fatherhood and at those times marveled over his own potency, crowing about what a mighty seed sower he was when male friends came over for dinner. Other days could drop me into a trough of despondency. These fetuses, already real people, provoked the most frightening dilemma of my life. Wandering through the orchard, galvanized by the sunlight, I would feel tiny arms and legs thrashing for space inside their palace of flesh, watch the fantails darting above my footprints in the grass searching for insects, and note how my heart now felt as hard and juiceless as a dried pomegranate. "Whose are they?" he'd yell, slamming the refrigerator and shoving me up against the wall. "Fucking admit it! You were married to that twin bastard before me. Admit it!—you fucked him before you went to London. You got pregnant. You're carrying his litter!" He couldn't have guessed just how ironic his accusation was, considering what Declan's and my sex life had turned out to be. Besides, I hadn't seen Declan or any other man for a long time; I could no longer meet men's eyes. It was as though I was now dead to them, a walking corpse neutered by Geoff's jealousy. As for the violence—those sessions had deteriorated into the predictable, as violence always does.

His mother had done this, I thought. She'd inspired this chaos. She was the creator of the entire situation: our messy marriage, the fact that the father of my unborn children writhed around in a batty paranoia. I was reaping a punishment meant for her. I hated her.

Every three days I could count on some verbal outbreak. Routine dictated it. I would be sitting at the dining table, laboriously typing a plot outline or a strangling sequence on my portable electric, when he would charge in from his studio shed and yell for me to stop that bloody tap-tap racket or he'd rip out the machine and throw it through the bloody window. But now he'd started saving the physical up for after the twins' birth.

And within a month following their premature delivery, he came into his full lion's rage.

THERE ARE CIRCUMSTANCES in our lives, Treatie, that forge our strengths. There are events that whet our certainties to their supreme keenness. Knowingly or not, we choose these conditions. Until they occur our self-knowledge is limited; we can have no idea of how firmly we might stand, how durably we might bend and spring back. Only adversity teaches this. Reaction proves we're alive.

But God alone can say whether such awkwardly gained knowledge is worthwhile.

THE WINTER BROUGHT pain such as I'd never known before. Once the twins recovered from their prematurity and the hospital released us from intensive care they both gave voice to the same exact needs at exactly the same time, and I began to forget what it was like to sleep. I breast-fed them. Diapers decorated every spare surface of our house.

Geoff's schedule, not surprisingly, didn't really change at all. He kept to the same list of tasks he'd followed while I was pregnant: get up late in the morning. Pull on his jeans. Drink a cup of tea. Eat a Moro bar. Go out to the studio with no word at all and start painting, then continue until lunch, with maybe a pause to wash a load of laundry and hang it up—his contribution to parenthood. Then back to the studio, with a break when you came home from school to waylay you for the mail the bus driver would have given you, and to stand in the yard and open any letters I might have received and scan them for evidence before turning them over to me. But this too you will remember.

Sometimes it seems that when the crest of awfulness has been reached, that some breakthrough, some searing cautery, must surely follow. Impossible to think that all this misery is for nothing; that it's infinite, it settles no debts; it will keep expanding like the galaxy and still not find its ultimate form. But such is the truth of violence. Which is why, in the end, it turns mundane.

The invisible wounds are the ones that persist.

ON AN AFTERNOON in early spring I made a decision to leave. It was a hasty moment, thrust by a realization that struck from nowhere. When a person is crazy, I'd thought for many months now, he can't be held accountable for what he does. You can't talk with him; his reality is too different from yours, and no matter how overbearingly he asserts it, you must cling to what you know as your own truth. Was Geoff, I kept wondering, truly crazy or just lethally willful? Was he responsible or blameless? I watched how he acted when some guest entered the kitchen while I was cooking a meal: he wouldn't eat afterward because he secretly believed they'd poisoned the food. I watched as he stopped short in the middle of the street and shushed everyone, cocking his head as if listening hard to dim voices. It wasn't long before another thought occurred to me: what if the ridged scar on his forearm wasn't caused by his mother stabbing him? What if all the terrible things he'd reported were lies? Even half lies?

And then, in the midst of grinding the steamed silverbeet and kumara in the Mouli and mixing bottles of soy milk while the twins jumped up and down in their Baby Bouncers and howled for their dinner, I knew.

Slowly I looked over at your little brother Jonathon. He was holding tight to the straps of his bouncer, laughing and trying to kick toy cars across the room. I looked at your brother Mickey. His petal face tilted, contused with hunger. Suddenly it didn't matter whether Geoffrey was just a selfish, mean son of a bitch who felt justified in bashing women, or whether he was as tortured and loony as Nietzsche on his deathbed. It no longer mattered what his mother had or hadn't done. The late-afternoon light broke brighter. I put the Mouli down on the counter and went over to the table and sank into a chair. My hands felt empty; my head seemed to be splitting open, light pouring in. There was no way to ever give him enough sympathy. It wouldn't buy anything, it wouldn't change his past or save him, it wouldn't even buy me virtue. No longer did it matter a jot what I'd been trying to prove, with all my endurance, my commitment to a lost cause—or what I'd been trying to correct, make up for, redeem. Sanity no longer mattered. Nothing mattered. What was crucial was to get us out, and make damn sure that the abuse stopped here.

As IT TURNED out, I never met Geoffrey's father, but I saw Cassandra one last time.

It was about a month before the eruption occurred that blasted us free of that nucleus forever. We were about to celebrate the twins' first birthday and she was flying over from Sydney to inspect her new grandchildren. Geoff seemed very pleased about her impending visit, even jaunty. "There's nothing the same as family when all's said and done," he declared. "Blood's the real thickener. It'll be good to have the old girl stay at last and lend a hand with the twins. After all, she was once a ward sister." Any comment he'd made about the past was now long-drowned by his focus on me: I was the Lilith of the present. Because he didn't know how to drive I belted the babies into their infant seats, left you with neighbors, waited until he got settled on the passenger's side to his satisfaction, and then headed down the road through green bush the one hundred forty kilometers to the Auckland airport.

SHE EMERGED FROM Customs almost immediately after the Qantas flight landed. Geoff had sauntered off to the newsstand for city papers so I stood alone with the stroller. I saw her first. A relaxed smile curved her face. Sleek-hipped and over-breasted, she paused at the doorway, smoothed her clothes, glanced around, and caught sight of us.

"There you are. Louise!" The little smile lifted slightly. Her skin seemed chalkier than it had in Sydney. Perhaps it was the flight.

"Hello, Cassandra."

"How are you?"

"I'm fine. How was your trip over?"

"You know, darling, you look tired," she said.

I no longer cared how repellent her poise seemed. Pushing the double stroller forward like a freight car, I came level with her and spoke through my exhaustion, "This is Jonathon and Mickey, in that order. Your grandchildren."

"Oh!" Instantly she knelt down and peered into their faces. "Oh, my."

"They've just had a long drive, so they might turn cranky any minute." But they didn't turn cranky. Whimpers and fretfulness that had filled the car now dwindled into silence. Instead they gazed up at her with fascination.

"You beautiful wee things," she murmured.

"They are kind of pretty, aren't they," I admitted.

"Of course!" She reached out and cupped Jonathon's hand. "Oh! Oh, my. They look just like Geoffrey. Isn't it amazing?" These days Geoff couldn't possibly dispute their paternity any longer; they were miniature versions of him, with his slanting green eyes, long lashes, and wide, chiseled mouths. As I watched, Cassandra's smile deepened. She ruffled through their curls in turn, chucking them under the chins. "I can't wait to cuddle them!" She lifted Mickey from the stroller. "Come here, darling. Come to Nana."

Mickey chortled and then smirked complacently at his brother still waiting his turn.

"Isn't he a treasure! Look at that cheeky grin. And look, he has truly red lips!"

"Yes." No grandmother, surely, could welcome these babies with such loving delight and be the calculating sociopath Geoff had described.

"Now, they're not identical, are they?" Something seemed to be happening to her expression.

"No, they're not. They're fraternal."

"What a darling love," she murmured to Mickey. Her voice caught a little. "Yes, you are. Oh, yes, indeed you are."

"*Hiii!*" yelled Jonathon, disgruntled.

"They don't even have the same size heads, much less—" But I realized I was maundering. "It wasn't one split egg. It was more a question of fertility," I added out of reflex.

"Or enthusiasm, perhaps." She smiled slyly. A shine filmed her eye.

I didn't know what to say.

"Let me take a look at this handsome chap," she relinquished Mickey to me, bending to hoist Jonathon into the air. Mickey let out a wail of indignation.

"*What are you doing?*" roared Geoff, snapping a magazine under his arm as he marched up.

"Oh, hello, darling!"

"*What did you just do to him?*"

"Oh, Geoffrey, they're gorgeous! Simply gorgeous!" She cradled Jonathon against her and gazed down at him, glowing. I felt as if I was watching ice crack. "I had no idea!" she said.

"Why's Mickey yelling?" he demanded, turning on me. Mickey let out another cry of abandonment.

"Your mother was just holding him and——"

"Oh, shh, darling. Don't whinge. I'll come back to you in a moment. Geoffrey, darling——I couldn't tell from the photographs. There just seemed to be so many of them at once, and——look at his big green eyes. He looks so exactly like you did when you were tiny. Isn't he beautiful? Isn't he absolutely wickedly sweet?" She was crying now. Tears spilled over her cheeks. Jonathon returned her damp gaze with all the ardor he could muster.

"Here, give him to me!" Roughly Geoff grabbed at him.

"You must be so proud," she said, letting go reluctantly. "He's got your same mischievous little grin." Longingly she caressed Jonathon's hair as if Geoff hadn't spoken, wiping her eyes with the other hand.

"Watch it!" Geoff barked, twisting Jonathon sideways out of her reach.

"Geoff, it's *okay*. It was just——oh, Mickey, honey, be still, you can go back to Nana in a minute——" desperately I hung on to Mickey, who was lunging from his seat in my arms toward Cassandra like a wild-eyed porpoise.

"Now this one again. Your turn! You come back here to me, you sweet poppet," she said to Mickey. "Come to me, darling. Come along, hurry!"

"*No!*" cried Geoff.

She paid no attention.

"Leave him alone!"

"That's the way, raise your little arms——" she was encouraging.

"*Do not touch him!*"

And at that she could ignore him no longer.

"Geoffrey? Darling, what is it?" she asked. "What's wrong?" Her cheeks were webbed with tears. All her coy control was melted, gone.

"Don't you lay a *finger* on my children!"

"Geoff——" I began.

"Hush!"

Jonathon shifted restively against his shoulder and offered a mingy bleat. Judging by its note it was merely preparatory.

"Geoff, listen. Everything's okay." People milled all around us or stood, discreetly glancing over. "Everything's fine. There's no problem." Even though I knew at this stage placation never worked.

"Mother." He wheeled back. "Where are you planning to stay?" His cheekbones and the saddle of his nose had stretched tight. His jaw turned to stone.

"Why——why, I——" She stopped.

"We're a little far north for your holiday convenience, I think."

"Geoffrey——"

"A bit bucolic. Unsophisticated. The Wap-waps."

"Well, but I——I want to——"

"Not much happening up there. Only farmers. No pubs."

"I haven't come home to New Zealand in fifteen years," she whispered.

"Perhaps you could stay with Judith. She still lives on the North Shore, doesn't she? Birkenhead? Devonport? Your old cousin Judith?"

As I watched her face seemed to crumble and then slowly, facet by facet, begin to recongeal into its porcelain slipcast. "Yes," she said.

"Well? Which?"

She didn't answer.

"Where the bloody hell is it?" he said fiercely.

"Devonport."

"Goddamn you. How *dare* you touch my son? Listen to him crying! That's *you, your* fault. How *dare* you act as if you never so much as—how dare you—*everything* you touch—" His voice burst. Its timbre carried through the crowd and on toward the airport doors. "I'll never forgive you," he cried, and with those words he crammed Jonathon back into the stroller, grabbed Mickey squealing from my grasp, stuffed him into the front seat without even fitting his legs through the seatbelt harness, and stormed off pushing the stroller ahead of him.

After a moment I said, "Cassandra."

She watched him leave, surveying what she had wrought. She bit her lip.

"Look. I'm sorry. I have to—I'd better go—"

Her glance was not so much blind as empty. It held a familiar, eerie likeness, like a mirror in a dimly lit room.

"Cassandra?" I said.

For the first time I realized how her mouth was by nature shaped like a smile. A trick of genetics. Musculature. Not intentional. "Look—Cassandra. Are you all right?"

"I suppose I'd better find a taxi," she said, and slowly bent and picked up her small carry-on suitcase.

I watched her a moment. "Listen. You've got our phone number. And our address . . . don't you?"

Slowly she nodded.

"I'll contact you as soon as I can. I don't know what he'll—I'm sorry. Please phone. I'll get your cousin's number from Geoff somehow and phone you—"

"That's all right, darling. You go along. I'll be all right."

"You can call us tonight. Please phone us tonight. Please."

"It will be fine," she said.

"I'll talk to him first—"

"It's fine. I'm fine, no worries."

"Listen," I said intensely, the insight that I'd arrived at just a few days earlier beginning to force its way urgently into the open. "Listen—"

"You'd better run, darling. Go along. Hurry. Geoffrey's probably halfway to Mangere Bridge by now." She gave a low, careful, brittle chuckle.

"You've got a lot on your plate," she said. "With those beautiful, beautiful babies."

"Yes," I said.

"So much to love," she said.

I stood for a second more, staring.

She met my eyes and smiled.

"Until later, then," I breathed, pressed a kiss against her cheek, and rushed toward the glass doors in search of the children. Through the years since I've often replayed that moment, the closing words she said to me, that last sound of her voice I ever heard.

TO THIS DAY the scars inscribe the history of that first night, written on my vertebrae under Marble Arch.

I no longer allow the memories of those final weeks in the Northland cottage to pollute my spirit or affect the present. There's not room. Besides, I forgave Geoff his dementia long ago. Most of those images I have finished with; they don't return and don't matter. The good ones I keep, the good moments: of the twins smiling and taking their first steps, the pair of them crawling around the front garden chasing the bantam rooster while you throw bread crumbs, of Geoff pointing out some commonplace thing, like the amaryllis in bloom, and making me truly see it, of you climbing to the top of the plum tree. The final few hours of that battle are erased almost completely. I can only recall walking across the paddock the day before we left, hearing a drone, and looking up to see a plane over the beach: a bone-white insect flying in a straight line across the blue sky toward America. Those upper zones of clear, empty air, the tropic of light, of thin oxygen. *Skylark, have you anything to say to me?* The tempting strata of flight.

1986: Ghost

A girl must marry for love, and keep on marrying until she finds it.
— ZSA ZSA GABOR

Three years later, when we returned to the United States, Dan the journalist was waiting to take me to lunch.

BETWEEN THE BREAKUP of my marriage and the day the Air New Zealand flight landed at San Francisco International I had from time to time mailed Dan Hambleman a letter. Often I would enclose a manuscript or a short story, and he would respond by criticizing my plots or praising some characterization nuance I hadn't realized I'd made. Throughout the four years in New Zealand after the twins were born we'd been living on the interest from my grandmother's legacy while I typed my way through my first completed mystery. Dan was always encouraging. "You have an ear and a good sense of suspense," he'd write. "Now get published." Periodically I'd receive a postcard picturing California bears rolling backward on their kiesters, or Spanish señoritas dressed in real inset satin and lace, or a road map of the State of Anxiety with a single line scrawled on the back: "Awaiting your return. Love, Dan." Sometimes, more wistfully, "What do you look like these days? When do you come home? Many XXXX and OOOO, D."

When I did it was with three children in tow, a truly finished mystery in my suitcase, and a crazy optimism romping through my bloodstream like a dose of speed. I was hyperactive with fatigue. The fourteen-hour flight (two-hour stopover in Honolulu, just long enough to wake the twins from a first-time sleep, get them buzzing until their eyes frogged out, and trudge through Customs before the next six-hour leg) had been delayed for eight extra hours while maintenance crews in Auckland searched for an electrical fault. During that time the twins ran up and down the departure lounge racing the courtesy wheelchairs. "Aren't they cute," said a stewardess dubiously as she came on duty with the second-shift staff. I said yes and called Mickey over so that I could scrape the chocolate and chewing gum off his knees.

DANIEL HAMBLEMAN WAS an only child.

Well, that says it all, doesn't it? No, it does not. He was tall, a middle-aged Jewish epicure who'd had no Bar Mitzvah because his father had declared himself an atheist. Once, when he was twenty-two he'd been married to a violinist/yoga teacher for a sum total of five months. His high intelligence was belied by a face like a cherub.

There's more.

Daniel, known to his family as Danny, was born multi-talented——a jazz pianist, Shakespearean actor, a tennis player who took up the sport in order to compete against his father and ended by pleasing him with his deadly skill, thereby thwarting his own bitter intentions. When he turned nineteen he was invited to audition for an off-Broadway play. This infused his father with so much pride that Danny renounced acting for the next twenty-five years. His father was a successful lawyer. The week after Dan acquired his first Master's Degree he founded an underground newspaper, working at a job selling vacuum cleaners on the side.

When Dan first married the yogi violinist his father cannily pretended to a deep craving for grandchildren. He even bought a silver-plated porringer engraved with an *H* that he found at a garage sale and presented it to Dan and his wife along with a wink and a comment about lucky coincidences. In truth (as Natalie Hambleman told Dan later) he hoped the happy couple would wait several years before even thinking about a baby, since he considered Dan too immature for parenthood. The result was that Dan not only practiced fanatical birth control but eventually stopped sleeping with his wife altogether. She packed her bags and filed for annulment.

Twenty years later Dan had not remarried. He lived alone, a man with very particular ways and a beautiful enunciation of the English language. The decor in his Pacific Heights apartment was light, spacious, and subtle. Serious romance he avoided like the plague.

But his relationship with his mother Natalie was legendary.

WHEN DAN AND I had lunch that day after I got back to America, and I described my marriage to Geoff, I saw his mouth twist with dismay and his eyes light up with interest. He reminded me over the *salade nicoise* of how long he'd held me in fond esteem, how good it had been to write each other across the oceans. He shook his head over the choices we make for our lives. In no way did he perceive me as a victim, which came as a big relief. I'd done this to myself, he agreed, and what's more, whether I realized it or not, there was some vital and perhaps arcane reason I had *had* to do it, I'd needed to pass through that annealing fire of dysfunction in order to become a more conscientious person. Personally, he viewed me as heroic.

Then I pulled out the snapshots of you and the twins.

"Good God," he said flatly.

IT TOOK US three months to start dating.

This was not because he wasn't eager to get going right away. I spent some weeks in Texas reuniting with the family, meeting with uncles, aunts, and cousins, catching up on everybody's news. But before long I was headed for the Bay Area. By the time the twins had lost their Kiwi accents I'd managed to find an apartment in Berkeley that fit in with my meager trust income, buy an old Volvo station wagon, and fly back to Bernice to pick you all up.

Meanwhile Dan kept telephoning Texas every few days, often from startling places.

"I just want to say hello," he'd say, and pause.

One night he called from the study of a friend of his who kept a pet Komodo dragon in the adjoining bathroom amid decaying gobbets of raw meat dragged from a tub marked "Lizard Chow." Another time he rang from the foyer of an S & M parlor where he'd been researching an article. He also phoned from the sauna room at his gym, from the backseat of a hired limo taking him up to a rock musician's cabin on the Russian River, and once, surprisingly, from his own breakfast table. "When are you coming back up here? Maybe go on a little spin together down the coast? Have you found someone to watch the kids yet?" he would say ingenuously. "When are you moving?"

BEFORE I MOVED us to Berkeley, Dan and I flew to the Yucatan to spend a long experimental weekend together.

We were strolling down the beach one morning with the rollers crashing and the sticky salt breeze whipping our faces when we paused to examine a peddler's straw hats. "What do you think?" Dan asked, trying one on.

"It's okay. A little short in the crown." His curls were receding by now, which revealed a tall forehead getting more sunburned every minute. "I'd go for the Panama type if I were you."

"Like this one, perhaps?" He tried another.

"Yes, definitely."

"Great." He counted out the correct number of pesos.

The peddler sighed philosophically; nobody had even haggled.

"I trust your taste," Dan said.

"You look like something out of a Bogart movie."

"Do I?"

"Yes."

"Marry me," he said.

I stood dazed.

"I beg your pardon?"

"We've known each other for ten years. That's a pretty good run."

"Oh. Ah. Um. Is it?"

For a moment the shine in his brown eyes sharpened like lacquer. On some deep level I knew he was committing an act that he admired, that he was in love with, a sprint of courage that thrilled him with his own magnanimity and tenderness. "I love you," he said. "I really *love* you!" caressing my cheek in rapture that he could surrender this much. "You're so—*good*."

I didn't know what to say.

"Yes. Yes, you are!" He cupped my chin, gazing down into my eyes.

"Oh, no, I'm not," I whispered, feeling my eyes widen but unsure of what else I felt.

"Which proves my point. You're so humble you don't even know it."

Which should have tipped me off to run like hell.

But of course—

• • •

WHEN I MOVED us to Berkeley Dan stood by with loads of good advice. He knew where the best daycare centers were, the best junior high, which pre-Kindergarten provided the best S.A.T. and college prep. He knew where to get deluxe housewares dirt cheap, which Junior League thrift shop had the highest incidence of Armani, and what hole-in-the-wall liquor store carried the largest selection of single-malt scotch. "I learned fastidiousness from my mother," he confided. "You would understand that. The first time I saw you exchange a sterling spoon for a stainless one before dipping it in the mayonnaise I knew you'd been well brought up. You didn't even know I was watching." He beamed.

Of course, what he didn't know was how I'd spotted my own lipstick print on the spoon.

THE TWINS FOUND it hard to settle into a new city.

"Mum," they would say, as I tucked them into bed each night. "Mummy, I want apple. You peel it for me. Mum, he took my pony. Mum, read another story. Make him give me the Leggo man, don't turn out the light. Mum, he bit me, Bring me some juice, don't leave. Don't shut the door, *no*, don't leave, stay here, *don't go!*" Tears slurried down their cheeks from their shiny, terrified eyes. "Sing, Mummy. Sing a song. Sing 'Blinken.'" I'd sing a lullaby, and another, and finally the same one over and over again, my voice thinning to a stop. Gradually they'd drop off into a doze. On some nights I felt barely enough energy to get up from the edge of one bed or another and tiptoe out of the room.

You may remember this, Treatie. I don't know. You were pretty busy yourself at that time, making new friends, listening to the Grateful Dead, discovering girls and California life, in that order. I wrote during the mornings; in the afternoons I'd shuttle the twins over to daycare and work as a part-time secretary for a temp agency. On the evenings when I scraped the money together to hire a pair of high school baby-sitters and go out with Dan, the twins would scream. "*No, no!*" Then they'd grip my legs, digging in and running my stockings with their nails. "*Don't go! Please, please, oh please stay here, no, please, Mummy, Mummy, Mummy!*" I'd kneel down to try and comfort them, especially Jonathon, who seemed the more desolate and shrieked the louder. The two high school baby-sitters, a pair of sisters, would stand there watching patient and mute. Dan always waited by the door. His hat perched back on his head. His white silk scarf draped around his neck, gleaming.

On the night I particularly remember he was smoothing his leather gloves as he spoke.

"The curtain rises in forty-five minutes."

"Mickey, go with Li-Yung to your room and show her your new puzzle book. She wants to see it. She's never seen a puzzle book that talks before. Have you, Li-Yung? Go show her where to press the buttons. Jon—honey—"

"Maybe it would be better if you just walk out now," Dan said as always.

This time I argued. "I can't do that. They're too upset. I can't just leave them."

"They know that. They're counting on it." He decided to elaborate. "Do you not see? You're conditioning them. Take a firm stand. Cut it off."

I blinked at him, stricken by my own betrayal.

"We still have to find parking."

"I'm sorry," I said. He stood in his cashmere overcoat with the Homeric set to his face. "Jon? Sweetie? Wouldn't you like to take Ming to the kitchen and get your froggy cup out for some milk?" I bent and hoisted him up and clasped him weeping miserably in my arms, dripping tears and snot on the black crepe sleeve of my dress. I gazed in appeal at Ming. She stared back, bewildered.

"Ming? Wouldn't you *love* to see Jonathon's froggy cup?" I asked with emphasis. "It's his ceramic *cup* with a little *frog* in the bottom. He *loves* to drink his *bedtime milk* and see the *frog peek out* when it's nearly all gone." Jonathon wailed louder.

"Oh, yes!" said Ming. "Of course! Jonny! Come here! Here! Come with Ming! Show me in the kitchen!"

"*No!*" screamed Jonathon, clinging desperately. I heard a crash from the bedroom. Mickey began to yell.

"No, no, Mickey," soothed Li-Yung. "No kicks."

"*Just go,*" said Dan.

I felt like tearing out my hair.

"Jonny. Come close." Ming drew near to his little red ear. She flicked me one stealthy glance. "I give you candy," she whispered, looking away.

Slowly Jonathon rose. He gulped. His next sob caught and stopped halfway up his throat.

"Ming——" I said, aghast.

"*Lulu*." Dan headed me off at the pass.

"Come," mumbled Ming, avoiding my eyes, and held out her arms. Jonathon knuckled his nose. Hesitantly he leaned toward her, then fell into her waiting embrace.

"Where?" he said.

"Shh. Pocket," she whispered, carrying him off to the kitchen, her forehead pressed against his red hair.

"Chinese candy?" I heard him ask. "Like the kind your mother sent us last time?"

"Mickey. Don't throw the truck, Mickey," wheedled Li-Yung from somewhere deep within the twins' room.

Wordlessly Dan took my arm and guided me out the door and down the stairs. "They've already brushed their teeth!" I railed as we hit the pavement. "They're not allowed sugar! It's too much! The girls know that! I've told them and told them! It's *bribery!*"

"Thank God for corruption," he muttered.

"They've been moved to a strange city seven thousand miles from where they were born and surrounded by total strangers who feed them candy to shut them up!" What had I done?

"Why don't you get in the car," suggested Dan, opening the door like a gentleman.

"I can't! I can't go off and leave them like this!" I was too exhausted to be rational. I was crying, my mascara bleeding black globs over my contacts.

"It's the best thing you can do. They stage-directed this

chaos the same way they do every time. Now you know what the girls have to resort to in order to do their job." I looked up at him with horror. "Lulu, listen. Those boys can't run your life. They've got to learn that. Otherwise they'll never gain a shred of self-reliance or autonomy. Besides, you need time to yourself." He gazed down at me, wisdom and benevolence glowing from him like radioactivity. Carefully he settled me into the front passenger seat, went around to the driver's side, and climbed in. "You need off-time, quality time. For replenishment," he added thoughtfully. Reaching over, he rubbed my shoulder. A certain hunger began to kindle behind his eyes. His left hand grasped the steering wheel. His right wandered down to caress my knee, squeeze lightly, and then slide casually up my skirt.

"Don't worry."

"I can't help it."

"When you come back tonight they'll wake up and discover you're there. Or else they'll find you in your own bed early in the morning. Either way they'll know for certain that you aren't really abandoning them."

"You know who you sound like?" I said.

"Who?"

"Your father."

He stiffened. His gaze twitched, turning to glass. I had never met his father. All I knew about him came from Dan's many stories.

"You've never met my father," he said icily.

"That's true. But Dan, tell me this: what would *your* mother have done if that had been you crying and begging for her not to leave?"

Very quietly he slipped his hand back down my thigh and out from under my skirt. His eyelids dropped.

After a few moments he said with crisp deliberation, "You are correct."

I waited.

"There was a time once when my father returned from a long business trip." He breathed deeply a moment. "When he got home his presence, for some reason, and I can only guess why, upset or frightened me. After I ran away from him and began to cry he came and found me, picked me up, put me in a room, and locked the door. He then ordered that all the women of our household, my mother and grandmother and my two aunts, on no account release me. I'd become spoiled, he said, and needed to be taught a lesson. I needed to learn who was boss." He paused. "Apparently from all reports I cried for the next three-and-a-half hours while the women huddled in the living room or wrung their hands, pacing back and forth through the hall, pleading with him to let me out. He stood against the door with his arms folded on his chest, ignoring them. My mother claimed afterward that she never got over it. Even when she was dying, she brought it up and recalled it all over again." He pressed his lips together. "I was, I believe, approximately two years old at the time."

Finally he softened.

"I will never be that kind of stepfather," he said, turning to me. "I will *not* force you to become like my mother, or go through what she endured. Ever. You have my word."

Then he took both my hands and pressed them with kisses.

Months would elapse before I recovered enough wit and vitality to realize that, no matter what his promise, he already had.

IT SEEMS TO me, Treatie, that so much of our lives are lived in reaction. Choices get made that seem balanced at the time, but all they really balance out is the thing we're turning away from. Our wasted energies could be plugged into a public generator (in my case large enough to light up Corpus Christi) so that the power would have been of some use instead of just trickling away into oblivion. We imagine we're choosing freely, but most often we're not; the opposite side of the same coin is still the same coin. I fell in love with Dan Hambleman's honor of me, his earnest wish to venerate me in spite of his history and mine, and his determination to fling off his former habits in order to do so.

Looking back, I can now say that second to Geoff, Dan was the angriest man I'd ever met. Once again I'd picked unerringly, drawn by the fumes of a fire I unconsciously recognized. But then, how does love ever start but with the old familiar territory? Don't we all veer toward what we know?

I can remember thinking after the second time he'd

proposed that I couldn't possibly dream of marrying any-one ever again. The few crimes I never wanted to be hung for were moral extravagance and cheap vulgarity.

Then I thought, Well, maybe it won't matter so much. This is California, after all.

And at least nobody will ask to display the sheets after the wedding night.

WE COURTED FOR some months. The path of true love never has run smooth, but with two children accompany-ing our walks in the park and testing Dan's mettle by dumping ice cream on each other's heads or screaming at the museum dinosaur, it looked as bumpy as a cobblestone alley in Romania. Several times when we were out alone at night he repeated his marriage proposal. Each time when morning arrived and he phoned me to dreamily say hello and heard the twins bouncing on my bed like a tram-poline, he would cough and murmur that perhaps we should think things through a little longer. After eight months of this game I grew irritated enough to finally break off with him completely.

"I CAN'T SLEEP with you anymore," I told him one clear February evening as we sat stuck in traffic on the Bay Bridge, creeping toward San Francisco for dinner at Stars.

"How is that?" he asked after a terse silence.

He'd made our reservations eight weeks in advance. Jer-emiah Tower himself was cooking a special *prix fixe* meal tonight to celebrate the restaurant's anniversary. We were dressed to kill.

"Your vacillations are making me crazy."

His eyes glazed over with the impassivity I'd come to know so well.

"Is this by any chance to do with my requesting you to install a lock on your bedroom door?"

For a split second I fumbled. "Well . . ."

"In the interests of privacy, I might add? And out of regard for normal, wholesome child development?"

"No. I'm sorry. It's just that you keep wobbling back and forth because you can't figure out what you really want, and I'm so tired—"

"Oh, yes," he said firmly. "I know what I want."

The sway of the bridge seemed to shift from hypothetical to perceptible.

"Unconditionally, I meant."

His mouth clamped tight. He did not reply.

"Well, then . . . I guess what I really mean is, whether you want a life with me or not."

"That's a little closer to accuracy, although not much." He was glaring straight ahead. A car behind us honked and he rolled his window down and shot the driver the finger.

"Considering, since you've asked me to marry you four times now and then backed off, it's only natural to conclude—"

He pursed his lips, unclenched them, pursed them again. His eyes took on that stubborn blinkless stare that exposed the whites. "I would appreciate it if you would not bend things in directions to which they don't belong, and assign to me motives I do not have."

I sighed. "Okay. A life with my children."

Glowering, he released the brake pedal as the cars began to inch toward the exit.

"Life with me means a life with my children, Dan."

"Are you always going to insist on stating the obvious?"

Love does not exist, I thought. There is no place for it in this vintage Karmann Ghia. The water far below us seemed to rearrange darkly, pointing and caving like flaked obsidian, the waves marching by in miraculous order. Overhead the sky expanded through unmarked cobalt. "You're right. I'm stating the obvious. And I did make the choice to have them."

"Indeed."

"So I guess it's up to me to sort out all these yeses and nos and shape something definite."

"I agree."

My heart faltered, then bucked up.

"What thing do you have in mind?" he said.

"Drive me home."

His head jerked. "What? *Now?*"

Dusk had fallen. Bridge lights carved vases out of the gloom as if they were arc welders. I shrugged my shoulders deeper into the wool of my coat. "Yes, please."

It had taken us forty-five minutes to reach the nearer zones of the city. The traffic was finally beginning to pick up. His anger felt as palpable as wet ashes.

"I don't want any more ambiguity in my life," I said. "From now on."

Gunning the car, he wheeled us down the nearest exit ramp. Then finally he answered, stacking the words like boulders one by one on a rising wall. "There is no such thing as an absolute. To believe otherwise is the naive hope of children. And you," he said, "are *not* a child."

"But I sure do spend all my time with them," I said; and only after he'd dropped me off in front of my apartment building did I register the full pith of this statement.

ONE MONTH LATER my phone rang at five in the morning.

"Lulu," came the low voice.

Turning over, I threw the blanket off my shoulders and bunched the pillow higher.

"I've been up all night. Walking the streets."

"Why?" I asked.

"Trying to get through the throes of a crisis."

After a moment I said carefully, "I'm sorry to hear it." We'd had no contact for weeks. Despite the hour and murkiness of my brain my pulse started lightly to hammer.

"I don't like not seeing you."

"Ah." Rubbing my eyes, I hoisted up on one elbow.

"I miss your generosity," he whispered.

"Oh," I said.

"And I want to share something with you."

"What?"

"I've made the leap."

His portentous tone made me wary. I started to ask what leap, but remembered the last time I'd asked him a simple question. Plainly I was supposed to know.

"I can do this thing." His voice began to ripen self-convincingly. "I can do it," he cried in elation.

"Oh—well, that's great, Dan. That's really—"

"I—*can*—*live*—with—your—*children!*"

It took a minute to catch my breath.

"*What?*"

"You heard me!"

"Is this—are you sure?" Are you feverish? I wanted to ask. The receiver seemed to emit heat.

"Absolutely!"

"But you said there were no such things as absolutes."

After a loaded pause he said, "I was mistaken."

I was flabbergasted.

"Could you actually, um, accept them?" I asked, swallowing. "All three? Are you sure? There's three of them, remember. Treatie may not be little, but he—"

"I can count," he said with fulsome patience.

"You—do you really want to do this? Really? And—and actually like them?"

"*Yes!*"

"I mean, Dan, it *is* a big job. There's no question. Could you really take on that much responsibility?"

"*I will do so.*"

"You're willing to share a home with a teenager? I mean, he's going to turn thirteen soon. And become a stepfather?"

"I welcome it!" he cried.

Lying under the smooth sheet I pictured him bounding to his feet, his rumpled, feathery hair on end, the fervor stretching his face, and felt a trancelike languor slide over my internal organs, a languor that had no bearing whatsoever on cold reality.

"Will you take me back?" he murmured deeply, with zeal. "Will you marry me? Will you forgive all the hesitations and cautions?"

"I don't know."

"Despite the fact that they could hardly be unexpected under the circumstances," he added wryly, and then caught himself. "But I'm over them. I've wrestled them down." He gave a little self-conscious chuckle at his own pomposity. "Lulu?"

"Yes?"

"Help me become a papa."

The word stunned. Suddenly I saw Dan swinging one of the twins up onto his hip while the other gazed up at him, saying "Papa! Papa! Me next!" I saw him squatting beside a short formica school desk, poring through crayon drawings and phonics exercises on Parent/Teachers Night. My pulse began to thump harder. "I need to think about it."

"May I please come see you?"

"When?"

"Now!"

"The kids will be awake in half an hour. I'll have to make breakfast."

"Well, then how about right after you deliver them to daycare?" he said quickly.

Over the past month I'd moved at last from the quagmire into a clearing. I was beginning to experience days that promised not only survival, but occasional glimpses of clear thought. But I still wasn't yet eagle-eyed enough to see what lay smack in front of my face.

"Okay," I said. "This isn't one of their scheduled mornings, but I'll phone and check if it's okay for them to come in."

"Thank you, my love," he murmured.

"It's going to take about three hours or so."

"That's all right. I can hardly wait to see you."

"Okay."

"Thank you," he said again. "These last few weeks have been—illuminating," and I have to admit the gratitude sounded sincere: absolute, in fact.

You WOULD HAVE liked my mother. A more intelligent, sensitive, loving person never breathed." Reflectively he hooked one arm around my shoulders and stroked my hair, and with his free hand poured himself a second finger of scotch. "She cared about everyone but herself. Most of her time was spent looking after people who didn't appreciate it."

I lay back against him. "What did she do otherwise? Did she work?"

He shook his head. "That was not an option in my father's household."

"Oh." So it had been one of those old-fashioned setups with rigid roles.

"What she wanted most was to write."

I looked up, a *frisson* quickening. "Write?"

He nodded. "Like you."

Quietly we sat as I pondered this. He chewed on the rest of his drink. "What she had left was books. Her favorite subject always revolved around whose work she'd discovered lately. All those years spent tucked up in a Cincinnati suburb, marooned far away from New York where she'd been born and reared, and kept company with highly accomplished people, all she could do was read. She'd lived in the Village while she attended NYU. She'd also been very involved in the theater. It was her dream to write plays. But then she became a housewife. Late nights during my teens after I'd come in from dates, we'd sit around the kitchen table, comparing fiction reviews. She was the person I confided in." He sighed. "She was my best friend. And I was *hers*. There were even a few rare moments when she talked about my father. She'd confess to me what—" he paused, gravely furrowing his forehead, selecting the *bon mot*, "—what she *forebore* within their marriage. Not complaining. She didn't whine. Always she was the soul of grace and generosity. But I could tell how she felt from the time I turned three years old. Our empathy made us a kind of—unit." He paused again. Then sadly he shook his head and smiled. "She taught me all I know about love. And I've never yet had the right context in which to practice it, until now."

For a month we'd been officially engaged. I'd broken the news to my parents. The fourth finger of my left hand sent out shivery, fractured light from a 1½-carat diamond set in a platinum shank. Most weekends we spent house hunting.

"Did you feel guilty when you moved so far away?" I asked. "From Ohio to Berkeley?"

"The bulk of any parent-child relationship is ninety-five percent guilt," he replied. "Either one party carries the freight or the other one does. Besides, I left home to go to college in Pennsylvania. There wasn't exactly a question of return."

"But somewhere you felt like you deserted her?" I persisted.

He shrugged. "I had to follow my destiny. She understood that."

"And so did you."

"But with regret." He shook his heavy head: with regret.

"That's too bad."

"My mother used up so many of her years trapped in remorse," he said, and his voice grew poignant. "I think in the end, that's what killed her."

"How?"

"She felt crippled by her love for my father and me, and didn't know how to resolve our differences. The sense of responsibility rendered her helpless. She thought she'd failed us both. She also felt very, very alone. By the time she was diagnosed with pancreatic cancer her sadness was almost impossible to penetrate."

The picture he drew made me want to deny, defy, to

blot out such terrible, familiar pain. "I don't believe in re-gret," I announced. "It solves nothing. All it does is eat you up inside."

"That's what I love about you," he murmured, stroking my hair even more tenderly than before. "You're such a fighter."

AT THIS TIME, while I was so busy not recognizing the starry quality to Dan's reverence, all I knew was that he behaved exactly as Geoffrey had not. He would hold me dear, respect every molecule of my being no matter how hard the struggle; he would keep himself reminded never, ever to deliberately hurt me; and all this because he had finally fallen for someone as valiant as his mother.

One man's twist is another man's warp. Between Geof-frey's bitter projections and Dan's idealized ones: in the final count, was there any difference?

OF COURSE THERE was one person to which my marital record mattered very much.

"It looks like it fits you with only a little room to spare," said Mr. Hambleman civilly to me as he handed Dan his dead wife's wedding ring to slip on to my finger during the upcoming ceremony. "Which is good, because it can't be sized." The ring had been made from Mr. Hambleman's own father's stickpin. It glittered all the way around with a thin rim of diamonds.

"Thank you," I said.

He smiled, his eyes crinkling at the corners. Despite

Dan's warnings I had yet to view his austere, controlling side. His voice was mellifluous and urbane. His compliments could coax a dead flounder back to life. He made witty puns. Over dinner he often carried on enthusiastic monologues about music. His beautifully tailored tweed suits looked straight out of Bond Street, even though he was now retired and could have dressed in something looser. We'd been visiting Cincinnati for two days so that I could meet him; now, as we stood outside his house, getting ready to climb into a waiting cab on our way to the airport, he took my hand between his own and patted it thoughtfully.

"Do me a favor."

"Of course. Anything." This man was accepting me into his household, accepting his middle-aged son's love for me, accepting my three children; he was accepting without demur the fact that between us Dan and I did not yet jointly earn enough money to negotiate a mortgage on a doghouse; and he was willing to help us out if we needed it. I was happy to oblige whatever he asked. "What?" I asked.

"When you get through with the ring, please make sure you give it back."

And with that he turned to his son, gave him a brief hug good-bye, and shut the cab door on us.

WE GOT MARRIED, as you'll remember, in the Claremont Hotel.

It was at the wedding breakfast before the ceremony that you tasted your very first champagne.

We were all excited. A climate of reunion permeated

the room. Dan's two aunts had arrived from New York only minutes before we sat down. Mr. Hambleman's plane wound up three hours late; for some reason he'd preferred to remain in Cincinnati until the actual day, since, as he pointed out, we weren't having a rehearsal dinner. I greeted him at the door just as the waiters began to serve the food. Miriam had flown up from Dallas to act as my maid of honor. Also present were my parents, Dyllis, my older brother and his wife, and a few of our most intimate friends.

"I'd like to propose a toast," called Dan's best man, holding his glass high like a sword of Damocles over Dan's curls.

"Go ahead," Dan said.

"To an act of vandalism masquerading as a state of optimism!"

"What's being vandalized?" asked Dan's Aunt Lydia.

"My faith in bachelorhood." The best man brought the glass down to his mouth and drained off the whole thing in one gulp.

"Who's performing the service, by the way?" Aunt Lydia turned to Dan. "Will it be one of your San Francisco friends? The Church of Free Thought or Rational Afterlife, or whatever those New Age mail-order organizations are?"

"No," said Dan. Surreptitiously he glanced in his father's direction. "We got a rabbi."

Mr. Hambleman lifted his head.

My father leaned across the table toward me with a conspiratorial murmur, "You've never been married by a rabbi before, have you, Lulu?" His sense of humor so rarely made a family appearance that it seemed a shame I'd want to kill him for this one.

"Oh, Hank!" scolded Mother, and slapped his hand as he grinned.

"A rabbi?" said Mr. Hambleman in a tone of wonderment.

"That is correct," Dan replied. Ominously his jaw tucked hard against his collar.

"Ah. Your chosen man of the cloth." Mr. Hambleman sat up straight and sipped a glass of champagne.

"What wonderful news! A rabbi! That would have made your mother so very happy." Aunt Lydia sighed. "Wouldn't it have made Natalie happy, Isaac?"

"I have no idea," said Mr. Hambleman, inspecting the jacquard design in the brocade tablecloth.

"That's what Lulu and I both concluded," Dan said.

"Well, of course! Oh, absolutely, no question. She'd have been delighted. Tell me, where did you find him? What synagogue is he with?"

"The one up in Sausalito on Larch Avenue," I told her.

"I see. They must be very liberal. That's Marin County, isn't it? Did he have any problem about doing—well, you know?"

"A mixed marriage, she means," said Mr. Hambleman coolly.

"No," said Dan. "Not at all. As a matter of fact he had no problem whatever with that. So long as we bring up our children Jewish." He thrust out his chin. "Oddly enough, when he first met us for the prenuptial talk he assumed Lulu was the Jew."

"Really? Why?" marveled his Aunt Rose, speaking up for the first time since she'd started grappling with her eggs Florentine. "She doesn't look Jewish. Do you think so? Does she look Jewish to you, Lydia?"

"No, she doesn't look Jewish to me."

"Does she to you, Isaac?"

Delicately Mr. Hambleman raised his napkin and touched his lips. Then he folded his hands on the table-cloth. "I couldn't say."

"Well, it's much better to go ahead and mention the subject than to sit around all stuffy and pretend it doesn't exist like a bunch of Episcopalians!" Aunt Rose said.

"What about you, dear? Are you Jewish?" Aunt Lydia diplomatically asked Miriam, who smiled and shook her head.

"No, I'm afraid not."

"I thought maybe as the bride's maid of honor, and with your name, which as you know is very traditional—"

"Your own *best friend* is Gentile, Lydia. What are you talking about?" said Aunt Rose. "Get back to the topic."

"There's no harm in asking." Aunt Lydia fingered her pearls.

"Maybe you have some Jewish ancestors and the rabbi saw their bloodlines in your face," Aunt Rose speculated. "Maybe he sensed something you haven't known about. Your forgotten heritage, for instance. Is this possible?" she turned to my parents.

"No. I don't *think* so," said Mother, earnestness wrinkling her forehead.

"On your side, maybe," Aunt Rose said to Dad.

"Well, I'm afraid that's not very likely," he chuckled in apology. "My folks have always been Southern Baptists."

"You never can tell. It's historically documented that a number of Jewish immigrants arrived in Texas from Russia early in this century. They disembarked at Galveston —that's your main port, isn't it?" Aunt Rose spoke as if of a very foreign country, which no doubt to a Brooklynite it seemed. "The whole plan was a kind of test alternative to New York, which was getting very crowded what with the sweatshops and work competition and neighborhoods bursting at the seams. Entire male populations of certain *shtetls* got transported all at once. They were pioneers on the frontier just like in the Western movies. We learned about it in B'nai B'rith."

"Was the test successful?" asked Mother timidly.

"*I* couldn't say. You tell *me*."

"Why, honey, you know it was!" chided Dad. "That's where the Cavits and the Brinches originally came from. Some of our dearest friends are descendants of that bunch," he explained to Aunt Rose. "Successful—why, I should certainly say they were. They've done very well indeed. Far, far more so than most."

"Oh, the Cavits! Of course!" said Mother, flustered but now visibly brightening. "Yes! And Anna Jane Brinch— she and I are in the same Literary Club—and Leo, and Rochelle, just a lovely sweet girl, a sophomore at Stanford next fall—"

"This is so very nice to hear," exclaimed Aunt Lydia.

"Very nice news. You have close Jewish friends, then, down there in Texas."

"Oh, yes indeed!" Mother agreed.

"Natalie would be so relieved." She smiled at the thought of her sister's vain years of hope.

"This still doesn't explain why the rabbi would mistake Lulu for a Jewish bride," retorted Aunt Rose. "You know what they say about recognizing. I would imagine he'd know."

"But then, Danny doesn't really look so Jewish either, do you, darling?" said Aunt Lydia. "Natalie was very blond. She and Rose and I all got the blue eyes, but she got the golden hair. Like a fairy-tale princess. They used to say that about her when we were in school."

"And I was the frog," Mr. Hambleman remarked glibly to the window casements. We all looked up, startled. For the first time I noticed how much Dan's eyes resembled his: same lids, same bulbous look, same urbanity, same guarded, mulish dispassion.

"Well," said Aunt Lydia. Gently she edged a puddle of hollandaise with her spoon.

"Oh, come on, Isaac. Don't always be the pickle in the barrel. Let's enjoy the day," said Aunt Rose, briskly changing key. "Excuse me, but isn't it nearly time for the ceremony?"

"You know, I believe you're right," said Mother, vigorously twisting her wristwatch.

"There you are! It's been such a pleasure meeting all of you for the first time. A beautiful breakfast. Now I'm sure the bride and groom need to go and get themselves dressed." Graciously Aunt Rose turned and smiled and bowed to my family, Miriam and our friends at the table's far end. "The rest of you just sit tight. Lydia, come with me. We'll go find the rabbi and make him feel at home."

"That's a good idea," said Aunt Lydia as we all pushed our chairs back.

"He may as well meet the real Jews. Isn't that right, Isaac?"

Mr. Hambleman straightened, his head tilted in dignity, as if considering.

"Natalie's representatives, you could regard us as," she added.

He regarded her inscrutably, a faint smile arranged on his thin lips. Suddenly I felt a wrenching compassion: in this old, old battle he was cornered at last.

"Lulu, you look gorgeous. Darling, we're very glad to have you join our family women." Aunt Rose wheeled around and gripped my arm.

"Oh, yes," cried Aunt Lydia, and they both gave me a quick little squeeze. "Now you run along and get ready."

"A good traditional ceremony," added Aunt Rose. "Personally I can't wait to see my darling Danny step on the glass!"

She reached up on tiptoe and gave Dan a resounding smack, leaving her lipstick rosebud printed just below his ear. "We're so proud," she whispered fiercely, patting his jawbone. "You've chosen very well."

I think it was the happiest wedding moment of my career.

OVER THE NEXT few months, however, I grew all too aware of the struggle going on inside Dan.

Since unfortunately I stood in the center of the problem—the hinge, you might say—I couldn't do much about it. Even heroines are sometimes stymied.

"I'm going to need to declare this room strictly off limits," he explained, watching as the locksmith screwed the brand-new deadbolt on to his study door.

"Really? How come?" I asked, although I already knew.

"Because, as we've already discussed at length, there are certain steps I have to implement if we're going to manage this transition."

"Off limits to whom exactly?"

He gave me a narrow look that said, Who the hell do you think? "Mainly people under twenty."

"Oh. You mean, not necessarily me."

"I perceive you as courteous enough to knock."

"Ah," I ruminated, feeling sarcasm creep up on me like a stealthy cat. "You perceive me, huh?"

"Bearing in mind that I have spent the last couple of decades accustomed to having an entire living quarters to myself, child-free, quiet, and clutter proof, I think this is a fair compromise," he added. "Don't you?"

"So you're saying that there are going to be, like, places within our home that some family members cannot enter?"

"No," he replied evenly. "Not places. A place. This place." He smiled. "My place."

"Correct me if I'm wrong, but wasn't there a story

about a similar situation that may ring a teensy bell? Concerning a main character with blue facial hair?"

"Venom is uncalled for, Lulu." He jerked his head toward the kneeling locksmith: at least in front of the help.

"I just don't happen to believe in whole areas of a private home being labeled *this* damn private. It sets a bad precedent. Of mistrust." And leaves a bad taste in the mouth, I thought, simultaneously wondering if within Dan there lurked a stronger emotion than mere nuisance resentment toward my children, such as disdain.

"I'm more interested in beginning this experiment with as clear a head start as possible," he reasoned. "The fewer handicaps the better."

"Experiment?"

"Well. Naturally. The challenge of merging two households has been written up in—"

I stared at him. "Wait just a second. Dan. This is no damn experiment."

He tucked his square chin tight, as when faced with a confrontation he knew was about to turn tedious.

"Is it?" I demanded.

"Any process of exploration involves an open-minded—"

"This is commitment for life. Permanent! That's what you said you wanted. That's what we agreed to."

"Of course. No one has implied anything else. I am now committed to exploring—"

"That's the only reason I married you in the first place." My neck was starting to grow hot.

"So I am aware." He stared back at me in a smooth, deliberate inspection.

"Do you honestly think I would have married again if we weren't counting on a lifetime?"

"I haven't questioned our permanence. Where do you get such a misconstruction?"

"Oh, great. Next you're going to tell me for the thousandth time that I've misheard you and misinterpreted your intent and that we're talking at totally opposite angles." The skin on my scalp was prickling; intensity dried my tongue.

"Look. Do you think we could perhaps postpone this?"

"This what?"

"Dialogue. For a *decent interval,*" he muttered, keeping his back to the locksmith who now rifled nonchalantly around in his toolbox for another part, looking as if he was ready to break into a carefree whistle.

"My children's home is their refuge," I hissed through my teeth. "Every part of it should be open to them. As a *policy!*"

"What about *my home?*" he said. The vein in his forehead began to jump.

"What about it?"

"Do you feel I have the right to a refuge?"

"You chose this! We're a family now. Integrated. You can't turn around and bar off some entire region of the house and turn the rest of it into a ghetto!"

"Since when does it hurt children to have a few clear boundaries drawn? Have you never heard of setting limits?" he shouted.

"So *now* you're going to attack the way I'm raising my children?"

"Well, since they're yours, yes!"

"Oh," I said frigidly. "Well, now. How interesting. Should I be taking that personally? As in 'mine,' Lulu's, the hopelessly bad parent? the perennial fuck-up on a transinternational scale—"

"I meant, *since they're not mine!*"

The locksmith dropped his electric drill. "Oops! Sorry!" he cried gaily.

Dan loomed above me like the Colossus of Rhodes, ears aflame, the tremors of his roar still oscillating on the air. Both his dangling arms ended in fists. His eyeballs bulged like fried eggs.

"We shouldn't have done this," I mumbled, and averted my face from the study doorway.

"When should we *ever* argue?" he inquired stiffly.

"I wasn't referring to arguing," I said. I trudged off to the kitchen to mash up some tuna-fish salad for lunch. Only when I stood morosely chopping celery did the logical question strike me, the one I should have asked him in the first place: Would your mother have done that to you? Locked you out of a room?

And why, this one time, should you have expected me to be any different?

But then, the guilt I bore toward you kids in those days tended to make me a little slow-witted. Besides, Dan was far too busy being his father to have listened.

• • •

MESS TENDS TO beget mess.

"Your children seem to have no idea of how to pick up their toys," Dan would say. "Do you think you could perhaps teach them that what comes down can also go up?"

"We pick up the toys together after playtime," I replied.

"And that ends at what hour?"

"There are two of them."

"So I've noticed."

"No, you don't understand. As soon as I get down on my knees with one to start him cooperating, the other races off and climbs the kitchen counter, hauls the Nutella jar out from the cabinet, and sneaks through the backdoor to feed the dog next door. It's like guerrilla combat."

"You're their mother. Make it a game."

"I've made it into as many games as you could dream up in a doctoral dissertation," I said. "Treasure Hunt. Tuscany Grape Harvest. Seagull Egg Gathering. Shipping the Toys to Neverland. Moon Rock Collection. You name it."

"It's not working."

"Maybe your idea of what's workable isn't realistic for a home with small children."

"Simple hygiene mightn't be such a bad start," he said.

"Dan, we're talking clutter here, not germs."

"Hm."

"Aren't we?"

"One eventually breeds the other." He pursed his lips, obviously trying to restrain himself from further comment.

"In case you hadn't noticed, the actual house is basically

clean!" Why, oh why couldn't I see that we had no business entertaining this conversation, stoking our efforts toward the impossible with such acrimony; that neither of us had any business being in a relationship at all? "I should know. I'm the one who either cleans it or pays for it to be done. And what's more, if your old apartment hadn't been kept so pathologically neat—"

"Pathologically?" he pronounced. His tone turned sepulchral.

"Oh, God." Suddenly I collapsed. We were sitting on his white couch which had bloomed over the past few months with soy sauce, ketchup, and cranberry juice. These days it looked like a bad floral print from Wal-Mart. Why did it seem to me that this marriage was so wrong and out of character that it must be bound to work?

"An obsessive/compulsive, which I am, is apparently not always the correct configuration for a hysteric, which you are," he said, his voice softening. The kindliness his mother had taught him surfaced for an instant, and all at once I realized that that was what I was really hearing; how much of that kindness had been present throughout our courtship, unruffled and disciplined, like a shadow? How much was his, and how much hers? As if reading my thoughts, he drew closer and wrapped an arm around me. He stroked the hair back from my face. "I love you, Lulu."

"I love you, too." Resisting the comforting scent of his aftershave I sidled away, scrubbing the tears off my nose, filled with mistrust. "I'm just so tired."

He watched me.

"I know we can do this somehow."

He didn't respond.

"I mean, there's so much good here. The Seder the other night with your cousins, and Chanukah. Teaching the twins about polar bears, and the visit to the Indian excavation. The Children's Theater performance concert last week. You were the one who bought the tickets."

Thoughtfully he kept watching me.

"The Columbus Day Parade in North Beach. That was good, wasn't it? When the mounted policeman let Mickey ride his horse?"

"Yes. I suppose."

"Things do click together sometimes."

"Sometimes," he agreed quietly.

"Well, I promise, I give you my absolute word, that I'm not going to walk out on this one. Never. Not like the others. But I'm really just so tired of all the strain."

"Yes," he mused, almost as if he was speaking to himself. "I know."

IT WAS ON a morning when Dan had gone away for three days on a magazine assignment that I happened to wander into his study—if you can call removing the spare key from the the sock drawer in his maple burl chest, climbing the flight of steps to the landing, turning a sharp left to continue the next flight up to the third story, and then unlocking the stiff latch to the only room that occupied that entire floor of our hillside home and gliding in on tiptoe, wandering. Throughout all the months we'd lived there so far I had never yet entered the study alone. Desire to respect Dan's privacy had reached almost superstitious proportions; despite my umbrage I had not the faintest wish to cross his line or tamper in his life's arrangements. It was a matter of principle.

But now something felt different.

"I need to remember to take that red porcelain lamp to the repair shop when I get back to the city," he'd said to me the night before over the phone when he'd called long distance from Florida. "Would you please remind me?"

"Which red porcelain lamp?" Usually he painstakingly wrote down tasks and reminders on a list that he kept inside his wallet.

"I only have one."

I ran a mental inventory: wedding present? bedside reader? living room? hall credenza? dining sideboard? "There's no red porcelain lamp here, Dan."

"Certainly there is. A Chinese oxblood glaze vase with a cream silk shade. It's in my study."

"Oh."

"It seems to have developed a crack down one side," he said, and for a moment the statement hung in the airwaves.

"How did that happen?" I said innocently, taking the bait.

"I have no idea. It wasn't there when we moved into the house. It wasn't there when I organized the furniture." He paused. The silence extended a fraction too long. "It looks

like it's received a blow of some kind. There's a small chip
at the lower end, as if the base had got struck with something—a peashooter pea, or a beebee, or a dart. Some . . .
less than casual projectile. The crack started out a hair
fracture, which is how I first noticed it. Now it's grown
into a fault line. I'm afraid if it isn't caught in time the
lamp will break."

As he spoke the dread that I knew so well from many an
argument swirled in its dark waters. I pictured the lamp,
crimson, glowing, sitting wherever it sat—on his desk-
top, the bookcase, the windowsill facing the park; before
my imaginary eye it split open like the two halves of an apple, the pieces falling apart, silently, in slow motion. The
shade toppled to one side, the lightbulb slid askew. The rim
of white below the glaze smiled like a bite from the apple,
the edge scalloped with toothmarks. Then, as if time suddenly jumped, fragments hit the floor beside Dan's Kilim
rug and a great long shatter sounded on and on.

"Have any of the boys been up to my room, that you
know of?" he asked neutrally.

"No," I replied. "Not at all."

"Hm."

"They know better. Neither of the twins would figure
out which key to use, anyhow," I added. "Or how to use it.
Or where you keep it. Or anything."

"Kids are far more adroit and observant than I think you
give yours credit for," he said.

"Oh, I know they're smart. Sharp, I mean."

"Mickey especially always impresses me, as you know.

His quick eye doesn't miss a trick," he said. "How are they, by the way?"

"They're fine. Somebody threw a birthday party at school today. Then they went to the craft show along with the big kids from the first grade. Very exciting."

"And Tristan? What's he up to this evening?"

My stomach lurched. "Doing his math homework."

"I thought I could hear some very loud Bob Marley in the background just now."

Carefully I picked up the phone from its table in the upstairs hall and began to inch step by step away from the immediate vicinity of your bedroom. "He says it helps him concentrate." A faint whiff of smoke leaked from under your door as I passed. The whiff was sweet, acrid, herbal. I felt the scorch as it hit my nose. Softly I pulled the cord into the upstairs bathroom behind me, closed the door, and hastened to another subject. "Um—how are *you?* Is the interview coming together with the child molester?"

"Unfortunately, yes. It's not pleasant."

"No." I rubbed a speck of dirt off the chrome tap with my fingertip. The smoke was scarcely noticeable in here; I must have dreamed it, I thought, it must be floating up from the street.

"I plan to take a few long walks on the beach before I get home to chase the toxic fumes away."

Fumes. "Where'd you eat dinner?"

"At a crab shack in Coconut Grove."

"That's where you used to go when you were little, isn't

it? When your parents took you on vacation in the summer?"

"Yes." Another pause.

"What's the matter? Was the food bad?"

"It was exactly the same restaurant with exactly the same menu as the last time I ate there. Which was when I went there for the final summer with Mom and Dad when I was seventeen."

I waited. "How uncanny," I said eventually. "Did that give you deja vu?"

"I ate fried scallops and conch salad. The same as last time." His voice was sounding more and more remote.

"I've never tried conch. What's it like? Rubbery?"

"Lulu, that lamp belonged to my mother." He stopped and cleared his throat.

"Did it," I said.

"Yes."

"Oh. I didn't know."

"Apparently you didn't know it even exists."

It wasn't from lack of interest, I wanted to say. It was more that whenever I entered the threshold of that room I grew afraid to look around. I felt like a burglar.

"Almost every single item in my study came from my parents' house after my mother died. Except for my metal filing cabinets and one or two bookcases."

"Oh."

"Everything *there* has a *history*."

"Dan—" Desperately I tried to think of what furnishings filled his vast space nudged against the sky. The big oak desk. The Eames chair with its black leather seat. The Swedish Modern teak end table stacked with journals and magazines. "Look, Dan. Couldn't you have accidentally knocked the lamp at some time? With some object or something?"

"No."

"Maybe one night when you were working late? A ruler? A brandy snifter?"

"Baccarat snifters don't leave little holes," he said.

"Well, I don't know *how* it could have happened. Especially when it was your mother's." Although what that had to do with it I didn't have a clue, except that as I thought about your teenage anarchy lately I cringed all the more.

"Perhaps we can figure it out when I get home," he suggested.

Then he sighed.

"Maybe." I closed my eyes. "I hope so."

"Give the kids my love," he added.

Now the third-floor door swung open on its silent hinges, and all at once it was as if I stood in a re-creation.

Before me lay a diorama depicting another woman's life—in miniature, it was true—correct in scattered details. There was the desk where she'd sat to pay her bills, the hassock she'd once reupholstered in avocado linen. Relics of her taste lay everywhere. They'd been transplanted to a far West Coast city not on her original itinerary, with a different, oceanic light pouring in through the bay windows across her oiled wood finishes and a different set of art deco glasses perched on her forties Mexican cactus coasters, the artful grouping set ready for use on the glass top of her white wrought-iron bar trolley under the white-framed East Village abstract she'd bought while a psychology major at NYU. Underneath the layers of dust and time these things smelled of her still. They received her ongoing, ghostly breath. Looking around at the world surrounding Dan's contemporary bookshelves, I understood for the first time what he'd meant: his refuge. His inner sanctum.

His real home.

I felt her shape occupy the blank in front of the desk, a glimmer of light on emptiness. Quickly I stepped back. She was now no more than a sunbeam filtered through bird-spackled panes. But the room's air trembled with her frail memory; I felt my shoulders echo her shoulders' curves: the same cock to our heads, the same swell of rib cage and link of spine, like a silhouette of my own shadow cast upon nothingness and poured with a faint dazzle. But also with subtle changes. I imagined the careful hairdo set in permanent waves as she raised her hand absently to check it. I imagined the smell of her pale Arpege perfume. From just beyond the corner of one eye I sketched a fine-boned thumb, reaching out and stroking the blotter's leather mount.

She was here.

Turning, I nearly ran. But then I stopped myself. I had to lean back and peer around the shifting absences in order to locate just where she might have stood.

The invisible presence moved. As light chases a track

across ruffled water, she melted and flowed sadly toward a goal. Was the goal a person? Each object in the room seemed encased in a separate atmosphere that could draw her with its mundane familiarity. But no; she wasn't aimless. Her form would have a core, a focus that I knew as well as I knew my own name. Even waiting in place, she would stand fixed with purposeful longing.

Was she here all the time? I wondered. Was it just my own loneliness and pain that conjured her memory from these sticks of furniture? Or did she come also for him?

On top of Dan's filing cabinet a hinged frame spread its brass wings. Two photographs side by side smiled out from it: Mr. Hambleman, very young and almost unrecognizable in an army uniform, and Natalie, about twenty-two. Even in black and white her full lips looked red as a pomegranate, the wide mouth of a pensive humorist. Her eyes were direct and frank. They seemed to invite mine, asking what I was doing here, what I was thinking, suggesting that I should perhaps sit down and have a conversation. Life had only just started for her when this photo was taken, I knew; Dan had not yet been born, she hadn't yet paced up and down that hallway, begging her husband to let the baby out of the locked room; she lounged frozen in time on a banana-leaf print davenport, one hand gripping the armrest as if ready to propel her any second toward the viewer. What shyness she'd possessed early on had by this stage already been overcome by a lively curiosity, and not yet grown renewed by solitude. It was only after I'd gazed at her for several minutes that I realized: this was the very first time we'd met face to face.

Which is why it seemed odd to recognize her so fast.

Stranger still was that no other snapshot of her had yet come my way. No other portrait had been shown to me. She looked so warm. Intelligence shone from her expression. It was as if I *had* known her for a long, long time, all the way back to this captured instant—known her as intimately as I knew my best friend. The presence slipped here and there through the stillness, tenuously, as if motile in that aqueous light. It was no accident that now she seemed to inhabit her son's working place. She'd gravitated here as surely as bubbles rise. Who, after all, was the one person she felt for most, the confidant who held her personality cupped within his own and protected it even as he'd tried to separate himself from it, and who'd sustained her spirit against its main challenger until he'd finally found another vessel into which he could let it go?

Whose is the connection that never ends?

It was at precisely that moment that I understood our real bond.

"You'd like her," Dan had told me, and I knew he'd spoken truth. Except he thought it was because we were alike. He thought that because we cared about the same books, the same music, our intellects would have meshed, our emotional grids matched. He'd assumed we'd both suffered and endured enough to share a common stoicism. But he was once more mistaken. There was no way for him to know the crossroads where we really met.

I stared deeply into her face. "Here is where I belong," she seemed to say. "You know why. We both occupy the same realm. We each have our function." And yet, I thought, perhaps not completely; for she had faltered and given hers up in the end.

"You must not do so," her young, hopeful eyes seemed to say. "Even if he is my son. You know who comes first. Just as he always did with me, no matter how much I bent to his father's will."

The oval face seemed to kindle like a pale moon in the picture, swimming before my eyes.

"Everyone has his limits. Each of us can only try to leap beyond them." Light shifted as a shadow moved across her and fell away. The thoughts wavered like water. "He's doing what he can. And that's all he can do," she seemed to say.

And I knew this was so.

Gently I touched the photograph with my palm. Whomever we'd married, whatever struggles we'd picked for ourselves, what we shared most was the love for our children, and our desperate wish that everything in life treat them well.

WARFARE DOESN'T END when a person dies. Its energies get passed down to the next heirs. A legacy of bafflement and striving make a pattern as real as any carpet design, and everybody has to tread over it until it finally wears out, which can sometimes take centuries. Who knows how many tough Hambleman fathers had preceded the one who fathered Dan? How can I even speculate why a soft girl like Natalie had been so attracted to the iron in his soul and the struggle a life with him would demand? Why do we do it over and over, go out and seek and seek, until we find that special mate that fits the fit? I stood in the shimmering sunlight beside the image of my dead mother-in-law, asking myself that question.

And then I realized what I should have been asking. Why on earth had I married Dan?

"I'VE BOUGHT SOME presents for the kids," Dan announced the next night when he came home from Florida. As the twins sat at the dinner table slaving through the rest of their mashed potatoes and cubesteak, he called, "Hey, you two! Hurry up and clean your plates, and you'll get a big surprise."

"What is it?" I asked.

"You'll see."

I envisioned little educational gimmicks like gyroscopes or perhaps subtraction flash cards. As seldom as Dan took it upon himself to interact with the children, he did like to keep standards up. Lately he was making as much effort as he could. I realized how fixed his eye remained upon the leap, and how far out of true bearing its direction lay. I also knew that this gift was in part a peace offering to me: we hadn't so much as gone out to dinner alone in quite some time, he'd already ostentatiously stowed the red lamp in his car the minute he got home from the airport to take to the repair shop in the morning, and our sex life was as dead as the mastodon.

"Is that the last of your vegetables?" he asked Jonathon, who grinned and nodded.

"That's the last of our steak, too. See?" cried Mickey, poking one shred of meat to the edge of his plate. "What do you got for us?"

"This!" He grabbed his hat from the sideboard, put it on the table, and pulled out two black eggs.

The twins huddled close around his chair.

"Whoa," said Jonathon.

"Rocks," Mickey said.

"It's black Silly Putty," said Jonathon.

"No," Dan corrected, cradling the eggs in his broad palm. "Look what I found in the magic hat."

The objects glowed like jewels.

"They're from Russia where my grandfather was born a long time ago. See the little paintings all around the sides?"

"What are they?" Mickey asked.

"That's a princess," said Jonathon, astutely pointing at a beautiful girl with blond hair streaming from beneath a tall crowned hat.

"Hey, she's riding a bird, and it's on fire!" Mickey cried, lifting the egg to the light. "Hey! Why isn't she burning up?"

"Because she's cool," Jonathon said waggishly, and smirked.

"Those are neat. Thank you, Dan," said Mickey. Jon repeated it after him.

Dan glanced around toward the stair. "You're very welcome. I have something for Tristan, too. Where did he get to already?"

"Let's see his!" Mickey said.

"No. His is a little box instead of an egg. He should see it first."

"What's on it?"

"Mine has a bad old witch," muttered Jonathon, holding it at arm's length.

"Oh, I know who she is. That's Baba Yaga. See? Standing next to her house with the chicken legs?" I said, at which Jonathon opened his mouth and Mickey started to laugh like a drain: Har har har.

"Chicken legs! Chicken legs!"

"Treatie's doing his history report," I said to Dan, hoping this was indeed a fact.

"I see." He handed his hat to Mickey, who put it on, blinding himself. Then, turning to me, Dan dug something out of his pocket. "Look at this."

I plucked a small colored tube-shaped bead from his palm.

"It's—what is this? Blown glass?" I thought he was offering me some treasure he'd come across in his travels.

"I wouldn't know."

"Millefiori? It looks like millefiori."

"I found it on the floor under my desk."

"Oh! Really?" The cylinder seemed to heat up between thumb and forefinger. My throat tightened. Could I have dropped something in there? Knocked some container over on his desk? "Nice. Is it something you've had a long time?" I asked politely.

"It's an African trade bead, I believe. I've never seen it before. At least, not consciously, not this particular one."

"Oh. Hm."

"Take a look at that spot. Right there." He took the bead back and pointed with his fingernail to a small crater on one end of the tube. The place was broken, the inside yellows bright and raw next to the dirty rind. Sheared wavy glass shone under the dining-room chandelier light. A tiny fissure laced through the stripes to the other end, splitting the hole where it once had been strung.

"I see," I said.

"At first I was perplexed."

"How did you happen to find it?" I watched the twins, who were rolling their eggs down the parquet hallway in a race. I should stop them, I thought. Rolling won't do that Russian enamel much good.

"From stepping on it through my slippers."

I turned. He was watching me.

"So what is it you want to say?" I asked finally.

"Do you recognize it? Does it remind you of anything?"

"Not really, no. I don't—" And then it came to me what he intended.

You were still in your Grateful Dead stage at this time, Treatie. Old hippie necklaces you'd bought in the Haight hung three and four strands deep around your neck.

"These things have been strewn all over Berkeley for the past twenty-five years. Street vendors sell them on Telegraph. Maybe you picked it up accidentally, or you were out somewhere and it dropped into your pants cuff," I said.

"I think it matches others on a string I've seen quite lately," he replied, cryptic.

I couldn't reply.

"You would have to throw something this size pretty hard with a lot of deliberate force to break a lamp. But it could be done."

"Dan," I suddenly pleaded.

"Yes?"

"Let's go upstairs. There are things about the children that I want to discuss with you."

"What kinds of things?"

"Family dynamics. Family issues."

"There's something missing from my desk drawer."

Silence dropped.

"What's missing?" I whispered at last, the cold increasing.

"Something I use to relax," he said, his eyes locked wide on me even as his voice skewed evasively. "For when I'm alone. A private—stash. For smoking."

I stared back, astounded.

"I cannot bear the sense of violation I feel constantly when I'm in this house, Lulu," he said, his tone just low enough to undercut the twins' sudden squeals as they argued over who'd won their race. "I can no longer tolerate it."

"I know. Look, I'm sorry, it's awful, being a stepparent is the hardest job in the world. We both know that. There

must be a way we can work things out. That we can handle
it so that you get what you need and we don't wind up feeling cut off and so alone from one another, and so under
seige and—and far apart and—let's go upstairs and—"

"I can't do this anymore."

"What 'this'?" I asked. "What 'this' do you mean?" I
tried to swallow. The lump in my throat seemed to have
paralyzed all my muscles. Unbelievable, I thought; it really can't be happening.

"The marriage." He waved a hand. "This."

"But you said it was what you wanted," I whispered.

He set his jaw, locking it tight. "I was mistaken."

And quick as a wink, all this was over.

May 12, this year: Ceres

Never a bridesmaid, always a bride.
——LULU PENFIELD, MYSTERY NOVELIST

So now maybe you can see why I got so upset when you phoned me from Montauk and said, "Mom, guess what?"

YOU'RE MARRIED. It's still hard to digest. Of all our little family, you're the one who's married now.

NEEDLESS TO SAY, to anyone who knows us it's obvious that I have more history than most small European countries. Well, you can't change the past. Certainly the years of work I put in trying to understand why I married so many times were worth it. There's no point in rehashing all that here; other private journals log that particular trek, and you won't be reading those any more than you will this one. I still remember the day, though, when we'd moved to Colorado right after the San Francisco breakup and you were starting your high school freshman year, that I swore to you I'd never do it again.

The devastation we all felt after Dan and I divorced manifested itself in different ways. Jonathon went into mourning, a pitiful sight in a six-year-old—can you remember how he curled up in a fetal position on his bed the night we told him Dan was leaving? Even once we'd found the mountain house and were starting another life far away from the site of his grief, for months he didn't want to come out of his room. It nearly killed me. Later he grew boisterous and angry, hitting out at everybody, getting into trouble at school. Mickey developed a fear of the dark and an anxiety level that hasn't entirely calmed down to this day.

And you, of course, felt guilty.

How often have we talked about your theft of Dan's marijuana? Heaven only knows. Of course, I understood instantly why you'd done it. The fact that you confessed so quickly and with such remorse left him looking a little foolish, to say the least; but he was the sort of man in whom foolishness spurred righteous indignation, so I've never been able to take his high moral stand too seriously. I mean, the man kept half a pound of dope in his desk! Besides, the implication he made about your deliberately hurling a tiny glass bead at his mother's lamp is in hindsight so ridiculous that it's almost embarrassing to remember it here. No telling what kind of guilty bad-stepfather dreams had been stewing around his head. Thank goodness you told him about knocking the lamp over before he could trot out his big picture.

Of course, the real miracle of it all is how you've never

once complained. I know it seems like my marriages are the equivalent of most women's flings, but if you look at it on a sociological level, you might conclude that I've just been acting out the paradigm for an entire culture—a paradigm I've hoped you wouldn't continue.

The first inkling I got that this could be so was way back in England. Geoffrey and I stood there in the town-hall office, listening to the registrar confirm our legal statuses for the wedding documents before tying our knot. "Louise May Penfield. Born *Texas* . . . United States of America. Married *two times* prior, all *decree nisi*—" He stumbled. His voice filled with a supercilious wonder. Peering severely down at the license in his hand, he glanced up from one of us to the other, frowned, and lifted his ferret lip in a sneer. "*Two times,*" he intoned. "Two divorces. At age twenty-eight," and his eyelids drooped and fluttered like tired window shades. "*In America.*" He turned back to Geoffrey, the raw innocent dupe from the colonies. "We don't want to have this happen again," he announced. "Do we?" and for a split second, as I stood there miserable and unwilling but ready to do what I'd promised, it seemed as though he was going to refuse to marry us. He coughed, shuffled the papers, and all at once began to drone out the civil service. A savage spite rose up in me. "Get used to it, Buster," I thought, baring my teeth. "It's the wave of the future."

But please, Treatie, I've wanted to beg. Please. Not yours.

• • •

When I published *The Haitian Hit* and started making money and finally knew I could pay the electric bill without wincing, my view of the world began to change. As you know, the success of that second book in the Gypsy Roland Lane series, *Cretan Coffin,* was what helped me decide to move one more time. Then came *Defenestration in Denmark.* Remember when the movie options started? At last I could buy us a decent house, stop renting apartments and jerry-built ski lodges, and send you and your brothers through college.

Returning to Texas just as the twins were hitting high school did seem an anomaly, I admit. In all my rovings I've maintained the same policy, whether I've forgotten important mail when pulling out of the driveway or left a favorite silk blouse behind in a motel only to discover the loss eight miles down the highway: Never go back. Cut your losses. Nothing is ever re-created, only renewed; each day means time to move on.

But going home, I finally had a different reason to move than a man.

My one big worry was you. Thank goodness you took our defection so easily, since you were at that time a junior at New Mexico State, having already racked up two whole years of living with Swalla.

Who is now my daughter-in-law.

Once in a bathroom once long ago when I was eight years old, as I lay in the tub lathering my stomach, I announced to Dyllis who stood at the sink brushing her smooth brown hair, "I'm never going to get married."

"Why?" she asked, smiling. She was then newly engaged for the first time and had a dreamy, knowing look in her eye.

"Because then I'd have to give up the family name."

"That's true. So what?"

"I don't want to turn into somebody else instead of a Penfield." At the time I was thinking of my grandfather: the climate of honor surrounding him, his humanitarian resolve, his joy, his love. Our association seemed too dear to forfeit through a changed name. My pride still depended on that sacred aura contained within its letters, on being connected to him and all his generations, and the moral privilege that conferred. I wanted my identity blessed.

"Oh," said Dyllis, whose goal it then was to become the first woman president of the United States, "when you really fall in love with somebody, you won't care what their last name is."

"I won't?"

"Uh-uh. You'll be glad to adopt it just because it's his."

Back then we didn't say, "You may keep your own name." Back then a girl would turn into a woman and assume her husband's full name automatically in the proper form: Mrs. Oswald Aloysius Murgatroyd.

"No," I said. Slowly I shook my head.

"Sure you will. It won't matter. It'll sound wonderful to you. Like in *West Side Story*."

I thought about Tony and Maria singing to each other. Then I blew some bubblebath off my kneecaps. "No one is ever going to have a name better than Penfield."

She laughed, snapped her barrette closed, and left the room.

Throughout the years since I've taken on more than one name. Vonick, Miller, Rutherford, Hambleman—at least after Miller I left their names alone and stuck with my own. But when I return to that Sunday morning bath so long ago I have to wonder how much of what I felt then was prophesy. And how much of that original stubbornness stuck.

I'm glad Swalla has kept Burrman, for your sake as well as hers.

TREATIE: I ADMIT here and now that on the day you first introduced us I didn't know how to be, I didn't know how to react.

"Mom, this is Swalla," you said as soon as I got out of the car on that visit, "Swalla, my mom Lulu. We're living together. We have been for six months now." You said it proudly, with your usual equable style, although I saw the tension tightening the skin around your eyes. Then you put your arm across her shoulder, and she stood there, beautiful and self-confident and exotic and wary, unsmiling, with the snake tattoo winding up her leg like a vine from her ankle to her inner thigh and disappearing suggestively under her miniskirt, and the red-dyed rooster tail above the short black hair, and the tiny sweater that rode high above her dragon-tattooed navel. And I felt scared to death.

"You're what?"

"Living togeth—"

"Treatie, how could you?" I cried.

"What?" You looked startled. Of all the things I might have said, you certainly didn't expect this. Or did you?

One of the strongest truths I've learned during my life is how quickly fear takes on the guise of anger.

"How could you? How could you *spring* this on me?"

"Spring?" you said stiffly. You, of all people. My ally.

"Living with someone! With—I'm sorry, I don't mean to be rude, Swalla, but he's only nineteen years old and all I've known about you is that you're a buddy who sometimes answers the phone."

She didn't smile. She didn't move, or blink, or speak a word. She stared.

"Mom. Have you had a hard trip down from Colorado?" Suddenly you were watching me as if I was a stranger.

"Considering that I've been driving for seven hours through a snowstorm only to be told that you've been cohabiting for *six months,* yes!" I snapped. Her nails were painted green. Under the turquoise contact lenses her eyes may have been gray. I couldn't tell, since at this point she looked uncomfortably in another direction.

"It's been casual. We started out as roommates," you explained. "That's why I haven't mentioned it to you before. It's only recently that things have developed into something more serious."

"Serious?"

"Maybe this isn't a good time for us to go eat," you said, closing the space between her body and yours, one hand gripped protectively on her thin shoulder. "You're obviously tired. Maybe you should go on to your motel and get settled in."

"Oh, thanks." I was on the brink of tears, so angry, so confounded by my own disorientation and pain and the knowledge that we had never, ever spoken to one another this way before that I could hardly spit it out. "Thank you so much, Treatie. So hospitable. To your *mother*."

"Look," and you spoke in that patient, distancing, careful tone I'd heard you use on so many friends and girlfriends through the years when they got out of hand, "this isn't about hospitality. It's about our lives."

And that is when, in a sudden flash of light, I remembered a front door swinging open on a warm December night in Bay City, Texas, and a woman decked out in Christmas baubles standing at the threshold, smiling with automatic welcome at a bedraggled nineteen-year-old hippie who must have looked to her eyes like Janis Joplin's street-kid sister.

THE TERROR THAT we feel as children doesn't diminish, Treatie, when we grow into adults. It just takes on different causes. Only when we pay close enough attention to the teachers life brings us can we sometimes, with luck, learn how to negotiate its labyrinths and transcend it.

If I was frightened the day I first met Hazel Vonick, what must she have felt about me?

My experience of living with Ted at nineteen and then marrying him, with all the subsequent disaster, triggered every nerve I owned. "Look at my example!" I wanted to yell. "Look at the mess I made! Don't do this!" I wanted to shake you both, shake you to your senses. Yet in that one moment of comprehension, as I saw Swalla's eyes widen defensively and your hand squeeze her shoulder, I grasped the true breadth of Hazel's aplomb. And in that same moment I recognized the irony: when the crunch came I had turned into my own parents, when all along I'd had another living model persisting, ready, right before my memory's eye.

"YOU'RE RIGHT, TREATIE." I swallowed. "You're absolutely right. This is about your lives."

You both glanced guardedly, blankly, at me.

"Hospitality and my own selfishness have nothing to do with it."

Still you held that noncommittal stance.

"I'm sorry," I said. "Honey, I'm really so sorry."

"Well," you said after a few seconds.

I turned to Swalla. "Listen. I promise you. I know better. This is not how I want to meet someone my son cares about. It's not even remotely how I really feel."

"Oh," she said.

"I'd like to start over."

"You always have, Mom," you said. But with so little inflection that I couldn't be sure whether you meant it as sarcasm, judgment, or mere historical observation.

"Well. Is it possible?"

You glanced down at Swalla. She looked up, all at once vulnerable, questioning, a young girl in love.

"Please," I said. And then words failed, and I did the only thing I could think of. Stepping forward I wrapped my arms around you both.

And by the grace of Hazel Vonick, that was enough.

"IT'S FUNNY YOU got so bent out of shape that day," Swalla said to me much later, when we were remembering our first introduction. "It wasn't at all what I'd anticipated."

"Really? How come?"

"I didn't imagine you'd go all conservative on us like that."

"I hope it hasn't made you nervous for good," I said, forking up a bite of the chocolate cake we were sharing. This was right before you both moved to Montauk. She'd taken me to her gym that morning as a guest, and now we were giving ourselves a postworkout treat.

"No, not at all. It just took me by surprise."

"Well, you can never count on anything when it comes to a mother's notions of her children."

"I guess. But I had this preconceived idea of you, and that kind of blew me out of the water."

"What kind of preconceived idea?"

"Oh, you know. What I know about your own past."

"Ah."

"And Treatie's always called you a sort of free spirit."

A shock rippled through me. For a few seconds I couldn't understand why. Then I realized that the words rang a chime deep in my mind, a vibration that went on and on, unending. But it took several more seconds to bring back where, and when, and from whose mouth, while the desert wind tugged at his long pale hair through the truck window, that I had once heard them said.

I HAVE GROWN to love Swalla's company. We always enjoy talking, both on the phone when you're not around, and during those rare holidays when we're all able to get together. But the true connection between us doesn't necessarily lie on the plane of chitchat. It lies somewhere much deeper: we've got you. With Swalla I feel as linked and as strange as Odysseus' mother must have felt with Penelope.

There's one thing I've learned for sure. Mothers-in-law possess power, whether we want it or not. Each phrase we speak carries a pressure. The revelation of this unsuspected role has sharpened my consciousness: you can't imagine the dismay I felt recalling that first day and realizing how I'd hurt you both. What horror to know one blurt can crush so. When I see you during our visits, I can bring in the shadow of my presence either good or evil; without even realizing it I might sweeten your morning or lace it with alkali. So now daily I learn a new kind of diplomacy: thoughtfulness, restraint.

The lessons my teachers have taught me.

As for the many other gifts this news of your marriage now brings—where do I start? It's as you silently told me so long ago, when you were still a baby: you are not me. Together you and Swalla have something that I never had. Just lately the pledge you both embody has, oddly enough, become my example, rather than the other way around. You've shown me the path I never took. Consequently it has awakened a dormant journey, the one I've avoided through years of marriages, divorces, and their handy spectacles. At last I'm on my own. An empty bed holds me each night. No distractions block my course. Each morning I begin, certain that herein lies the way to enjoy the vision you and Swalla offer, and through it, all the other manifold possibilities of love in the world. For how could I have anticipated the greatest gift of all: seeing my son grow truly happy?

Thank you, Treatie, for making me a mother-in-law.